CHIVALROUS RAKE, SCANDALOUS LADY

Mary Brendan

First published in Great Britain 2010
Harlequin Mills & Boon Limited,
Eton House, 18-24 Paradise Road, Richmond, Surrey TW9 1SR

© Mary Brendan 2010

ISBN: 978 0 263 87603 1

Harlequin Mills & Boon policy is to use papers that are natural, renewable and recyclable products and made from wood grown in sustainable forests. The logging and manufacturing process conform to the legal environmental regulations of the country of origin.

Printed and bound in Spain
by Litografia Rosés, S.A., Barcelona

'It seems to me you need someone to protect you.'

'You'll help me at a price, you mean?' Jemma whispered.

'It's a price I believe you'll be willing to pay. We suited once, you and I. In a basic way we suited very well indeed. Do you remember how I could make you want me?'

He closed the space between them in a single, prowling pace. She was tugged back against him and his mouth slanted hot and hard on hers, demanding, yet breathtakingly seductive.

'You may name your terms. I'll be attentive and generous in every way, I promise,' he added with gentle, laughing coercion. 'As my mistress you'll have *carte blanche*. Anything your heart...or body.. desires.'

Her lashes fluttered, her eyes focused, and she glimpsed what moments ago she'd been blinded to. He was watching her scientifically, to gauge whether she would let him ruin her.

'I have an answer for you, sir,' she choked, knocking again at his hand as it sought to bring her back to him. 'It is no. A man as egotistical as you may find it hard to believe, but I find you quite resistible. And please be assured that being degraded by you is not, and never will be, a price that I am willing to pay.'

Author Note

Regency Rogues
Ripe for scandal. Ready for a bride.

A roguish gentleman can be devastatingly attractive to a genteel lady, especially when she's already had a taste of loving him, and regrets losing him.

In *CHIVALROUS RAKE, SCANDALOUS LADY* the heroine is unwilling to succumb to a rejected suitor's offer to be his mistress, despite being sorely tempted to do so. The vengeful rogue has a fiancée, and the heroine has a secret that should remain hidden if she is to salvage what remains of her reputation.

The second book in the duet, *DANGEROUS LORD, SEDUCTIVE MISS*, finds the heroine under threat from a gang of local ruffians. Then she is unexpectedly reunited with the hero many years after their youthful romance ended in a bitter parting. But is he a villain too, and does he present a greater danger...to her heart?

I hope you enjoy reading about how the couples overcome scandal and heartache to eventually find love and happiness.

CHIVALROUS RAKE, SCANDALOUS LADY

Mary Brendan was born in North London, but now lives in rural Suffolk. She has always had a fascination with bygone days, and enjoys the research involved in writing historical fiction. When not at her word processor, she can be found trying to bring order to a large overgrown garden, or browsing local fairs and junk shops for that elusive bargain.

Novels by the same author:

WEDDING NIGHT REVENGE*
THE UNKNOWN WIFE*
A SCANDALOUS MARRIAGE*
THE RAKE AND THE REBEL*
A PRACTICAL MISTRESS†
THE WANTON BRIDE†
THE VIRTUOUS COURTESAN**
THE RAKE'S DEFIANT MISTRESS**

The Meredith Sisters
†*The Hunter Brothers*
**linked by character

Chapter One

Quality loved to tattle, Jemma Bailey knew that. She knew too that her parents' disastrous marriage had provided ample reason for her and her sisters to suffer spite and speculation. But over time the tabbies had grown bored of worrying at an unresponsive prey. One of their victims had gone overseas; the other had escaped their clutches for good by shuffling off this mortal coil. The couple's two elder daughters had married and now lived blameless lives in the shires with their husbands. Jemma was the youngest girl, and the one least affected by her parents' *mésalliance* as she'd been but nine years old when her father was granted a divorce. She had remained single and had kept house for her father until he died, whereupon she'd been astonished to learn that her parsimonious papa had been far flusher than he'd let on. He'd left her a tidy amount of cash together with his brace of properties.

For the past two years Jemma Bailey had lived as a young spinster of independent means, spending a good proportion of the year in a neat town house on the out-skirts of Mayfair. When the tawny beauty of the countryside beckoned she would set off with her housemaid to her small estate in Essex. In London she socialised with people of moderate means, and she'd mellowed into accepting that her parents', and her own, behaviour had cast her to the fringes of polite society.

As far as she was aware, years had passed since a Bailey had transgressed. Jemma therefore felt at a loss to comprehend what might recently have occurred to cause such lively conversation to cease the moment she'd entered Baldwin's fabric emporium. Such *grandes dames* as those Jemma had caught whispering about her were usually too lofty to notice her quiet, modest existence. Eyes that were long-lashed and an unusual, deep shade of green flitted over the female assembly. Flustered gestures and colouring cheeks were everywhere as the ladies picked and stroked at lengths of cloth to cover their confusion at her sudden appearance. A slight figure at the back of the group stepped towards her with a blush and a constrained smile. It was Jemma's cousin Maura Wyndham. The young women were of similar age, and in their prime had gone about together. Maura continued to enjoy inclusion in social circles that now were denied to Jemma, but they remained on friendly terms and visited one another quite often. Jemma sent a speaking look at her cousin. She was dismayed and not a little annoyed to think that one of her own kin had been involved in tattling about her behind her back.

'Shall I go out and come in again?' Jemma suggested in a dry undertone once Maura was within earshot.

Maura quickly linked arms with Jemma and turned her about so they were heading towards the bolts of cottons and away from the knot of mothers and daughters busying themselves amongst the silks and satins.

'I'm sorry you came in and caught us,' Maura began breathily, 'but I'm not sorry I was in that group and heard what I did.' She slanted Jemma an earnest look from wide eyes. 'I was going to come straight to see you and warn you of a ridiculous rumour that will certainly be doing the rounds by this evening. We…' she took a glance back over her shoulder towards the ladies '…we all agreed, even Lucy did, that it must be the work of a mischief-maker, though why anyone would bother doing any such daft thing—'

'And will you ever tell me what that daft thing is?' Jemma interrupted close to her cousin's ear. She gave Maura a faint, encouraging smile. Her indignation was mounting, and she was impatient to know what had been said about her.

Maura cleared her throat, and her tongue-tip slid nervously over her lower lip. 'Did you notice Lucy Duncan amongst the ladies?' she asked.

'I did,' Jemma confirmed evenly.

'She told us…but it's not her fault really as she was just repeating a conversation she overheard between her brother and one of his cronies. So you can't blame her except for being indiscreet. I wish she'd only told me so I could have privately spoken to you…'

'Spoken to me of what?' Jemma implored whilst raising her expressive jade-green eyes heavenwards. She knew Lucy's brother, Philip Duncan, of course, because the fellow had offered for her hand in marriage when she'd been a débutante. Jemma had always thought Philip had taken the rejection reasonably well at the time; she hadn't imagined he'd brood on it for five years before retaliating and slandering her to his friends.

'Philip Duncan has been boasting that you are trying to extract from him another marriage proposal.'

A hoot of genuine amusement escaped from Jemma and was swiftly smothered by a shapely, gloved hand. 'I don't for one minute believe that he would broadcast anything so utterly idiotic and false,' she spluttered through muffling fingers.

'I'm only repeating what Lucy said.' Maura sounded quite miffed that her courage in divulging the grave news had been rewarded with hilarity.

'I'm not disbelieving you,' Jemma said gently as a few of her fingers lazily tested the quality of striped dimity. The other hand was busy wiping mirthful tears from her eyes. 'Some misunderstanding has occurred. I haven't clapped eyes on Philip in months, and last time I passed him in Pall Mall he was no more than polite. He was escorting Verity Smith and looking quite her lapdog too. Any hankering he had for me is very much in the past.'

'Apparently that's what he said to Graham Quick,' Maura blurted. 'Lucy heard Philip telling Mr Quick that you are the one hankering and chasing after him.' Maura had noticed that a dangerous glint had replaced the humorous twinkle in Jemma's eyes. Quickly she sought to defuse her cousin's temper. 'I don't know what Lucy's brother is thinking to invite such a fellow in to his lodgings. Mrs Duncan and Lucy often visit him there. Philip was furious when he discovered his landlady had let Lucy in alone and she'd been loitering in his hallway, listening to every word they'd said.' Maura paused, added with an excited shiver, 'Lucy nearly came face to face with Graham Quick! When she heard him coming she had to hide in a cloakroom till he'd gone. But Philip guessed she'd been eavesdropping all along.'

Jemma knew what had prompted such a thrill in her cousin. Graham Quick was an infamous reprobate and shunned in polite society. Most young women only knew of him by reputation and had never met him in the flesh. Their parents and brothers made sure of that. The fact that Philip Duncan had mentioned her name, let alone discussed her with such a blackguard, had stoked Jemma's disgust to such a degree that she felt rather bilious.

'Lucy said Philip mentioned having received a letter. It invited him to renew his proposal to you. By all accounts he thought it comical. He showed Mr Quick the letter and said he had no intention of rescuing you or any other...' Maura's fluid, whispered account came to a halt as her teeth sank in to her lower lip.

'Or any other...?' Jemma prompted, with a fierce frown, her eyes shining with suppressed temper. She was very aware of the group of women close by.

'Or any other uppity chit destined to be an old maid abandoned on the shelf,' Maura recited on a regretful sigh. She shot Jemma a sympathetic look. 'As if you would be interested in Philip now! He's going bald and he's grown too fat to get his waistcoat buttons done up properly, whereas you are still as trim and lovely as ever you were at seventeen.' Maura patted her cousin's slender arm in a show of solidarity. 'Why, you're not yet twenty-three and could outshine any of the girls out this year.'

Her cousin's extravagant compliment did nothing to ease Jemma's sense of outrage. Her fingers had stiffened on the crisp fabric beneath them. The healthy bloom in her cheeks had reduced to two high spots of wrathful colour on a complexion that resembled parchment. 'He said *what*? He did *what*? How *dare* he talk about me! How dare he even mention my name to a vile libertine such as Graham Quick!'

'You might not like Mr Quick, but he seems to admire you,' Lucy blurted thoughtlessly. 'By all accounts Lucy heard him praising your figure and its… best points.'

'Did he, indeed!' Jemma's soft mouth thrust in to a rosy knot. 'I have to tell you I don't regard that as a compliment.'

'You didn't send Philip Duncan a letter, did you?'

Such an audacious act was outside the role of any gently bred young lady, yet a shade of doubt had tinged Maura's tone and drawn a wintry look from Jemma. Maura's timid hazel eyes flinched away from her cousin's stormy stare.

'I did not,' Jemma enunciated through perfect pearly teeth perilously set on edge. 'Send him a letter?' she scoffed. 'Propose to him? The man must be addled in his wits.'

'He had a letter. Lucy saw it being waved about. I don't think he is lying about that. Someone is being very mean, aren't they?' Maura chewed anxiously at her lip. 'Who would do such a vile thing?'

'I don't know, but unfortunately now I must find out.'

Maura knew that her cousin Jemma had a formidable temper once she was roused to action by a sense of injustice. She cast an anxious glance back at the ladies she'd recently been with. Thankfully, the older women had decamped, probably to regroup in the shop across the street where they might continue to savour this latest tale unobserved by its central character. Only Lucy Duncan and Deborah Cleveland remained and now seemed more interested in shopping than gossiping as they unravelled shimmering sapphire satin to cascade over the counter.

The two young ladies also drew Jemma's ferocious feline gaze. As she frowned in their direction it was Deborah Cleveland who raised her flaxen head and met her stare. She could tell that the young woman was attempting to signal with her eyes that she was sorry for what had gone on.

Tension tightened Jemma's stomach. She had always thought Deborah very pretty and had no reason not to like her. In fact, on the rare occasions they'd met in the past they'd exchanged a few cordial words that had hinted at a fledgling friendship, but Deborah was several years younger than she was. At eighteen, an heiress, and one of this season's top débutantes, Deborah inhabited a different world to Jemma. Deborah had just become engaged to a handsome and most eligible bachelor. She was accordingly very popular and much fêted by the *beau monde* despite the fact that many of the young ladies striving to be her friend were envious that she'd netted such a catch. The most eligible bachelor, now spoken for, was another reason why Jemma and Deborah might elect to keep at a polite distance.

Jemma had received several proposals during the Season she'd made her come out. Philip Duncan had been just one of several gentlemen who'd offered for her and been rejected. Few of her suitors had made any lasting impression on her; in fact now, just five years later, Jemma struggled to recall all of their names.

But one had intrigued and very much attracted her. When a novice socialite of just seventeen, he had drawn her in to a glittering, sophisticated world now denied to her. He'd taught her to dance properly, given her the confidence to converse with his aristocratic friends and relatives. Her little inexperienced gaffes were never mocked, but gently corrected or smoothed over. When she'd nervously enquired if he'd heard the scandalous talk about her family, he'd mildly replied that her parents' problems were not hers. Utterly relieved that he knew, but had elected to dismiss the Bailey stigma as irrelevant, she'd abandoned herself to enjoying being with him, aware that other débutantes watched, green-eyed, whilst he lavished on her his amusing, charismatic company. He'd made her laugh…and sigh when he'd taken her out to the garden during Lady Cranleigh's ball. There had been other occasions too when he'd managed to manoeuvre her, quite willingly, into a seductive setting, but she'd remained faithful to Robert, her faithless sweetheart.

So she'd rejected Marcus Speer's proposal too and gone home to Essex unattached with her father's disapproval growling in her ears. Now Marcus was betrothed to Deborah Cleveland. No doubt later today he would be told by his fiancée of an amusing bit of gossip she'd heard whilst out shopping with her friends. Jemma swallowed the painful indignation that threatened to close her throat and eject water from her hot eyes. She had done nothing shameful and didn't deserve to be laughed at by anyone. She could not bear that he, of all people, might find her risible. Would he believe her so desperate now to get a husband that she'd stoop to sending a letter to a fat, balding fellow, known to keep company with the worst kind of people, to beg him to renew his proposal? Shaking off Maura's restraining fingers, she marched towards the young women, determined to impress on them both that there was no truth in any of it, no matter what Lucy had overheard her brother telling his repulsive friend.

'Sir…please, sir…you must attend to some of your pressing affairs. It will take but a quarter of an hour of your time. If you will only join me in the library, we can clear the worst of it.'

Marcus Speer strode on into the house, his handsome features tautened in preoccupation. Adroitly he relieved himself of his coat and hat without slowing his pace. The butler fielded those garments wordlessly and made off towards the cloakroom with them.

Marcus's secretary, Hepworth, was less easily dispatched than Perkins had been. He doggedly bore being ignored and skipped behind his master, trying to keep up with his long stride whilst repeating his pleas to make him deal with his correspondence. 'Some social invitations for this very evening must have urgent replies,' he huffed.

Marcus came to a halt and pivoted about with a frown. 'What?' His thick dark brows were knit together in a mix of irritation and concentration. He had just arrived home from visiting the Earl of Gresham, his uncle, who, having relapsed overnight, was now deemed by his physician to be on his deathbed. The Earl had been called an old fraud before when he'd clawed his way back to health from a lung infection virulent enough to see off a man half his age. But on this occasion his nephew, and Dr Robertson, had offered no gentle banter to encourage the septuagenarian to stop coughing and take a spoon of gruel. It was plain to see that the Earl of Gresham had taken his last meal and was close to taking his final breath. He was mortally ill and drifting in and out of consciousness. Dr Robertson had sent Marcus home to rest. In his professional opinion he estimated that his patient might battle on for a day or two yet, for his pulse was still quite strong. He'd advised Marcus to return to Grosvenor Square in the morning, and if he were needed sooner at his uncle's bedside to be with him at the end, he'd swiftly summon him.

So it was a deep and sombre melancholy rather than bad manners that had made Marcus ignore his secretary's pleas to go with him to dictate some correspondence. Marcus cast a look down on Hepworth's sparse pate. The man pushed his spectacles up over the bridge of his nose and myopically returned his gaze.

'Just fifteen minutes of your time, sir, and we can at least deal with those matters pertaining to the next few days.' Hepworth's tone was wheedling.

Marcus gave a brisk nod and, turning on his heel headed towards the library. Whilst they walked he started on the business in hand the quicker to get it over with. 'With regard to any social invitations that fall within the next fortnight, you may decline all on my behalf.' He stooped to retrieve a document that had fluttered to the floor despite Hepworth's contortions to catch at it.

'I have that, sir. All to be declined.' A look of enlightenment suddenly crossed Hepworth's features and his mouth drooped sadly. 'Oh…your uncle, sir…beg pardon, I omitted to ask how he is,' Hepworth whispered, aghast. 'He has rallied before and I've always believed the Earl to be indestructible, you know.'

A half-smile softened Marcus's thin lips at the genuine distress in Hepworth's tone. As the Earl of Gresham's rightful heir, Marcus understood that he now had important matters to attend to. He'd been quick to slip away from the sick-room in order to begin the inevitable business with undertakers and lawyers. It wasn't his inheritance or the ambition of having a title that had hastened his departure from Grosvenor Square, but the need to escape the distressing truth that he was soon to lose someone who'd treated him as a son. He'd been unashamed to love the Earl in return. No man ever had a better guardian and mentor.

A combination of Marcus's innate pride and ambition and his uncle's guidance and excellent connections meant that by the time he was twenty-five he'd achieved wealth, status, and popularity. With his thirty-second birthday only a few months away all he'd lacked until now was a title and a wife. Soon both would be his, yet he desired neither. Slowly he became aware that his secretary's bleak gaze was still fixed on his face. 'There is no hope this time,' he told Hepworth gruffly. 'He is dying.' He cleared his throat to continue. 'Dr Robertson has sent me away for the Earl is slipping in to a coma. He thinks that I should return in the morning, although he cannot say for sure how long he has.'

Hepworth bowed his head, shook it, and murmured his regrets. He had clung to the hope that the old boy might surprise them all by springing back to life as the weather became more clement. It was early April and outside gloriously mild and bright for so early in the year. The daffodils had been showy for weeks beneath radiant light and cloudless skies. In contrast the atmosphere within this grand mansion on Beaufort Place was depressingly gloomy and grave.

Having entered the library, they headed for the large table and took their customary seats: Marcus at the head of the table and Hepworth positioned to one side of him. Briskly Hepworth spread out papers on tooled leather. He sorted them into piles. 'Those I have an answer for,' he muttered to himself, putting a stack of gilt-edged invitation cards to one side and flattening them with a pat.

He came to one letter and unfolded it. 'Ah…this one…' He coughed and a finger worked inside his cravat to ease it from his flushing neck. He did not relish broaching this subject. 'Umm…it seems a delicate matter, sir, and I would have left it to you to open had I known the nature of its content.' He pushed the paper over leather towards his employer. 'It had nothing on the outside to mark it as personal, I'm afraid.'

Marcus idly picked up the paper, quickly scanned it, let it drop, and for a moment made no comment. His expression remained inscrutable, yet, as though in disbelief at what he'd seen, he stared into space before snatching it up again and rereading it. Aware that Hepworth was discreetly regarding him over the rims of his spectacles, he let the paper fall back to the table. 'I think it must be a joke in very poor taste. You may ignore that one. I will personally deal with the matter.'

'Indeed, sir,' Hepworth agreed with a sage nod whilst diplomatically keeping his eyes on the documents he was shuffling.

Fifteen minutes later, and true to his word to be expedient, Hepworth had all the instructions he needed for the time being and told his employer so. Politely he took his leave and exited the room, quite aware that once he had gone his newly betrothed master would remain a while and again study the shocking note from Theodore Wyndham that invited Mr Speer a renewal of a marriage proposal to his cousin and ward, Miss Jemma Bailey.

Chapter Two

A rustle of skirts disturbed the quiet in the hallway. Marcus turned his head to glimpse a shimmering banner of chestnut hair waving behind a willowy figure dressed in blue. His harsh dark features became cruelly sardonic. He might not have seen Jemma Bailey in some while, but he'd immediately recognised her before she'd slipped out of sight. So the shameless chit was here, too, and so eager to discover if she'd hooked him that she'd been patrolling the hallway to spy on his arrival. Moments after she'd disappeared from view Marcus heard a door click softly shut as she concealed herself. His eyes remained riveted to the far end of the empty corridor as he battled with an urge to go after her, drag her from her hiding place and demand to know what in damnation she thought she was playing at. She'd turned his life upside down once before, and he wasn't about to let her do so again.

'Mr Wyndham will see you now, sir.' The butler had returned and, by repeating himself, drew Mr Speer's narrowed silver eyes from glaring into the distance.

Manwell led the way to a room adjacent to the bottom of the stairs and, conscious of the hostility crackling in the atmosphere, promptly withdrew. A moment later he crept back, putting his head to the mahogany panels. After a moment of intense concentration, as he strained to listen with his good ear, he realised he was being observed by one of the parlourmaids. Shooting upright, he stalked off.

'Please, sit down, you will feel calmer in a moment.' Maura tried to gently ease Jemma down into the chair by the window in her bedchamber.

Her cousin resisted any such attempt to be seated or to be calm and continued to stamp a channel in the rug's pile as back and forth across its width she went. Her face and manner betrayed her anguish, but failed to fully describe the maelstrom of conflicting emotions that kept her fists curling and uncurling at her sides. Her eyes were tightly closed to prevent tears of rage and mortification from again dribbling on to her cheeks.

'How could he do this to me!' Jemma gritted out for what seemed to be the hundredth time. 'That my own kin should humiliate me in such a way is…is insufferable! Abominable!'

Maura's hands were agitatedly twisting in front of her. Up until a short while ago she had maintained that there must be some mistake or misunderstanding. Her brother surely could not be guilty of such underhand behaviour. Of course, Theo had made no secret of the fact he wished to see his cousin Jemma wed before she got much older, or much poorer. But to go to such lengths as to try to arrange a match behind her back was indeed outrageous, as was his choice of prospective bride-grooms. Contacting spurned suitors from Jemma's past was undeniably embarrassing for her.

In her brother's defence Maura conceded that Theo had a point in thinking Jemma ought to pay more attention to getting herself a husband and children and less to squandering her time and money on charities for ruffians. Since Jemma had had her heart broken by her childhood sweetheart she'd shown no interest at all in a romantic involvement or a family of her own. 'Perhaps my brother believed it all to be for your own good.' Maura knew her loyalties were divided, so she decided she might as well side with her closest kin. 'I expect he hoped to help you,' she ventured diffidently, then shrank beneath Jemma's violent green gaze.

'Help me?' Jemma ejected the phrase in a strangled gasp. 'He wants to help himself, and well you know it. He's so desperate to get his hands on what is mine that he is careless of making me appear the most ridiculous creature in the whole of London.'

A crimson stain spread from Maura's neck to the roots of her mousy brown hair. It was well known in the family, and probably in wider circles, too, that upon marriage Jemma would forfeit her inheritance to the next male heir. Theo was the beneficiary and would take two properties and whatever else Jemma had left from John Bailey's original bequest.

Niggling doubts over her brother's motive had pricked at Maura's consciousness as soon as she'd learned more about the sorry affair that afternoon. But she'd chased them away. Theo would never stoop to act in so mercenary a fashion. He had simply grown impatient and impulsive because Jemma refused to encourage any gentleman to court her.

'I should not have run away.' Jemma marched across the room to swiftly snatch at the door handle. She held on to it while attempting to steady her breathing and boost her courage. 'I should go back downstairs now and tell Mr Speer that I had no hand in this. What will he say, do you think?' Trepidation trembled her tone. 'I cannot believe that Theo didn't know of his recent engagement,' she cried. 'If by some chance he did miss seeing it gazetted, Mr Speer could have remedied his ignorance in a letter. He didn't need to come in person to tell Theo what a fool he is. Oh, why is he here?'

'I remember he was very much taken with you. Perhaps he has come to offer for you after all.' Maura's tone veered between disbelief and optimism.

'Of course he has not!' Jemma disabused her pop-eyed cousin in a croak. 'He is going to marry Deborah Cleveland.' Her cousin's blunt suggestion had made Jemma's heart leap to her throat. Maura had touched on a very raw nerve by forcing her to acknowledge an idea that had already wormed its way into her own mind.

A poignant yearning had gripped Jemma's insides as soon as she'd heard the butler announce Theo's visitor. What if he *had* come to agree to her guardian's outrageous proposal? It was a thought that had refused to be ejected until the moment she'd caught a glimpse of him as she'd fled to the stairs.

Jemma cast her mind back to the terrifying sight of Marcus in the hallway. He had thankfully been too far away for her to properly read his expression, but every prowling pace he'd taken over the stone flags had impressed on her that he too was very angry indeed. Her stomach churned with the nauseating certainty that Marcus might believe, as had Philip Duncan, that Theo had been acting with her encouragement when he'd written those letters inviting gentlemen to renew their proposals to her. She'd had that awful information just an hour or so earlier, from the man himself.

Following a frosty confrontation with Lucy Duncan in the fabric warehouse, Lucy had been ashamed and repentant at having spread gossip about Jemma. However, she was adamant she had not told lies and had offered to take Jemma immediately to her brother so Philip might vouch for her honesty. At the lodging house they'd found Philip about to climb into his gig. Ushering them in to his lodging house hallway so they might be private, he'd rather sheepishly admitted that he *had* shown Graham Quick a note he'd received from Jemma's guardian. Jemma had demanded he go and get it so she could see the revolting evidence, but Philip had said he'd already thrown it on the fire. As Jemma had turned to leave he'd found the grace to mumble he was sorry for mentioning the matter to Graham Quick. Moments later he'd diluted his apology by adding that the message had clearly implied it came with her full agreement.

Following that awful revelation there had been nothing Maura could say that would deter Jemma from immediately confronting Theo about what he'd done. At the Wyndhams' town house in Hanover Square they'd found Theo looking very smug. Without a hint of remorse he'd told his enraged ward that he'd not only sent a letter to Philip Duncan, but to every one of the fellows he could bring to mind who was still unwed and had offered for Jemma in the past. In all, four letters had been sent. He'd even had the cheek to try to turn the tables on her and put her in the wrong. In a martyred tone he'd added that she'd put him to some considerable trouble by not dealing herself with the matter of getting off the shelf.

Before Jemma could properly express her disgust and outrage Mr Speer's arrival had been announced by Manwell. That information had stunned Jemma into silence. A moment later she'd bolted with just one horrifying thought in her mind: she had discovered the identity of another recipient of her guardian's scandalous letters.

'Mr Speer has simply come to tell Theo what he thinks of him…and me…' Jemma finally told Maura on a heavy sigh. 'One cannot blame him for that.' A moment later her spirit had again rallied. 'I wish he had just discarded the stupid, stupid letter and forgotten all about it as Philip Duncan did.'

'Ah…do come in, Speer. Glad to receive your message and your prompt visit, sir.' Theodore Wyndham's voice held a high note of confidence as he continued to nonchalantly pose against the high mantelpiece with an arm slung along its marble shelf.

Theo now appeared so indolent that it would have been hard to imagine a more docile individual. Never would one have guessed that just moments ago this gentleman had been simmering with temper whilst listening to his ward violently berate him for interfering in her life.

Jemma had discovered, sooner than Theo would have liked, his scheme to get her married before she com-

pletely ran through the Bailey inheritance. She'd turned
up like a whirlwind, moments before Marcus Speer was
due, making Theo fret that she might erupt in hysterics
just as the fellow arrived. He'd been worrying needlessly.
When his butler had announced Mr Speer's presence in
the hallway it was as though an invisible hand had dashed
a bucket of water over her. She'd drawn a shuddering
breath, taken on a ghastly pallor, then quietly fled from
Theo's study via the connecting door to the library as
though the hounds of hell snapped at her heels.

Now, as Theo watched his very welcome visitor close
the door, then begin to bear down on him with a startling
speed and purpose, he surged upright and fiddled at the
knot in his cravat. He could tell, before a conversation
had passed between them, that he'd misjudged this man's
reaction to his bold suggestion. Speer's swift steps
cracked against the boards like percussion pistol shots
and his expression looked lethal. Marcus's refusal to
return a greeting, or say anything at all, added to the air
of menace emanating from him, and Theo strove not to
betray by look or manner his alarm and disappointment.

So far he'd received just one reply; it had come from
this gentleman and had been delivered just hours ago.
From its few lines he'd only been able to glean that
Marcus demanded an audience that very afternoon.
Theo had been happy to grant him his wish and had,
whilst pacing to and fro excitedly awaiting his arrival,
persuaded himself that the fellow was eager because he
still harboured a *tenderesse* for Jemma despite the fact
that, in five years, she'd turned from a saucy minx in to
a tiresome bluestocking.

Along with the rest of the *ton*, he'd seen gazetted

Marcus Speer's engagement to Deborah Cleveland. Theo had dismissed it as an irrelevance. His letters had been ready, and he'd despatched every last one. Now, with Speer within striking distance of him, he belatedly paid heed to two vital facts: the fellow had a far superior height and breadth to his own and was renowned as a talented pugilist and, secondly, Deborah Cleveland was, undoubtedly, younger, sweeter, and richer than was his cousin Jemma.

'How do I look?' Jemma asked breathlessly as she pulled her coat this way and that to straighten it. Her hands next darted to her abundant locks to try to bring some order to the ruffled chestnut waves. 'Am I presentable? Are my cheeks stained with tears?' Jemma was of above average height for a young woman and of necessity dipped her head to gaze at her reflection in the glass on the dressing chest. Watery jade eyes were rapidly blinked to clear them and briskly she rubbed at her complexion with her fingertips to erase any sign that she'd been crying. Her appearance had suffered during the past hours due to her acute distress. But now, having conquered the worst of her shock, and brought her wrath under control—for the time being, she certainly had not finished with Theo!—she was ready to set another gentleman straight on the matter of her guardian's shocking plot, and her lack of a part in it.

'I don't think you should do that!' Maura whispered with a throb of foreboding. To her mind Jemma was still in a stupor over it all and not thinking straight. Having listened, drop-jawed, to Jemma's determination to loiter somewhere outside in Hanover Square in order to ambush Mr Speer as he left the house, Maura could only foresee such an action bringing more trouble down on her cousin's head. She could sympathise with Jemma's need to immediately set the record straight, but such a highly irregular scene was bound to be spotted by a chinwag who later would gleefully pass on what they'd witnessed.

Graham Quick had no doubt already passed on in the gentlemen's clubs what Philip Duncan had told him. Soon those fellows' wives would know too that negotiations were underway to get Miss Jemma Bailey a husband. If it was reported that Jemma had accosted a gentleman known to have once offered for her, and one who had recently become engaged to another lady, her name would be mud. The Clevelands were an important and popular family at the heart of the *ton*. Jemma would be labelled a shameless hussy who was trying to steal Deborah's fiancé. She would be cut dead by everyone, and her disgrace would haunt her for very many years.

'If you think waiting quietly outside to state my case the greater risk to the Bailey name than making a scene within these walls I shall simply go back to Theo's study and say what I must now. It will be a nasty argument with your brother, I promise you. If Theo is made to look a fool in front of his visitor, so be it. He deserves all that is coming to him.'

'No! You must not do that! It would never do to act so disrespectfully.' Maura gulped in panic. 'Theo is your guardian...your family, after all.'

'Indeed he is,' Jemma agreed bitterly. 'Yet he has shown me no respect or consideration in acting so sly and underhand.'

Now that Theo had started scheming to arrange a marriage of convenience for Jemma it would be wise to leave it to him alone to finish it, so Maura thought. People would consider it an appropriate duty for a guardian to try to arrange his ward's future security by marrying her off, especially when the woman in question had her début a good few years behind her. Maura relayed that advice to Jemma, then let out a doleful sigh when it simply caused her cousin to frown and violently shake her head.

'Oh, you're too late,' Maura cried joyfully, interrupting her cousin who had been ready to quit the room. Maura had been standing close to the window and, twitching the curtain aside, she peeked at the top of a dark glossy head and impressively broad shoulders as Marcus swiftly descended the stone steps and strode off.

'He is gone already?' Jemma cried in disappointment. She darted to the window and craned her neck to check for herself that her quarry was on the move.

Maura's sigh of relief that the immediate threat was removed only fired Jemma's determination to impress on Marcus the truth. Now that she felt more composed, she regretted having let shock and humiliation cow her. She ought to have stayed in Theo's study instead of scampering away like a frightened little girl. She'd had more courage at seventeen, she inwardly scolded. Then she'd brazenly borne the brunt of her papa's chastisement, and the disapproval of the *ton*. She'd deserved both, too, for she'd believed her heart, her loyalty, belonged to another man when she'd flirted outrageously with Marcus during that heady Season when she'd made her début. She had led him on, taken everything he had offered as her friend and suitor, and now, older and wiser, she felt thoroughly ashamed of her selfish behaviour.

This time she was innocent of any wrongdoing, yet she had crumpled and cravenly run away instead of immediately mounting her defence and protesting against the injury done her. She should have stayed and made her scheming guardian admit that he'd acted without her knowledge or consent. She should have made it clear that she had no intention of entering a marriage of convenience with any man, no matter how convenient it might be for Theo that she did so.

With Maura's groan of dismay echoing in her ears Jemma impulsively darted to the door. Within a moment she was down the stairs and out in to the street, heedless of Manwell's dropping jaw as she sailed past him in a whirl of chestnut curls and swirling blue skirts.

Once on the pavement she squinted against the sunlight. She pivoted on the spot, hurried many yards one way, all the time looking here and there, then retraced her steps and rushed in the opposite direction. She paused on the corner and looked about. Of Marcus there was no sign, and he would be easy to distinguish amongst the strollers out enjoying the spring sunshine. With his lofty height and devilishly dark good looks he was an outstanding specimen of a man.

Marcus watched from the opposite side of the street as Jemma searched for him. And he knew it was he she was after as she flew hither and thither. She was retracing her steps along the pavement towards the Wyndhams' house and he wondered if she would mount the steps and go in again. His mouth twisted cynically as he wondered whether Theo Wyndham had, as a last resort, sent her out to try to lure him back. She passed the Wyndhams' door and kept to a slow pace, her head lowered as though she was both disappointed and distracted by her own thoughts. His narrowed silver eyes kept her in their sights as he moved a little away from the parasol his mistress seemed intent on twirling over them both whilst they stood beside her barouche.

'Will you come with me to the theatre tonight?' Lady Pauline Vaux repeated. A delightful dimple appeared in one cheek as she tilted her head to give Marcus a persuasive smile.

'I'm afraid I can't. My uncle is now mortally ill. I await some bad news from his physician,' Marcus told her.

He made to hand her back into her transport, but it seemed Lady Vaux was not yet ready to say farewell to her lover. She murmured her sympathy at knowing that the Earl of Gresham was on his deathbed. The fact that Marcus was soon to become an aristocrat, and a good deal richer, was neither here nor there to her. He'd made it plain at the start of the liaison that he'd never marry her, so there was no status to share, no future son to groom to be worthy of his earldom. As for the rest, Marcus was already rich and powerful enough to satisfy any young impoverished widow's yen for a pampered life.

Earlier that afternoon Pauline had been visiting her friend, Cressida Forbes, who lived on the edge of Hanover Square. Having quit her friend's company after a delightful episode taking tea and sharing gossip, she'd travelled just yards when she'd clapped eyes on Marcus striding along and instructed her driver to stop the

barouche. Having beckoned him, but failed to persuade
him to get up with her, she'd alighted to delay his departure and try to charm him in to escorting her to the
theatre. But he'd seemed too stern and preoccupied to
talk or tell her much about his reason for being in the
vicinity. Once or twice Pauline had glanced about to see
what had taken his interest for it seemed something was
causing him to stare off in to the distance.

'I shall come and see you soon,' Marcus cut in to
Pauline's musing, making her dimple her thanks at him.
Taking his mistress's arm, he guided her firmly towards
the barouche and helped her alight. He raised a hand in
salute as the conveyance pulled off steadily into the traffic.
Then his eyes swooped to the willowy female figure,
some way off now. Crossing the road, he started after her.

Chapter Three

A strange sensation prickled at Jemma's nape, making her absently scuff her fingers over it. She half-turned, sure she was being fanciful in imagining someone was following her. Out of the corner of her eye she glimpsed a tall male figure, darkly dressed. Her heart vaulted to her throat, and she came to a spontaneous halt before twisting fully about. In petrified silence she stared at Marcus Speer as he continued his lazy powerful pursuit of her. Instinctively she wheeled about and hastened on. The next instant she was inwardly berating herself for having so obviously betrayed her fright at the sight of him. Beneath her aching ribs her heart continued thudding erratically, making her softly suck in air. Slowly she brought some order to the chaotic thoughts whirling in her head, and her pace became less frantic.

A short while ago she had wanted to find him, had flown from Theo's house like a wild hoyden to look for him in the street. Now he was deliberately…temptingly…within reach. An awful suspicion occurred to her that he might have observed her fruitless efforts to

ambush him in Hanover Square. He was close enough
for her to have read his expression. It was mortifying to
acknowledge that he'd every right to that slanting,
sardonic smile. By touting her about to any fellow
who'd take her as a wife, Theo had made her seem weak
and risible. She'd not helped disperse that perception by
cravenly turning tail not once but twice this afternoon
in Marcus Speer's presence.

He knew she wanted to speak to him so he was pre-
senting himself to her on a plate, taunting her to swallow
her pride and approach him. Indignation ignited fire in
her veins, strengthening her composure. She put up her
chin, took a deep breath and, confident her blush was
fading, pivoted about. Purposely she marched towards
him and halted just in front of him. She flicked up her
face to boldly meet his gaze. Immediately her eyes
darted aside. She hadn't been prepared for the over-
whelming effect being this close to him had on her.
Silver eyes that looked forbidding yet achingly familiar
had been ruthlessly watching her mouth making the
first words she had uttered to him in almost five years
emerge in a strangled gasp.

'Why are you following me?'

'Why were you looking for me?'

'I was not!' The spontaneous lie sent a fresh burst of
betraying blood to stain her skin, and her eyes to swerve
back to glance on his.

'Were you not?' he drily enquired.

'You were just at my cousin's house,' she rushed on,
hoping to cover her confusion.

'So were you.'

'Surely you arrived in a carriage? Why are you not in

it instead of dogging my footsteps?' She recalled attack was said to be the best form of defence and certainly it seemed to be boosting her confidence and courage.

'As you were spying on me and saw me arrive, Miss Bailey, I suspect you know I arrived on foot in Hanover Square.'

'I was not spying on you, sir. And I certainly was not awaiting your arrival,' Jemma fumed in righteous anger.

'What a happy coincidence then that we both were within your guardian's house when I told him, amongst other things, that I won't marry you,' Marcus drawled. 'I imagine he passed that message on, and that's why you were outside searching for me to try to change my mind.' An insolent grey gaze slipped over her lush figure. 'I'm intrigued to know how you intended to persuade me to do that.' His voice was sultry with amusement, his eyes darkening dangerously behind long, concealing lashes. 'If you use the right approach, Miss Bailey, I might hear you out.'

A fiery blush raged from Jemma's throat to her hairline. She'd winced on hearing his scornful rejection; now she visibly flinched for a second time. How dare he mock her so! Any thoughts she'd had of offering her apologies for Theo's despicable behaviour were expelled from her mind. This hateful brute now owed her an apology for speaking to her, looking at her as though she were some dockside wench!

'I think I must put you straight on several things, sir,' she finally blurted in a suffocated voice. Her fingers formed fists and were held rigidly quivering at her sides. 'Firstly, indeed it was a coincidence that we were at the Wyndhams together, but a happy one…

never! Secondly, I've not received any report from my cousin of the outcome of your visit. I do not require one, for it is neither here nor there what you said to him. Theo has had the disgraceful impertinence to attempt to meddle in my life, but I will not allow him to do so. *I* shall decide if and when I marry.' Jemma drew a deep breath and threw back her head to slam her eyes on his impaling steely gaze. 'I was at his home just now to impress on him that fact and for no other reason that concerns you. Secondly,' she uttered on a shuddering breath.

'Thirdly…' Marcus corrected softly.

'What…?'

'I've heard your second point,' he reminded her with studied solemnity. 'You weren't aware of the outcome of my visit…'

'Umm…oh…yes…thirdly…' Jemma stuttered. 'Thirdly…' she resumed in a muted tone, the wind temporarily sucked out of her sails. A darting glance at his cynical expression soon had her temper again simmering. 'Thirdly,' she snapped icily, 'there is nothing of which I care to persuade you except perhaps this: I find your arrogant assumption that I wanted to extricate a marriage proposal from you most unpleasant. I believed I had already made it clear some years ago that I had rejected you as a husband. Nothing has happened since to change my mind. Good day, sir.' Jemma had managed just one triumphant pace away from him when a firm grip on her wrist arrested her, spinning her neatly around.

'Are you sure nothing has changed your mind?' he taunted softly. 'Wyndham seemed quite taken with the notion of having a Countess in the family. He implied the idea appealed to you, too, now you're slightly less immature.'

'Let me assure you it does not,' Jemma hissed, whitening with wrath at his insulting implication that she was ambitious for a title and childlike to boot. 'And let me assure you of something else. My guardian is also quite taken with the idea of laying his hands on what is mine,' she informed him acidly. 'It makes no difference to him if I marry a noble or a nobody, just as long as he has the marriage lines as proof that he can legally claim my property.' With a wrench she had her wrist from his grip. A phantom touch of firm fingers tingled warmly on her skin, making her rub in irritation at the spot. 'I believe, sir, that in your arrogance you assume you are the only gentleman who received a letter from my guardian.' She could tell by the hardening of his features that he had not heard rumours in clubs about the others, nor had Theo put him wise to it. A harsh little laugh bubbled in her throat. 'You may or may not recall that you were just one of many gentlemen who offered for me five years ago. Every one of those fellows who lacks a wife has been invited by my doting cousin to renew his proposal.' Jemma elevated her shapely little chin, looked up boldly into eyes that were glittering dangerously. 'I fear I must go on to dent your ego, Mr Speer…' she sighed with mock regret '…but say it I must: there is nothing special about you.'

'Except perhaps that I am no longer unattached, and well you and Wyndham know it,' Marcus returned quietly.

His answer was calm, and undeniably correct, yet oddly it disturbed Jemma more than a scathing outburst from him might have done.

* * *

Marcus could feel his temper rising, as was a part of his anatomy over which, it seemed, he had no control when in this little vixen's vicinity. She could infuriate a saint with her acid tongue, and he was tempted to haul the infuriating chit against him, but whether to kiss her or throttle her he wasn't sure. He hadn't been so close to her in five years, but he remembered well enough how she could stir his blood with just a saucy smile or a deliberately subtle scuffing of her skin on his. Once she'd captivated him to such an extent he'd risked ridicule when she'd rejected him. Inwardly he'd pined for her for a year; outwardly he'd seemed to become polite society's most predatory rake.

But he could admit to himself what he'd been keen to keep from others. At the time a girl barely out of the schoolroom had brought him to his knees—quite literally—he'd proposed in traditionally humble pose. Then she'd gone home to her swain to find a broken heart awaited her in Essex. When he'd heard about it he'd briefly felt a sense of malicious satisfaction that she'd tasted her own medicine. But much as he might have wanted to continue using the balm of vengeance, it had lost its efficaciousness, leaving him simply feeling bereft. He'd hoped her father might bring her back to London during the following Season. But she'd not appeared, and he'd wondered whether he might find the humility to travel to Essex and propose for a second time.

During those twelve dark months when his moods were unpredictable and his business dealings neglected, his uncle Solomon had watched quietly from the sidelines, keeping his own counsel on the matter of Miss Jemma Bailey. But Solomon had had no hesitation in taking him to task over bad business deals and impatiently had guided his nephew's investments back on course. Thus it had been left to Marcus alone to decide whether to swallow his pride and follow his heart or to salve his wounds in customary male fashion. His pride had won. He'd stayed in town and submerged his sorrows by carousing nightly with licentious friends and promiscuous women. After two years had passed he'd been sure he'd forgotten all about Jemma Bailey. At Christmas time, he'd travelled through Essex to see his mother and new stepfather in Norfolk and not once had it occurred to him during that trip to take a minor detour from his route and go past Thaxham House, John Bailey's small estate. His healthy ego had helped him survive his first disastrous encounter with falling in love. He'd been determined not to appear a maudlin fool in front of his family and friends. Thankfully he had not. And now he was over her.

Jemma fidgeted as the tense silence between them lengthened. She'd been very rude and regretted it. Yet she wasn't sure why she felt guilty when his implied insults had equalled her spoken ones. A moment ago she'd been ready to sweep away from him, feeling victorious. Now something about his attitude held her quiet and still. Instinctively she knew what was in his mind. He was brooding on what had happened between them five years ago.

She glanced about. Passers-by were starting to take an interest in them. Sidelong glances and sibilant whispers alerted her senses to potential trouble. The last thing she wanted was to stir more gossip.

'Shall we walk and talk, Miss Bailey?' Marcus had also become conscious that they were under observation. With studied gallantry he offered Jemma his arm. 'It might be wise if we do not appear to be involved in a tiff in the middle of the street.'

Jemma hesitated but a moment later nodded. She knew he was heading home, and so was she. Her small town house on Pereville Parade was not fashionably situated, whereas his mansion on Beaufort Place was in a prime spot. But they had to walk in the same general direction before their paths diverged. It would be silly for one of them to stay a step or two in front or behind to avoid the other's company. She knew too that it was sensible advice to maintain an appearance of civil acquaintance rather than one of being at loggerheads. Her small fingers hovered over the crook of his arm as a poignant feeling fluttered in her chest. Once she'd adored having the feel of his clothed muscle beneath her hand when they'd danced or promenaded. Yet all the while she'd felt so terribly guilty that she'd found him attractive for she'd believed Robert to be patiently awaiting her return to Essex so they might elope.

'What did you say to Theo?' Jemma forced her eyes up to his and her mind away from painful memories. She looked at him, *really* looked at him, and the ruggedly hewn, handsome features close to her made icy fire streak through her veins. He looked only slightly older than he had at twenty-six. There were a few silver threads in the thick blackish hair springing back at his temples and the grooves bracketing his thin yet sensual lips seemed a mite deeper than when last she'd studied his face. Her eyes diverted to the long firm fingers close to her own and unwanted images of being intimately touched by them made blood fizz beneath her skin. She'd been wanton—at such a tender age, too! It was little wonder that a moment ago he'd looked at her, spoken to her with such lustful amusement. He hadn't forgotten her lack of restraint either.

She hadn't been wholly to blame! The excuse ran back and forth in her mind, calming her embarrassment. She'd been a naïve young débutante under the spell of an older, more experienced man. He'd known exactly how to tease a response from her on those nights she'd allowed him to take more liberties than any young innocent ought. Had her papa known what he'd done to her beneath intoxicating moonlight on midsummer evenings he'd have called for his pistols. She recalled the whispered cautions from envious young friends when Marcus had invited her to step outside for a little air at the Cranleighs' ball: *He's a rake...a terrible flirt...tell him no...he'll break your heart.* In the event he had, but she'd had no one to blame but herself and circumstances had forced her to lick her wounds in private.

At seventeen she could have been married to the dashing heir to an earldom. Instead she had yielded to her conscience and gone dutifully back to Essex and to Robert Burnham, whereupon she'd had her loyalty tossed back in her face. But by then it was too late to contact Marcus and humbly say she'd changed her mind. She'd known him only a matter of a few months but during that time she'd learned enough about his character to understand he'd refuse to be her second-choice husband.

Within a week of returning home she was thankful she'd not written to him, abasing herself with pleas and promises and the laying bare of her soul. She'd had a letter from her cousin Maura describing the latest tattle doing the rounds. It had concerned Marcus and a new opera dancer who had been the toast of Drury Lane. It seemed to Jemma that for many months after that first awful communication every letter she received from her cousin contained a fresh tale of Marcus Speer's debauchery.

Finally Jemma had accepted that he hadn't fallen properly in love with her, as she had with him. He had never told her he loved her, and now she knew why that was—for him it had been just an infatuation and he'd settled too quickly on her to fill the role of his wife. She'd thanked her lucky stars she had not married a man who would doubtless betray her with a string of mistresses before they'd reached their first wedding anniversary.

A dispiriting truth had then settled on Jemma: Marcus would never come, in true romantic style, to Thaxham House and rescue her from her sorrow and loneliness. He would, at some time, be an Earl, but he wasn't the noble hero of her wistful dreams.

As though Marcus could guess at her memories his mouth tilted into half a smile and a smouldering grey gaze was slanted at her softly skewed mouth.

'I thought it was neither here nor there to you what I said to your guardian.' His smile deepened as she looked away with a regretful frown. She'd been so lost in her private thoughts that she'd forgotten she'd announced herself uninterested in the outcome of the heated meeting he'd had with Theo. 'I said nothing to your cousin that could be repeated to a demure young lady.'

'In sending those letters Theo acted outrageously and without my knowledge or consent.' Jemma's voice was hoarse and forceful, her cheeks burning. His mocking levity made it clear he considered her far from *demure*. If he was hinting at her wild behaviour at seventeen, he'd a right to his scorn. But she wouldn't have him think her a brazen hussy now because she had designs on trying to steal him from his fiancée. 'Do you believe me?' Jemma gazed earnestly at him.

'Why should I?' Marcus enquired casually. 'From past experience I would say you hardly inspire me to put trust in you.'

It was out! The first heavy hint from him that he had not forgotten or forgiven how she'd led him on like a common tease. Annoyingly she felt spontaneous tears start to her eyes. She swung her face aside so he might not see them.

Marcus slanted a look down on the top of a bonnet from which tumbled an artless array of thick chestnut curls. He felt the embers of desire within him become hotter. She looked little different to how she had as a teenage débutante. Perhaps her figure was fuller and her face slimmer, honed to classical perfection. But her little gestures, the tone of her voice, the success she'd had in rousing him, enticing him—those bittersweet things seemed the same. She was beautiful, spirited…and he realised with some irritation that he still wanted her.

Marcus dragged his eyes from Jemma's alluring presence as a familiar sight at the edge of his vision drew his attention. Beneath his breath he cursed. From the moment he'd read Wyndham's astonishing letter this afternoon, thoughts of his mortally ill uncle had been pushed to the back of his mind. Now he could see a carriage bearing the Gresham crest slowly patrolling the street as though the coachmen were searching for someone. He knew they were looking for him. Dr Robertson had sent for him earlier than he'd expected and he'd been away from home when the message had arrived. He'd told Perkins, his butler, he'd be visiting Wyndham and would be no more than one hour. The coachmen had doubtless been despatched to Hanover Square to find him.

A feeling of deep remorse washed over him, yet still, to his shame, he felt reluctant to quit Jemma's side. Abruptly he removed her arm from his. 'I think we must continue this conversation another time, Miss Bailey.' He executed a curt bow. 'Unfortunately I have pressing matters to attend to.' With that terse farewell he forced himself to take two crisp backward paces so a space was immediately between them. A moment later he'd stepped past and was striding towards the carriage, raising a hand to hail it as he went.

'Indeed, there is no need to talk further about any of this, sir.' Jemma felt mortified to be so abruptly abandoned. But he was moving with such speed and purpose she could tell that the sharp words she'd sent after him had gone unheeded. A knot of sorrow tightened in her stomach. She had a feeling that if they'd continued walking and talking just a little longer perhaps they might have gone their separate ways more contentedly than they'd come together. As it was, nothing about the situation had improved. Pulling her bonnet brim low to shield her hot, watery eyes, she plunged her hands into her coat pockets and moved swiftly on.

Chapter Four

Marcus paused on the threshold to his uncle's bed-chamber to dart an astonished enquiring glance at the physician. A glimmering hope that his uncle had made a miraculous recovery was dashed as Dr Robertson slowly shook his head. The prognosis was the same despite the fact the Earl of Gresham was once more conscious and propped up on a sumptuous array of satin bolsters and pillows.

On one side of the bed, ensconced in an armchair, was an elegant, elderly lady. Marcus had expected Mrs Paulson would still be here. She had been sitting quietly embroidering in the very same position when he had quit the sickroom earlier that day. He gave her a nod and a wonky smile, hoping that it adequately conveyed that her constant presence pleased him.

Victoria Paulson had been his uncle's mistress for three decades and was a similar age to Solomon. At times Marcus had wondered whether, if the couple had come together sooner in life, when Victoria was young enough to bear children, she might have given Solomon a son. They would then have married to legitimise the union and the child, and the course of his own life might have taken a very different turn.

Having pressed Solomon's hand and returned Marcus a hushed greeting, Victoria rose from her chair and left the gentlemen alone.

Solomon's exhausted smile for his nephew was curtailed as a cough rattled out of him. On hearing his master gasping, a servant sprang forwards, thrusting out a beaker of milk. Solomon flapped feebly at the fellow. 'If you've got nothing stronger to offer me, then go away,' he wheezed and tugged a burgundy velvet coverlet against a chest that was pumping erratically. 'Might as well let me have a brandy,' he threw peevishly at Dr Robertson. 'Ain't as if it's going to kill me.'

Dr Robertson relented, gesturing to the footman to carry out his patient's request. At that Solomon found enough energy to weakly grin and brush together his dry palms.

Marcus swiftly approached the dais at the centre of his uncle's bedchamber upon which was set a huge four-poster bed. He stopped with one hand splayed against a square mahogany post, feeling as awkward and apprehensive as he'd been at eight years old when introduced to his noble guardian for the first time. Instinctively he knew that this was to be their final meeting in this life.

Solomon beckoned him closer with a fragile-looking finger but, when Marcus immediately extended his hand, it was gripped with surprising strength.

'You look much improved, sir,' Marcus began. 'Perhaps cognac is not wise as you are a little better.'

The old boy exhaled a breathless chuckle and set free his nephew's fingers. 'Looks ain't everything, y'know,' Solomon imparted in a droll whisper. 'I'm still dying. I'm still able to appreciate a good brandy, too.' Marcus's hand had dropped to rest on the velvet coverlet and he gave it a fond pat. 'Don't look so miserable, m'boy. I'm ready. I've had a good innings. I saw off three score years 'n ten eight years ago. That's six years more'n Patricia achieved.' An increased glitter appeared in his sunken black eyes as he recalled his spinster sister. Patricia had pre-deceased him just last summer despite being in fine fettle up until two weeks before her maid had discovered her dead in bed. 'And it's a deal more years than your father saw.'

Marcus bowed his head, nodding it slowly in acknowledgement of the sorrow they shared at Rufus Speer's unconscionably early demise at the age of thirty-two.

His father had been a military man and away on campaign for a good deal of Marcus's early childhood. Major Rufus Speer had been killed in action a few days after his only child's eighth birthday. Thereafter, Rufus's brother, Solomon, had taken Marcus under his wing and treated him like an adopted son. It was widely held that Solomon Speer, Earl of Gresham, had felt it unnecessary to marry in order to produce an heir. In his eyes he'd had one since the day his younger brother had died with a Frenchman's bullet lodged in his chest.

'I know I've said it before,' Solomon whispered, 'but he'd have been mighty proud of you, m'boy.'

'He'd have been equally proud of you, and grateful for what you've done for me, as I am,' Marcus returned simply. 'I should have told you that more often than I have.'

'Don't get maudlin on me.' Solomon clucked his tongue in mock irritation. He gave the hand resting on the bed another affectionate pat. 'As for Rufus... I would have expected as much from him had our stars been swapped. He was a good brother. He wouldn't have let me down. So, like it or not, I had no choice but to take you on and make the best of things.' Solomon's doleful tone was at odds with the twinkling eyes that settled with paternal pride on his beloved nephew.

Marcus mirrored his uncle's wry grimace. Solomon was requesting that the full extent of his dues stay, as ever, unuttered. No fuss, no fanfare, no expression of the great affection that bound them as close as father and son. If that was how Solomon wanted it to be to the end, so be it. Marcus simply wanted to grant this finest of gentleman everything he desired during their precious final moments.

The branched candelabra set on a dressing chest was throwing wavering light on his uncle's face, highlighting the patches of feverish colour on his parchment-like cheeks. As Solomon sank back further in to his downy pillows, Marcus could tell that his little show of strength, his lively conversation, had sapped his vitality. A piercing glance at the doctor, grimly vigilant, answered Marcus's unspoken question. His uncle was unlikely to rally from unconsciousness a second time.

'Had a visitor this afternoon—no, I had two,' Solomon corrected himself with a flick of a finger.

Marcus found a suitable spot on the bed and, careful not to disturb his uncle, perched on the edge. He felt tightness in his chest and a lump forming in his throat, but he would not allow mournfulness to mar what little time was left. There would be days a-plenty to indulge his grief. 'Let me guess on that,' he said, mock thoughtful. 'Munro came to chivvy you in to letting him have the chestnut while you're still able to sign the sale sheet.'

Solomon's desiccated lips sprang apart in a silent guffaw. Finally he knuckled his eyes and gasped, 'The old rogue would, too—he knows I'm about to pop off.' He wagged a finger. 'Don't you sell that little mare to him either, when I'm gone,' the Earl instructed his heir with feigned anxiety. 'Cost me a pretty penny and it's your duty now, y'know, to maintain the Gresham reputation as the finest stables in the land.'

'And so I shall,' Marcus promised and gripped at his uncle's hand to lend him support as he fidgeted and tried to draw himself up in bed.

Once settled again, Solomon opened his beady eyes and regarded Marcus with brooding intensity. 'Cleveland came to see me this afternoon; so did Walters.'

Marcus knew that his future father-in-law was an acquaintance of his uncle's. So was Aaron Walters, who was also the Earl's stockbroker. Aaron was known as a stalwart of White's club and an incorrigible gossip whilst in his cups within its walls. Marcus had a feeling that his uncle was about to recount to him something of interest that Walters had told him. He further surmised he might have an inkling of the tale's content. But Solomon approached the matter of the gossip surrounding Theo Wyndham's outrageous letters from a different tack to the one Marcus had been anticipating.

'I know I said that before I turned up me toes it'd be nice to know you'd continue the Gresham line…. What

I didn't expect was that you'd settle on the first pretty lass you bumped in to at Almack's.'

'And nor have I done so,' Marcus replied lightly. He was aware that beneath his uncle's heavy lids his old eyes were fixed on him.

The footman appeared and gave the Earl a glass half-filled with brandy. A moment later the servant and the doctor discreetly withdrew to a corner of the room, leaving uncle and nephew in private.

'You courted Deborah Cleveland for a very little time… Could've filled it to the brim…' he tacked on whilst rotating his glass to eye its mellow contents from various angles. Despite his grumble he sipped, smacked his lips in appreciation, then nestled the glass in a gnarled fist curled on the coverlet.

'I knew straight away she would be suitable.'

'Suitable…?' Solomon echoed quizzically.

'Yes…' Marcus corroborated mildly. 'Do you think she is not?'

'I think it is not for me to say what a man needs in a woman with whom he must share his life and his children.' Solomon took another careful, savouring sip of brandy.

'Is Gregory Cleveland having second thoughts about marrying his daughter to me?' Marcus asked. He recalled that his uncle had said the Viscount had visited the sickroom earlier and wondered if doubts had been voiced about the match. Marcus knew without any conceit that he was worthy of being regarded as a good catch, but so was Deborah Cleveland, who would bring her husband a large dowry and equally impressive connections to his own.

'Gregory seems pleased as punch with the arrangement; he says Julia is equally delighted and eager to have you as her son-in-law.'

Marcus nodded, his mood little altered on knowing that his in-laws thoroughly approved of him. He was, however, glad to know his uncle hadn't been bothered by any aspect of the forthcoming nuptials. His relief was short-lived.

'Yet something is not right,' Solomon murmured, his lids falling over sunken, watching eyes.

'Perhaps the Clevelands suspect Deborah might change her mind.' It was a level statement, no hint apparent that Marcus had a suspicion why his fiancée might want to do so. Neither did the possibility of her crying off seem to bother him.

'Cleveland said nothing of the sort to me,' Solomon answered. 'Do you think the lass might get cold feet?'

'My offer was accepted quickly. Perhaps a mite too quickly.' Marcus shrugged, added mildly, 'She is very young; perhaps she would have liked to enjoy more of her début unattached with her friends and the gallants doing the rounds of the balls and parties. I don't want to spoil her fun. A betrothal of about a year is quite acceptable to me if that's what she wants.'

'You sound besotted by your lady love,' Solomon offered drily. 'Cleveland did say he hoped you might find the time to turn up and join them at another of the grand functions soon.'

Marcus smiled at the irony in his uncle's weak voice. So the Viscount had made a little complaint after all—damn him!

When his engagement had first been announced, Marcus had shown his commitment to it by accompa-

nying Deborah and her family to several notable occasions. But once they had been properly established as a
couple he'd discreetly withdrawn to the company of his
friends and his mistress. He had little liking for the
vacuous social whirl that was a part of the annual
London Season. Usually he would not be seen dead in
such a place as Almack's ballroom, but this year it had
proved its point even to a hardened cynic such as he. He
had found his future bride there. With that in mind he
realised he would be grateful if Deborah remained satisfied with the arrangement between them. He hoped
never to again set foot in the place.

About a month ago Dr Robertson had confided in
him that the Earl would probably not see Michaelmas.
Marcus had immediately set out to find himself a wife
of whom he was confident his uncle would approve as
the mother of future Gresham heirs. Deborah was the
daughter of a gentleman Solomon liked and respected.
His intention had been to content his uncle by starting
the process of continuing the Gresham line with a lady
of quality.

'So you're happy, then?' The Earl casually swirled
the amber liquid in his glass.

'Do you think I'm not?'

'I remember a time when you were not,' Solomon
said softly. 'Strangely I was reminded of that time just
this afternoon, by Aaron Walters.' Again his uncle's
hooded gaze fixed on him. 'Tell me, did you receive one
of Wyndham's strange letters that begged for marriage
offers for his ward?'

There was a slight pause before Marcus murmured
an affirmative.

'I sent a message that Dawkins was to look for you in Hanover Square if you were not at home,' Solomon informed him. 'I thought you might head straight off to Wyndham's house to have it out with the chump.'

'He's always been an idiot.' Marcus's muttered contempt emerged through splayed fingers supporting his chin.

'Maybe so…but he'd have been your kin had Jemma Bailey agreed to marry you.'

'I recall I thanked my lucky stars she'd had the decency to refuse,' Marcus said exceedingly drily.

'Eventually you might have done that,' Solomon gently reminded him. 'But for a long time I think you considered the lass worth the burden of her strange family. I never gave you my opinion on that child, did I?'

'It doesn't matter now,' Marcus said mildly.

'Maybe it does,' the Earl differed in a hoarse whisper.

Marcus could see his uncle again tiring as his bony head slumped back to be bolstered by plump pillows. 'That's all forgotten,' he soothed, gripping at Solomon's hand in emphasis. 'I simply went to see Wyndham to tell him that I thought his impertinence and his timing atrocious. I wouldn't want Deborah or her parents to be upset by ludicrous gossip. Wyndham claimed he'd not seen the engagement gazetted.'

'Did you land him a facer?' Solomon croaked, his eyes alight with mischief.

'Nothing quite so severe—he's smaller than me.'

Again the Earl wheezed a laugh. 'The gossip has it that Miss Bailey was in on it.'

'The letter made it seem that way.'

'Do you think she was?'

'No,' Marcus answered. 'I think Wyndham lied about that too.'

'He sent four, you know.'

'Do you know who were the other recipients?' Marcus immediately asked.

Solomon gave him a look that bordered on being smug. 'I do. And my guess is that one of those fellows will take up the offer. Walters tells me she's still a beauty, if a bit stand-offish and getting on in years.'

'She's only twenty-two,' Marcus mildly protested, making more brilliant a knowing glint in his uncle's dying eyes. Marcus looked at the ceiling, casually repeated, 'So which other gentlemen have been approached to take Wyndham's ward off his hands?'

'Matthew Hambling and Philip Duncan are contenders. Neither, so I hear, have a notion to take on a wife at present. But Stephen Crabbe has my money on getting past the post. I remember the two of you nearly came to blows over the girl.'

Marcus glanced away to where the doctor was sitting in a chair, his head bowed towards the hands clasped in his lap as though he was dozing.

'I don't think she had a hand in it either,' Solomon remarked. 'Wyndham's after her inheritance, you know. She'll be penniless before the ink dries on the marriage lines. And if Crabbe thinks Wyndham'll settle a dowry on her he'll be disappointed.'

'I know he only wants her money.' A mirthless smiled moved Marcus's mouth. 'Yet Theo Wyndham is arrogant enough to think he's concocted a convincing tale of onerous moral duty.'

'I rather liked Miss Jemma Bailey.' The earl's quiet

opinion drew Marcus's eyes immediately to him. 'I liked her mother too and never held with all that scandal-mongering talk about the Baileys years ago. Eccentric, indeed they were. But one cannot condemn a couple for wanting to escape the hell of a bad marriage.' Solomon fingered the rim of his glass. 'Do you recall when we visited Paris some years ago and spotted Veronica Bailey strolling by the Seine with her Count?'

Marcus nodded.

'It was the first occasion I'd seen the fellow close up. Handsome devil, wasn't he?'

Again Marcus gave a nod.

'I thought he had a look of you about him,' Solomon suggested. 'Different colour eyes, of course.'

'Are you saying you think he took an interest in my mother, too?'

Solomon guffawed so abruptly it made him cough, but he flapped away the doctor who'd sprung, startled, from his chair.

'You always did make me laugh, you know, m'boy.' He sobered, took a deep breath. 'I think you know what I mean so I'll say no more on it. I recall that Veronica was a good-looking woman and still in her prime when she went off with him. I can understand why John Bailey felt so bitter.'

'He was hardly in a position to moralise considering he'd kept Mrs Brannigan in comfort before and after his marriage to Veronica. The tragedy of it was for their daughters rather than for them. When Jemma Bailey made her début she was not always wanted everywhere because of the scandal they'd caused.'

'I recall you tried to compensate for that by showing

everybody just how much you liked her. You took very little notice of the family's calamities or its sullied name.'

'It made no difference to me what problems her parents had had. It was she I—' He bit off the words and finished quietly with, 'It made no difference to me.'

'Ah…but it would make a difference to a lot of people—people who marry for status and convenience rather than love,' Solomon said forcefully, leaning forwards to emphasise his point. The exertion made him collapse back on to the pillows, and with a start Marcus was on his feet, his soothing fingers at his uncle's face, moving back the wispy white hair from his forehead.

Silently the doctor had come up behind. He tried to ease the glass from his patient's rigid grip, but the Earl refused to let it go.

'Pull me up!' Solomon insisted weakly, trying to use his elbows to manoeuvre upright in the bed. 'I'll finish m'drink before lights out or be damned.'

Marcus gently eased his uncle's wasted body up to nestle on feathers once more.

'Off you go now,' Solomon sighed out. 'Robertson will see to me.'

'I'll stay…' Marcus croaked, attempting to swallow a burning lump lodged in his throat. He knew the time now was very near.

'No!' Solomon gasped. A smile quivered on his purplish lips. 'No,' he repeated gently. 'Some things a man must do by himself. Dying…choosing a wife…' He gulped back the small amount left in his glass and, satisfied, gave it over to the doctor. Then he lay back and closed his eyes. 'Go…' he told Marcus on an exhalation. 'Marcus!' the faint, urgent cry arrested his nephew at the foot of the bed. 'From the moment you came to me,' Solomon ejected the words with difficulty, 'your future happiness was the purpose in my life.' He sucked in a ragged breath. 'Now our journey together is done…I go on alone.' He panted rapidly, striving for the breath to finish, 'But you know where happiness lies…'

A groan of pain seemed to issue from deep within his uncle's being and it made Marcus instinctively rush back to clasp one of his freckled hands in support.

'I shall make him as comfortable as I can,' Dr Robertson promised gravely. 'Please, you must go or he will fret and try to struggle on if he thinks you still here. Mrs Paulson will stay until the end.'

Marcus nodded, his eyes feeling gritty and afire with grief. He stooped to kiss his uncle on both sunken cheeks, then in instinctive obeisance he lowered his forehead to touch together their brows.

Chapter Five

'If it wasn't for the respect I had for the old Earl I'd go right now and offer the new one his choice of weapons.'

Theo Wyndham continued gingerly fingering the bruise on his neck. It had been almost a week since Marcus Speer had turned up in Hanover Square and gripped him by the throat whilst informing him in awful tones what he thought of him, and what he'd next do to him if he had reason to return.

The gentleman to whom Theo had directed his remark was lolling against the window frame, ogling a housemaid's swaying posterior as she scrubbed the step of a house opposite. Theo's ludicrous boast caused Graham Quick to snort in derision, but his attention remained riveted on the girl's jiggling buttocks. Finally he turned to slant Theo a laconic glance. 'I suppose you do know that Speer has winged at least three fellows who've annoyed him.' Graham's heavy-lidded eyes dropped to the livid mark on Theo's neck. 'God only knows where he'd aim in your case.' After a last leer at the buxom servant, who was on her way to the side of the house with her bucket, Graham turned to face Theo with an impatient sigh. 'It takes you an age to get ready, dear chap. Are we off to White's some time this afternoon...or not?' A pinch of snuff was deposited on the back of a foppish white hand and immediately sniffed into a fastidious nostril.

In Graham's opinion Wyndham was fortunate not to have on his person a more severe sign that he'd incensed one of the gentlemen he'd solicited to marry his cousin. Graham unashamedly flouted convention, yet he wasn't sure even he would have found the effrontery to solicit proposals from fellows who had suffered the ignominy of being spurned by a saucy schoolgirl. In a drawling tone he told Theo so.

'Nothing wrong with a fellow trying to get his ward wed,' Theo testily defended himself. 'It's my duty, like it or not, to get her settled before she gets any older. Besides, there was only one of them took it badly.'

'And with good reason, considering he'd just announced his betrothal to the sweetest heiress imaginable,' Graham interjected ironically. 'Miss Cleveland has a very tempting dowry.'

Theo's complexion turned florid and he muttered something about being unaware of any of that. The stale lie only served to elicit another snigger of disbelief from Graham.

In exasperation Theo tugged this way and that the linen he was winding about his neck. At last he seemed satisfied that the intricate bow at his throat hid the worst of the damage and he turned from his reflection to give Graham a smug look. 'This, I think...' he waved a note he'd picked up from the desk '...adequately proves my point. The chit needs a husband, and I've got her one.'

'I wonder if Miss Bailey will agree with you on that,' Graham suggested with a hint of malice. 'You might march her down the aisle, but you can't make her say her vows. Besides, Stephen Crabbe has his pockets to let. Have you settled on her a juicy portion?' At Theo's sullen silence he goaded slyly, 'Come, tell me—perhaps if the price is right I might be interested in her too.' His idle remark seemed to amuse him and he erupted in a guffaw. ''Spose you'd want me to lend you that cash, too, just so you could give it back to me to take the wench off your hands.'

'I wouldn't wish you on any female, let alone my own kin,' Theo replied scathingly, ignoring the reference to the loans he'd chivvied out of Quick.

Graham grinned. He revelled in his reputation as an insatiable libertine. He found Wyndham a tiresome dolt and a constant drain on his pocket. But Theo had got himself an odd notoriety and Graham liked to be in the thick of things, so had become chummy with him. Unwittingly Theo had managed to worm his way to prominence by creating a drama and casting himself as a central character. Once the debate in Mayfair's clubs and salons over whether Wyndham had impertinently interfered, or sensibly intervened, in his ward's life ceased, he would drop him like a hot brick.

Theo was also aware that employing desperate measures to get the Bailey inheritance had turned up a wondrous benefit. He'd gained a little in popularity. He had realised the situation wouldn't last, so was intending to milk his moment for as long as possible. With that in mind, he released the note advising him that Stephen would be happy to be re-introduced to his ward with a view to making an offer. It floated back to his desk to rest atop the one his ward had sent to him earlier in the week. That communication had arrived the day after Jemma had confronted him at home like a deranged harpy and contained no welcome news. She had not spared his feelings or her adjectives describing her disgust at his behaviour. She had also made it plain she had no intention of succumbing to any plot to get her wed. Theo frowned; Graham Quick had touched a raw nerve when he taunted him that he could not force the obstinate minx to marry against her will. But there was always a way, and he would set his mind to finding it in due course. For now a pleasant afternoon spent holding court at White's beckoned.

It was no surprise to Jemma when her maid, Polly, announced that Miss Wyndham was pacing back and forth in her parlour awaiting an audience. Maura had been a visitor to Jemma's home on Pereville Parade every day since the furore erupted over Theo contacting her spurned suitors. As far as Jemma was concerned the whole idiotic matter was unworthy of such attention, and she was becoming irritated that Maura would not let it wither naturally away.

Jemma had been potting seedlings in the small conservatory set at the back of her neat town house. Now she wiped the soil from her fingers on to a cloth and with a sigh set off towards the parlour to see her cousin. Usually Jemma was pleased to have a visitor, but she suspected Maura would again want to hear the details of her meeting with Marcus Speer, and she had nothing new to tell her. Neither did Jemma want to be constantly reminded of that episode. Since it had occurred, every thought of Marcus made an ache of unbearable poignancy ripple through her. It was impossible not to remember their tense conversation without the memory of his lazy lustful look rushing heat and colour to stain her cheeks. It did so now and she put a cool palm instinctively to her skin to soothe it. Her mind darted to recall how, when a little less hostile to one another, they'd walked side by side as civil companions, if not friends, and she'd felt her uneasiness starting to evaporate. She'd been sure he'd believed her when she'd said she was unaware of Theo's disgraceful behaviour. But, only a few minutes later, and without any warning or proper farewell, Marcus had abruptly walked away and not once looked back. The memory of having been so rudely abandoned still made her inwardly squirm in indignation.

Within five minutes of having joined Maura in the parlour Jemma's ivory complexion had darkened in annoyance. Just as she was about to screw up the paper she'd scanned in disbelief her cousin deftly whipped the letter away from her quivering fingers.

'No, you mustn't do that!' Maura gasped and thrust it back in her pocket. 'I must put it back where I found it before Theo returns.' She gave Jemma an apprehensive look. 'I looked for him in his study to ask for my allowance, but he'd gone out. I lingered, thinking he might return. Then I saw this and on impulse took it to show you.' She shot a look at Jemma that begged a comment on her selfless bravery.

Jemma was still too distracted by what she'd read to

remember to thank Maura for warning her that Stephen Crabbe was preparing to renew his offer to her.

'I hope Theo's gone to his club, then he'll come back drunk and go straight to his chamber. I must put this back. If he realises it's missing, there will be dreadful trouble.'

Maura led quite an uneventful life. She knew her gay society friends—apart from Deborah Cleveland, who was genuinely kind—tolerated her presence in their heady circle because their sweet looks and vivacity were heightened by her lack of such charming qualities. She had therefore found this family drama oddly exhilarating for, like her brother, she was enjoying a temporary elevation in status because of it. None the less, she was already regretting having impulsively taken the letter. The reason she'd gone to Theo's study was not to speak to her brother—although she had planned to soon corner him about handing over her overdue allowance. She'd headed there hoping to see a very different gentleman.

Earlier that day, from the top of the stairs, Maura had overheard a visitor arrive and state his name to Manwell. Immediately she had been scandalised. Her brother had few friends and Maura knew that this reputedly wicked philanderer was not one of Theo's usual cronies. As one transfixed by a dangerous reptile, Maura had settled silently on to a high step to spy on devilish Graham Quick through the banisters. Of course she'd heard of him, but never actually seen him as he socialised, for the most part, in places and with people innocent young ladies knew nothing about.

She'd observed a man of below medium height with an excessively spare frame, flamboyantly clothed, who was blessed with blond good looks. Being a young woman of plain appearance with no experience of stirring interest, let alone passion, in a gentleman, she'd found watching him, unobserved, whilst wondering, acutely thrilling. As she'd gazed down on the top of his flaxen head, she'd recalled hearing a whisper that even the members of the Hellfire Club couldn't match Graham Quick for depravity.

After a moment the object of Maura's frenzied imagination had tipped back his blond head to inhale snuff and spotted her. With a sly smile he peremptorily beckoned her to come to him.

From the moment he'd seen her Maura had been petrified. That thin, demanding finger had finally jerked her to her senses and she'd jumped up and fled in a jumble of skirts with her cheeks aflame and his rough chuckle following her along the corridor.

The sanctuary of her room had done nothing to calm her; in fact, once a safe distance had been put between them, Maura had begun to relish her adventure and to find Mr Quick irresistibly interesting. He'd looked wonderfully handsome with his fair face and angelic curls and nothing like a wicked libertine. She'd known that Theo's visitor, once received, would be shown to his study and had, after a while, boosted her courage sufficiently to decide to go there on the pretext of needing to speak to her brother on a matter. But she'd tarried too long and by the time she'd tiptoed with hammering heart to timidly tap on the door, they'd gone out.

'I suppose I ought to go home now,' Maura murmured morosely. She still felt disappointed at having missed the chance to satisfy her curiosity about Graham

Quick by seeing, perhaps conversing with him, at close quarters. She also now felt quite miffed that, having sped here to warn Jemma that the plot to marry her off was progressing very fast, she'd not even been offered a cup of tea for her trouble.

'Oh…I'm sorry, Maura. Will you take tea?' Jemma belatedly recognised her cousin's mood and offered her hospitality.

'Yes, please,' Maura said immediately and sat down.

Having given the order to Polly for a tray of tea and cinnamon biscuits to be brought to the parlour, Jemma returned to giving the awful matter at hand her full attention. 'I ought to write to Mr Crabbe and let him know that his prettily stated intentions towards me are unfortunately unwanted.'

'No!' Maura shot to her feet. 'Please don't do that. It will give the game away that you have seen this letter. Then I will be in trouble, for Theo will guess I have meddled in it.'

With an unsteady hand Jemma pushed back the stray wisps fallen against her pale forehead. Her fingers remained tangled in those chestnut tresses as she slowly walked to the window and stared sightlessly out on another glorious spring day. She certainly did not want Maura to pay for being a good and loyal friend to her, but neither did she want Stephen Crabbe to remain under any illusion that she might agree to marry him. She had hoped that the two gentlemen who had received a letter from Theo—and whose responses she had not known—would have had the sense to treat the matter with the contempt it deserved. Then the whole stupid affair might have faded away with no need for her to do anything at all. But now it seemed she had no option but to quickly state her case before Mr Crabbe paid her an unwelcome call.

Five years ago she'd stirred gossip because she had trifled with Marcus Speer's affections and led him on like a common tease. Then she'd deserved the opprobrium for her silly flirtatious behaviour. On this occasion she'd done nothing to encourage a suitor's attention. Once she'd broadcast the truth of the matter, her guardian's motive would be rightly judged to be claiming the Bailey inheritance. As much as Jemma didn't relish seeing Maura upset by her brother's greed being exposed, she could see no other way to proceed.

Jemma's troubled thoughts were interrupted as Polly arrived with the tea tray. Having settled on the sofa opposite her cousin, and handed Maura her tea, Jemma was surprised to hear a tap at the door and see Polly again hovering on the threshold.

'A gentleman caller, Miss Bailey,' Polly announced in her soft Devon burr.

The hand that clutched a teacup froze halfway to Maura's mouth. Swiftly it was deposited back on its saucer, rattling together the crockery. 'It's Theo,' she hissed, pupils dilating in fright. 'He must have discovered the letter is missing. He's guessed I've taken it to show you. He's come to get it…and me…'

'Shh, it is not him,' Jemma soothed, quickly standing up. Polly was familiar enough with her mistress's guardian to have announced him by his name.

'Who is it Polly?' Jemma's heart had plummeted to her stomach. Had Stephen Crabbe come to visit without the courtesy of first sending a card, and before she had properly decided how she must attack such a delicate matter as rejecting him for a second time?

'It's a Mr Speer, Miss Bailey,' Polly announced, her eyes suddenly alight with admiration, her lips compressed to hide a smile. 'He's waiting in the hallway. Shall I show him in?'

'No!' Jemma blurted in a gulp. 'That is…yes, of course. Please show him in. No, one moment…' She again arrested her servant's departure, but gave Polly an apologetic look for the confusion. 'Ask him to wait just a moment, please.'

Polly nodded and slipped away to do as she'd been bid. As she skipped along the corridor towards the vestibule she inwardly chuckled. She'd be in a dither too if such a grand-looking man came a-calling on her unexpectedly.

'What do you think he wants?' Maura whispered, her eyes as round as the saucers on the table. Now she knew that her brother had not come in high dudgeon to chastise her she looked quite comfortable perched on the edge of her chair, and agog with curiosity. 'Surely he is not still furious at having received Theo's letter? Do you think that he is here to again quarrel with you?'

'I…I don't know,' Jemma croaked. And that was the truth. She had no idea why he'd come. The last time she'd been in his company his parting words to her had been that they should finish their conversation another time. She'd imagined it to be just an empty phrase tossed at her as a substitute for a proper farewell. She felt quite light-headed at the prospect of receiving him at home without knowing the purpose of his call. She knew too that she regretted having delayed her cousin's departure with the offer of refreshment. Of course it was best for her reputation that she did not see him alone but—etiquette be damned!—she would sooner hear whatever it was he had to say in private. Closely following that thought came another to reassure her. Marcus Speer was a sophisticated gentleman. He would refrain from discussing anything of a delicate nature in front of Maura.

After a moment Jemma realised that she would be no better prepared to deal with the situation after ten minutes of brooding on it than she was now. In fact, it would be bad manners to make him wait. She recalled the glimpse she'd had of him pacing impatiently in the hallway of Theo's house. She guessed Mr Speer was not a man who gladly wasted his time, and she didn't want to annoy him for no good reason. Quickly Jemma went to the door, opened it and gestured to Polly, hovering in the vicinity, that she was ready to receive him.

Chapter Six

'Will you take tea with us, Mr Speer?'

In her willingness to appear genial, Jemma realised she had barely allowed him to set one expensively shod foot in to the room before bursting out with her offer.

'Thank you. I'd like that,' Marcus replied lightly and, having allowed Polly to scuttle beneath his braced arm to fetch another cup and saucer, he proceeded to close the door.

Jemma then received a smile that made it clear he knew she was flustered by his unexpected visit. His amusement, though veiled, was aggravating enough to subdue some of her nervousness. 'I should like to introduce you to my cousin, Miss Wyndham,' Jemma plunged on thoughtlessly. A moment later she realised that an introduction was surely unnecessary.

Five years ago, for some weeks, Marcus Speer had paid regular calls to this house. Then her papa would receive him in his study and the two gentlemen would pass the time of day over a tipple before she was allowed to greet her visitor. Her father's sister, Aunt Cecily, would then act as chaperon whilst Marcus sat with the ladies to politely take tea. There had been occasions when the weather had been clement and they'd gone for a drive in his fancy phaeton. She remembered how she'd adored feeling the breeze catching at her bonnet as he set the horses to such a brisk trot that her elderly aunt would clutch doublehandedly at the side of the vehicle, her eyes clamped shut, her lips shivering in silent prayer. Delving into her store of memories, she recalled that Maura had enjoyed at least one exhilarating trip sitting beside her. Her cousin would have been present, too, when Marcus and his friends joined their party at an evening gathering. More recently her cousin had been invited to socialise in the Cleveland's elite circle. As Deborah's betrothed, it was likely that Marcus would accompany his fiancée and his future in-laws.

'I believe we have already met,' Marcus said amiably, confirming Jemma's thoughts. 'How are you, Miss Wyndham?'

His greeting to Maura had sounded relaxed and sincere and that pleased Jemma. Theo's despicable behaviour didn't seem to have coloured Marcus's attitude towards all the Wyndhams. Of course, what he really thought of her she had yet to discover.

'I'm very well, sir, thank you. Deborah has invited me to go with her party to the concert at Vauxhall later this week.' It was rattled out breathlessly before Maura had fully recovered from the little curtsy she was making.

'How charming,' Marcus replied. 'Do you like the pleasure gardens?'

An immediate nod answered him. 'But I haven't been for years, not since I made my come out. We were a

small group on that occasion. Jemma was there, and
Uncle John and my papa and Aunt Cecily. We—' Maura
dipped her head in Jemma's direction, too engrossed in
telling her tale to heed a cautionary glint in her cousin's
eyes '—we made our débuts during the same season, but
were not as fortunate as Deborah has been in finding a
husband…' Her voice faded away. Maura's enthusiasm
to spin out a conversation with this handsome paragon
had made her forgetful of how badly things had ended
for Jemma, and for Mr Speer. 'It's a long time since we
went to Vauxhall,' she mumbled awkwardly, then gulped
from her cup.

'A very long time,' Jemma endorsed with forced nonchalance. 'I barely recall it.' That fib caused Jemma to immediately blush and Marcus to slowly smile at his shoes.

Oh, she remembered that scented summer evening
beneath the twinkling lights strung in the trees. And,
from his sardonic reaction, she knew that he recalled the
sultry night too.

With the assistance of his friend Randolph Chadwicke, he'd managed to manoeuvre her away from her
friends and into one of the secluded walkways. He'd led
her by the hand to a shadowy spot where boughs of
whispering leaves almost disguised the sighs of secret
lovers, but through the dense dark hedges could be
glimpsed fragmented silhouettes. In her tender inex-
perience, it had seemed incredibly exciting, also reassuring to Jemma, to know that just a few feet away other
young ladies were being wooed by handsome gallants.
She felt her breath catch, her pulse accelerate with the
memory of the sensual delight that Marcus had awoken
within her.

Swiftly she began to collect the teapot and used china and put them back on to the tray. But the stimulating thoughts bombarding her consciousness would not be put to flight. She felt her breasts begin to throb, her legs to weaken and put a hand to the table as she swayed into it for support. She'd too generously allowed him to take liberties on that occasion just as she had at the Cranleighs' ball.

'How is your friend Mr Chadwicke, sir?' Jemma turned from shuffling cups to blurt that out. 'I don't recall seeing him in town for quite a while.' The question had been spontaneous, designed to eject memories of her bodice buttons being slowly slipped from their hooks and his fingers gliding inside… Of course the distraction was ill devised. The steady intense glitter in his silver eyes, the hard smile, made it clear he knew what was on her mind and how it had led her to remember his friend.

Marcus felt the tightening in his loins as he sensed anew tender flesh swelling to fill his palms, tasted again the sweetness of her novice kisses, her tongue-tip touching his with alternating ardency and wonder. He thought of Randolph too, and his welcome assistance in creating a diversion that evening. Then he wondered if the two of them might manage to remain friends for much longer…

'I danced with Mr Chadwicke earlier in the week,' Maura chirped up helpfully. It seemed to her that Mr Speer was taking rather a time to find an answer to Jemma's simple question about his friend. 'He was at Almack's on Wednesday. He made a point of coming over and speaking to us. He danced with Deborah too. Oh, he is so charming.'

Marcus dragged his mind from memories that were making him feel increasingly uncomfortable. 'Indeed he is,' he drawled. 'There, you have your answer, Miss Bailey,' he said in a voice roughened by lust. 'It seems Randolph is doing well.'

'That is good to know,' Jemma murmured, casting about in her mind for an innocuous topic of conversation. She could not find one. But she knew the matter of his betrothal stalked silently between them. The closest Marcus had come to referring to his fiancée was when he'd said that she and Theo were aware he was no longer unattached.

Now, with several mentions of his future bride's name hovering in the air, Jemma knew she should say something to acknowledge Deborah's position in his life. She would hate him to think that his impending marriage bothered her in any way. 'I must offer my rather tardy congratulations on your betrothal to Miss Cleveland, sir.' It was a light remark coupled with a sweet smile and then the tea tray, replenished with a fresh set by Polly, who'd whizzed discreetly in and out, again had her attention. Belatedly she recalled having offered him refreshment. She snatched at the pot and watched the stewed brew stream out of the spout. Jemma frowned at it; she feared the beverage might now be unpalatably strong and cool. She handed him his tea anyway with a polite, 'Please do sit down, sir, if you would like to.'

Marcus took a seat and then a sip from his cup. His expression gave nothing away, but he placed the cup and saucer down on the table and looked at Jemma with rueful humour far back in his eyes.

'Are you going to Vauxhall Gardens with the Clevelands later in the week, Mr Speer?' Maura looked hopeful of hearing an affirmative.

'I'm afraid not,' Marcus replied.

'Oh, that's a shame.' Maura's small mouth twisted in disappointment. She peeked under her lashes at Jemma as though expecting her to contribute something to the conversation.

'Will you be going to Vauxhall with the young ladies, Miss Bailey?' Marcus asked.

'I won't, sir. I have been invited to the Sheridans this week,' she truthfully told him, but omitted to pinpoint the exact day.

Mr Sheridan had dealt with her father's bank affairs and had given her guidance on financial matters since John Bailey's death. Once in a while he and his wife invited her to their neat villa outside Marylebone to enjoy cosy at homes with their growing family.

Jemma was sure she'd detected a hint of challenge in what had seemed to be an idle enquiry from Marcus. When he relaxed back in his chair, and continued regarding her steadily, she knew for sure he was keen to gauge her reaction. Jemma felt her indignation rising. He was obviously aware that invitations to join the Clevelands' lofty circle did not come her way. Her parents' openly adulterous marriage and subsequent divorce had put paid to her and her sisters becoming popular as débutantes. Never the less Monica and Patricia had found husbands to love them. But neither of her sisters had added to their infamy by acting like shallow flirts in their youth.

If Marcus's intention had been to embarrass her in to admitting she was *persona non grata*, he was to be disappointed; she gave him a look designed to tell him so. He returned her a smile that told her he wasn't fooled for a moment by her bravado. He knew that being excluded and lacking friends was wounding.

'I believe Bert Sheridan has recently retired from his position at the bank and is now a keen gardener.'

That casual, unexpected comment made Jemma dart at Marcus a surprised glance. She had not expected him to be on first-name terms with Mr Sheridan, who had held quite a modest position up until his recent retirement. She imagined Marcus Speer, heir to an earldom, and independently wealthy to boot, had the undivided attention of the highest official when he went to do business at Coutts in the Strand.

'Yes, he is just retired and tending to his plants. I did not know you were well acquainted with Mr Sheridan,' Jemma added.

'I have known him for some years. We spoke quite recently when I had occasion to go to the bank,' Marcus informed levelly. A corner of his mouth tilted when Jemma continued to look at him, an unspoken, rather impertinent question in her stare. 'Oh, I asked after his family and he returned the courtesy. He was kind enough to convey his sympathies on the death of the late Earl of Gresham.'

Jemma's rosy lips parted a little in a soft gasp of dismay. 'Oh…I… Oh…please forgive me, sir,' she stuttered, frowning in confusion. 'I had no idea the Earl had passed away. I had heard a rumour that he was poorly some months ago, but had thankfully recovered before, so I thought…expected to hear…' Her regrets tailed away.

'It is not widely known. The obituary is not yet published,' Marcus soothed. 'My uncle wished to be taken home and buried in a plot at Gresham Hall. The funeral was a quiet affair, carried out very quickly following his death in Grosvenor Square. Now the wake is over I've returned from Surrey to deal with his affairs.'

'I'm very sorry to hear of it,' Jemma repeated in a whisper. And she was. Marcus had introduced her to his uncle at the Cranleighs' ball. They'd met on only one other occasion when Marcus had been escorting her. She remembered the Earl, in his gruff, abrupt way, had been quite kind to her and she'd quickly decided she liked him. She told Marcus so.

For a moment Marcus studied his hands, lightly clasped between his knees. Slowly he raised his head and a storm-grey gaze tangled with troubled jade eyes. 'I recently discovered that he'd liked you too.'

A desire to know more was prompting a question to hover on her tongue, but it withered there. His revelation had been totally unexpected, and she was unsure what to say. She glanced at Maura, who had been silent since the news had been broken of the old Earl's demise.

It was not so much knowing of Solomon Speer's death that held Maura spellbound as her struggle to digest the enormity of his nephew's new status. The idea that she was sitting taking tea with the Earl of Gresham had rendered her quite in a daze. She continued to quietly goggle at Marcus. 'Deborah will become a Countess as well as a bride. How wonderful,' she finally croaked.

'We must not keep you, sir,' Jemma said hoarsely. On hearing her cousin's comment it was as though a blade had been plunged into her chest. Yet the reason for the piercing pain was unfathomable. She had never knowingly coveted riches or harboured an ambition to marry a title. She was content to have enough to cover her needs, and the husband she'd initially wanted had been a squire's son. She was sure it was only recently, thanks to her hateful guardian bringing chaos to her life, that she'd again given a thought to Marcus Speer.

After her disastrous début, and once more than a year had passed, her father had eventually allowed her to again visit town. She'd taken cab rides she could ill afford from the little allowance he gave her, past fashionable spots Marcus might frequent, hoping for a glimpse of him. Her plan had been to quickly alight and casually bump in to him. A little blush registered her thankfulness that nothing had come of such youthful folly. Had she been successful in tracking him down on one of those trips, she probably would have, at the last moment, tried to flee, or would have stood before him tongue-tied whilst enduring one of his hateful, mocking looks. She might, when still so very vulnerable to wanting him, have fled in tears when he sauntered past without a backward glance. But since her papa had died she had become tougher. Or perhaps it was just a natural maturity that had protected her with the passing of the years. At some point she'd accepted that they would always inhabit different worlds, and she'd let go of the need to fruitlessly yearn for him.

But since Theo's interference had thrust them back together it seemed she could not put the dratted man from her thoughts! Jemma decided that putting some distance between them might be the first step to presently regaining her equilibrium. It seemed he was reluctant to take the hint to leave, already given, so she repeated it. 'I'm sure you must have pressing matters to attend to, sir.'

'Indeed I have much to do,' Marcus concurred. 'But perhaps nothing is quite as important as apologising for having rudely abandoned you in the street.' His athletic frame was freed from the confines of the dainty armchair as he lithely stood up. He moved to the window to stare out and a hand splayed across his chin, covering his mouth before being abruptly removed. 'As a rule it is not in my nature to act discourteously. I called this afternoon to offer my sincere apologies. Also I recall we did not finish our conversation on that day. But now is not a good time to resume it as you have Miss Wyndham's company.' He again approached the centre of the room as though to leave. 'I'm sorry to have interrupted your tea.'

'I must be going home now,' Maura garbled. 'I have something urgent to do.' She instinctively felt in her pocket for the note she'd pinched from her brother's study. She was then abruptly on her feet and sinking in to a low curtsy. As she skittered past Marcus to the door, shock and awe still widened her eyes. With barely a few muttered words of farewell for them she was gone.

'I didn't intend to frighten her off,' Marcus mildly joked to ease the tense silence that ensued after Maura's departure.

An exceedingly quizzical look was slanted at him, and Marcus acknowledged it with a grunted laugh. 'Very well, I admit I'm glad your cousin has gone and we may speak in private.'

'So am I,' Jemma endorsed on a sigh. 'Although her absence is less necessary than I deemed it to be at first.'

His thick black eyebrows were elevated in imperious enquiry.

'I imagined you had come here to again browbeat me over Theo's scheme to trap me a husband,' Jemma breathlessly rattled off part of her answer, then regretted having instinctively yielded to his tacit authority. In an attempt to balance power between them, she paused deliberately before calmly continuing, 'I did not want us to bicker in company. But you've said you're here to apologise for going off so abruptly.' She looked earnestly at him. 'I saw you get in to the Earl's carriage on that afternoon. Had you been summoned to his deathbed?' Gruff sympathy resonated in her voice.

'Something like that,' Marcus confirmed quietly.

'Well, in that case, no apology is necessary, sir,' Jemma immediately said. 'I realise now that you must have been extremely anxious, knowing that at any moment you might receive such grave news about your uncle.' Her soft gaze was as forgiving as her words. 'It makes your behaviour, your feelings towards me on that day, more understandable.'

'I think, Miss Bailey, you understand very little about my feelings towards you.'

A low, liquid note had again entered his voice. His silver eyes too had taken on a slumberous quality and, as they slipped from her face to roam her figure, fire began coursing through her veins. Swiftly she turned away. The brief harmony gained when she'd commiserated on his loss had been whipped away. Now she sensed agitation, and anger, stirring her blood.

It was barely ten minutes since she had congratulated him on his engagement. He had dipped his head, casually acknowledging her reference to his future bride, yet now he was gazing at her as though he would very much like to touch her. And, to her shame, she knew she ached to again have his mouth bruise hers while slow hands scalded her skin in the magical way she remembered.

As she clattered spoons on milky porcelain to occupy her nervous fingers, her mind battled with disturbing thoughts. Perhaps he was deliberately toying with her for his own amusement. Perhaps he found an amount of malicious satisfaction in this situation. Once, when little more than a schoolgirl, she'd been able to wind the new Earl of Gresham about her little finger; now she had no such power. He was soon to marry a beautiful young heiress and she…she had become a figure of fun because her guardian was keen to marry her off to any fellow willing to take her. Well, she might not find the audacity to march in to the gentlemen's clubs and roundly declare that she was happy to remain a spinster, but she could impress on the Earl of Gresham that, despite her guardian's best efforts, she was not at such a disadvantage that she was fair game for lechery. Perhaps, if he knew honourable intentions were in the offing, he might act less like a big cat cornering its quarry.

'I was pleased to see my cousin Maura today,' Jemma breathily began, noisily stacking saucers, 'but not so glad to have the news that brought her here.' She tilted up her sharp little chin, pivoted about to meet his preying eyes. 'My cousin very kindly came to warn me that one of Theo's odious letters has turned up the required result for him.'

'Stephen Crabbe?'

A nod from Jemma confirmed that he had correctly guessed which fellow still wanted her for a wife. 'When Polly announced a gentleman caller I immediately thought he had come to pay a visit.'

'And were you disappointed to discover it was me instead?' Marcus asked drily.

A green gaze was flicked up at him. 'I...I was certainly surprised to know it was you instead,' she answered truthfully. 'Never the less, I am appreciative of your apology and in return I should like to offer mine.' Her slender hands disappeared behind her back to conceal their tremor. 'I believe we both said things in anger that day that are best now forgotten.' She forced a little laugh. 'There. It is done. Perhaps we might both at some time find the generosity to forgive my guardian for arrogantly assuming that he had a right to disrupt our lives. And, of course, he deserves our pity for being an idiot. It was a pathetically half-baked plot.'

'Yet it has turned up the required result for him,' Marcus reminded her of her words whilst plunging his hands in to his pockets and watching her from beneath preposterously long black lashes. 'Wyndham's an idiot, I'll agree, but a successful one it seems.'

'Theo might think he has forced my hand, but he has not,' Jemma returned stressfully. 'If Mr Crabbe had come here today, I would have had the unpleasant task of rebuffing his advances once again.'

He looked quite impressive, Jemma obliquely realised. Even his lazy stance could not detract from the aura of power that surrounded him. Dressed in an immaculately tailored black suit of clothes that moulded perfectly to his broad masculine frame, he looked every inch the affluent aristocrat. Why did I not realise he is wearing mourning? she wondered. A moment later she regretted having stared at him for too long. That smile crooking a corner of his mouth warned her he had noticed her unladylike gaping. Quickly Jemma attempted to cover the lapse with brisk dialogue. 'So, obviously I am glad it was not Mr Crabbe who'd come calling for I am not quite sure how to deal with this matter. I have considered writing to him. But Maura is rightly concerned that, if I do, her brother will guess straight away that she has been meddling in it. He will hate to be thwarted, and I would not want her in trouble on my account.'

'It seems to me you need someone to protect you from your guardian.'

'And my guardian wholly endorses that opinion,' Jemma countered with a sour laugh. 'I imagine he considers that the more determined he makes me to slip his yoke, the sooner I might accept the first fellow who proposes marriage.'

'It is not just husbands who provide young women with the protection they need,' Marcus drawled dulcetly.

'Indeed, fathers and brothers do too. Unfortunately I have only a grasping cousin to guard my interests.'

'Are you wilfully misunderstanding me, Jemma?' Marcus asked with a hint of amusement.

'I don't know, sir. Am I?' she immediately parried.

Their eyes clashed, grappled, before hers darted away. 'I can only again imagine that you must have much to attend to. Please, do not let me detain you here.'

'Indeed I will not,' the Earl of Gresham informed ironically. 'I think you know I stay because I want to.'

'Then I must ask you to go because I don't want you to— Don't!' she squeaked in alarm as he reached for her so suddenly she was sent in to a stumbling retreat. 'Don't…don't you dare!' she stammered angrily, her full bosom straining tightly against the loops that held her pearl bodice buttons. 'You are soon to be married and yet you—'

'My marriage need not concern you,' Marcus soothed.

'It need not concern me?' Jemma echoed in suffocated outrage. 'You have tried to kiss me and—'

'No, I haven't, not yet,' Marcus said, his mouth curving in hard humour.

'Well, let me make it unnecessary for you to attempt any such thing,' Jemma spluttered. 'Perhaps because you are now an Earl you feel you are entitled to ride roughshod over other people's feelings.'

'As you rode roughshod over mine?' Marcus suggested in a voice of subtle sarcasm. He smiled but in a way that missed his eyes and chilled her heart. 'Don't look so frightened, Jemma. I am not about to act vindictively because once I was slighted by a schoolgirl. Most of what happened between us then is forgotten, but not all; something vital remains and it is because of that that my offer of help is genuine.'

'You'll help me at a price, you mean,' Jemma whispered.

'It's a price I believe you'll be willing to pay.'

'I have listened to more than enough of your arrogant assumptions about me. Please leave.'

'If I'm wrong I'll leave.' A hand snaked out to manacle her delicate wrist with five lean, tanned fingers.

Despite her efforts to fling him off she was slowly, inexorably, drawn towards him on dragging feet.

'We suited once, you and I. In a basic way we suited very well indeed. Do you remember how I could make you want me? Why don't you let me look after you?' His voice sounded hypnotic; the warmth of his skin smoothing hers was soothing.

'And why would you do anything for me?' she asked in a tone that was both knowing and fearful.

'Because I can,' he murmured, his metallic eyes pitilessly pinning her down.

A small pink tongue-tip slipped moisture to Jemma's arid lips. She rotated her arm in his grip, to no avail. 'And you expect something in return?' she eventually croaked.

Marcus gave her an impenitent smile. 'When a gentleman offers his protection to a lady, it is usual that she rewards him in a way he likes.'

'It is fortunate indeed, then, that I have no need of your assistance in this matter,' Jemma cried, tugging against his restraint. He let her go abruptly, and she stumbled against an armchair, eagerly grasping it as support. 'I think we have now concluded our unfinished conversation,' she hissed icily. 'I shall ask Polly to show you out.' She elevated her chin and made for the door so quickly that she omitted to choose a path that avoided him. When she realised she would again come too close she halted abruptly, just out of his reach. 'Please go.'

'Are you sure you want me to go, Jemma?' He closed

the space between them in a single prowling pace. A finger unfurled from his fist to brush seductively against a pink cheek.

She shot back as though he'd scalded her, but within a moment his hand had curled on her nape, preventing her escaping far. She was tugged back against him, and his mouth slanted hot and hard on hers, demanding, yet breathtakingly seductive.

A small cry of despair broke in her throat, for she knew she couldn't resist the fierce flame of passion that had ignited at her core. From the moment he'd touched her she'd felt a coil of tension tightening within. Now the spring was slowly being released, yet she craved more sweet torment. It had been so long since she'd tasted a sensation that could enervate and melt her bones. Her hands balled against his chest, striving to push him away, but the sorcery of soothing movements along her spine, the skill of a stroking kiss, had her impotent fingers forking rigidly before clutching at him. A moment later her arms had slipped to his shoulders, her fingers had linked at his nape where ribbons of long ebony hair swept her skin. She moaned pleasure and pleading into his mouth and, as he slowly cupped, then caressed, a full breast, she arched against him, filling his artful fingers with tender pulsating flesh.

Marcus raised his head a little, looked down into a beautiful face tautened by desire. She wanted him. And God knew he wanted her. Until a moment ago when he'd touched her he wasn't sure how much. She was ripe for love now; a young woman awakened to sensuality by him, but still, he guessed, a virgin. His loins felt afire, thickened with a rush of blood, and he eased his stance as her need made her whimper and fidget and fit her hips to his tortured pelvis.

Jemma's lids fluttered up and, as bashfulness tempered her passion, she blushed. The bliss had been as frantic as she remembered. He'd kissed and caressed her as he had before with intoxicating persuasion rather than the spiteful lechery she'd been expecting. The culmination of that previous shared pleasure had been his marriage proposal. A foolish fantasy that nothing had changed seemed plausible in her present dreamy mood. A wave of guilt washed over her as she realised that he must break his engagement in order to wed her instead. 'Have you already spoken to Deborah? What did she say?' she murmured drowsily.

'Say?'

Jemma frowned, moved her head agitatedly on his shoulder in regret. 'Is Deborah upset and about to jilt you?'

Marcus smiled and touched his mouth to slick parted lips that clung eagerly to his.

'It's not the done thing, sweetheart, for a gentleman to worry his future wife about his mistress.'

Chapter Seven

A haze of drugging languor was slowly dispersing, and Jemma blinked heavy eyes to clear her vision and read his expression.

'You may name your terms. I'll be attentive and generous in every way, I promise,' he added with gentle, laughing coercion. 'As my mistress you'll have *carte blanche*. Anything your heart…or body…desires.'

Her lashes fluttered, her eyes focused, and she glimpsed what moments ago she'd been blinded to, whilst pining to believe honour was behind his seduction. He was watching her scientifically to gauge whether she would let him ruin her. As though to tease her consent out of her, his long fingers began expertly flipping free pearl buttons from their hooks. She was undone to the waist by the time she had garnered enough energy and willpower to dash the tears from her lashes and slap away his cunning touch.

'I have an answer for you, sir,' she choked, knocking again at his hand as it sought to bring her back to him. Her fingers flew over her bodice, clumsily refastening it. 'It is no. A man as egotistical as you may find it hard to believe, but I find you quite resistible. And please be assured that being degraded by you is not, and never will be, a price that I am willing to pay to get from under my guardian's thumb. I would sooner marry Mr Crabbe,' she spat scornfully, although the dew was back blurring her eyes. 'And that is something I swear I shall never do.'

'Of course it will be a discreet affair,' he murmured as though soothing a fractious child. 'People may guess at it, but there will be no ostracism or disgrace for you as the Earl of Gresham's mistress.' Hard humour curved his mouth. 'I admit I'm arrogant, but acquit me of conceit when I say some might consider it a privilege to be chosen for the office.'

'I am not one of those people,' she bit out icily. She had successfully dampened the delirium that moments ago had made her stupidly suppose he might reject a Viscount's daughter to marry her instead. Now she was more rational. And she hated him. She hated his repressed amusement; she hated his cool confidence; mostly she hated him because he was right. Whilst he wanted her, in the eyes of the *haut ton* she would be acceptably sullied. Once he'd done with her, of course, that would change. Polite society would turn a blind eye to the most outrageous behaviour if the perpetrator had power and influence enough to dazzle them.

She had been right, too. Her first instinct had been that he might use her predicament to wreak some sort of spiteful revenge for the way she'd treated him years ago. She had been just a silly, impressionable young girl! Had she not been, she would have known better than to imagine that eloping with a neighbour's son, when just turned seventeen, would be an exciting adventure.

But then she had believed herself to be in love with Robert. She had been determined to stay in love with Robert, and marry him, despite the spectre of Marcus Speer's sensuality haunting her mind. She had trusted Robert would remain true to their secret pact while she obeyed her father's wishes and made her début. In the end they had both obeyed their parents' dictates and in doing so had forfeited the bond of affection that had endured since their childhood. But hers was not the ultimate betrayal; she had not pledged her future to another as had Robert Burnham.

As though Marcus's thoughts were treading the same path, he asked softly, 'Are you still pining for Burnham?'

Heat bled into Jemma's cheeks. Her throat bobbed as she attempted to swallow the lump lodged there. 'It's none of your concern whether I am or I am not.'

Marcus's eyes narrowed shrewdly. It was obvious she was not immune to the memory of her feckless swain. He knew the fellow had a house in town as well as a country retreat. He also was aware that when Burnham used his Mayfair property his wife stayed at home in Berkshire. It had not occurred to him before that the young lovers' relationship might have endured through upset and betrayal and the callow youth's marriage to his cousin. Perhaps Jemma already was a mistress—Burnham's. The idea of it sent an unexpected, savage jealousy that rocked Marcus on his feet. He might be wrong in thinking her a virgin; not that it mattered to him if she'd lost her maidenhead—in fact, it was preferable. The only innocent he'd ever

intended to take to bed was the one chosen to bear
Gresham heirs.

'I want you to go.' Jemma issued that demand in a calm
voice, yet she turned away to shield the sheen in her eyes.

'Don't cry,' he said softly. 'It wasn't my intention to
upset you.'

'Go away!' She'd been determined not to weep in
front of him. She felt angry with herself for allowing his
ruthless seduction to bring her so low. She'd been sure
she had the inner steel to now deal with an opportunis-
tic lecher such as Marcus Speer. 'Please, leave me
alone!' Jemma's composure again crumpled and her
muffled shriek held enough volume to bring Polly's
peeking face around the door.

Without another word Marcus strode past her,
stony-faced, and, with a cursory murmur for Polly,
quit the parlour.

'Are you all right, m'm?' Polly whispered treading
tentatively in to the room.

Jemma nodded, knuckling the wet from her eyes.
After a moment she gurgled a chuckle. 'It's nothing. I'm
overwrought—but soon I'll again be myself.'

'Miss Wyndham said to me on her way out that Mr
Speer's uncle has passed away.' Polly looked closely at
her mistress for a reaction to that comment. Had learning
of the old fellow's passing made her so sorrowful that
she'd angrily send away the charmer bearing bad tidings?
Polly knew her Miss Bailey could be a soft-hearted soul,
what with her giving money to foundlings and so on
when what she should be doing, in Polly's opinion, was
buying pretty new frocks and going out on the town to
find herself a husband. Someone like the swell fellow

who'd just left would suit her mistress just right, so Polly thought, especially now she knew just how high up the perch he was. 'Miss Wyndham said as Mr Speer should've been announced as the Earl of Gresham. He didn't say that name to me, honest, ma'am.'

'It doesn't matter,' Jemma murmured, firmly brushing the last drops of water from her lashes. An ember of hysteria sighed into life and she suddenly giggled. After a moment Polly joined in the infectious laughter. 'It doesn't matter at all about him,' Jemma eventually said with a sniff and a smile for her maid as she again calmed down. 'Even if he should return and announce he's the Prince Regent himself, you may still tell him I'm indisposed.'

Whilst staring moodily out of his carriage window, Marcus focused on a familiar tall figure loping along on the opposite side of the road. The sight of his closest friend dug a furrow in his brow and reluctantly he allowed brooding thoughts of Jemma to be edged from his mind. There was a pressing matter that needed airing between them before it was allowed to fester and poison a close relationship that had existed since they both were boys. Marcus raised a hand, ready to rap for the coachman to pull up. A moment before his fist hit the roof it froze in mid-air and then was withdrawn. He'd noticed a blonde woman he also recognised promenading on the same stretch of pavement in Pall Mall, and he had no desire for an impromptu meeting with her.

It was obvious that Pauline Vaux had spotted Randolph Chadwicke, for she raised a gloved hand in greeting, then speeded up her pace towards him. Behind her trotted a young maid awkwardly carrying a bundle of purchases. A cynical smile touched Marcus's lips as he watched the girl juggle her parcels and scamper to keep up. No doubt later this week he would discover, when the bills hit his desk, just what trinkets and fripperies his mistress had been keen to have today to oust those chosen last week. He knew that Pauline had sensed he was about to end their relationship. He had not complied with the demands issued in her frequent little notes that he must promptly visit her. Doubtless his silence and absence had given a fair indication that he'd grown bored with her indiscretions and silly attempts to make him jealous. He guessed, too, from the laden maid, that before the end was announced Pauline was keen to make him pay one way or another for his ennui.

He slumped back in to the squabs, feeling irritated. Not that the money squandered bothered him; he was invariably generous to his women, even when he knew that it was time to put them off. What was annoying him was that he wanted very much to speak to Randolph, but didn't relish being saddled with Pauline's company whilst he did so. He knew she would resist being sent on her way and would try to extract a promise from him that he would later call and spend the evening with her. He therefore chose to stay in his coach and delay the matter with Randolph. Presently a problem existed between him and his friend, and between him and his mistress, and he would sooner tackle those issues individually and in private.

A glance through the window told him that, just as he'd thought, Pauline had halted Randolph by clinging to one of his arms. Marcus's lips twitched. He imagined his ears ought to be burning. He'd learned from another friend who'd been similarly buttonholed that Lady Vaux had been making unsubtle enquiries as to his whereabouts since he'd returned from Surrey. As the coach edged ahead of the couple in sluggish traffic, he glanced back at her, noting the way she was taking flirtatious peeks up at her reluctant escort. A rueful chuckle scraped his throat. She was wasting her time there, too. Marcus had suspected for some time that his friend was falling hopelessly in love. It was the reason why he needed to urgently speak to him.

Pondering on star-crossed lovers led him to again think of Jemma. Marcus exhaled heavily, dropped back his dusky head and closed his eyes. Within a moment the redolence of her skin's scent, the sweet taste of her lips had overwhelmed his mind and senses, blocking out all else. Even some vitally important things concerning his uncle's estate were erased whilst he eased back into the velvet memory of a soft mouth parting eagerly beneath his and pearl-pale flesh being exposed as her bodice gaped invitingly. A maddening throb in his groin, quiescent since he'd left her, burst again in to life, ejecting a groaning laugh from Marcus and making him shift restlessly on the seat. He was no longer sure if Theo Wyndham deserved his thanks or curses for having brought the two of them together again. What he did know was that this time he wasn't going to give up on having her as easily as he'd done before.

He'd not intended to go today to proposition her. He'd simply intended to say sorry for having so boorishly abandoned her on the day his uncle had died. But once in her company his desire for her had become insistent and impulsive. From the moment he'd stepped into the room and sensed that behind her quiet agitation was secret pleasure at seeing him he'd wanted to know if he could re-ignite the passion she'd shown him as a débutante.

He hadn't lied to Jemma when he said he would not exact retribution for the way she'd cruelly led him on years ago. He had no subtle punishment in mind. All he wanted from her was the raw sensuality promised to him every time she responded like a wanton to his touch. In a decade and a half of womanising he'd not found even the most practised courtesan could compete with her artless ability to arouse him. And it would be no selfish coupling. He had enough experience in bedding women to know shared pleasure was heightened pleasure.

The coach had become stuck in a knot of vehicles and after a moment the length of time they'd been stationary penetrated Marcus's lust-filled mind. He flicked aside a corner of the blind and tilted his head to see what the problem was—and spotted Randolph. His friend was again on the move and walking alone in the same direction as before, obviously having shaken off Pauline Vaux. Spontaneously Marcus rapped out an instruction for his driver, then leapt from the unmoving carriage and sprinted, in a weaving path through carts and carriages, to the pavement.

On hearing his name being called Randolph spun about and continued walking backwards whilst Marcus strode up to him. 'You owe me a favour,' Randolph told him mordantly as the two fell in to step together.

'I know,' Marcus returned with a smile at his shoes. 'As soon as I've dealt with some pressing matters I'll go and speak to Pauline.'

'Please make it soon,' Randolph begged sarcastically. 'I'm running out of excuses, as well as moral fibre. I've lost count of the number of times I've dissembled on your account.'

'You have my sympathy and my gratitude,' Marcus returned in the same ironic tone.

'I've been after you, too. So, where have you been?' Randolph asked and levelled a direct look at a pair of grey eyes.

The two men were of similar height and breadth, but whereas Marcus was quite swarthy in looks, Randolph had hair of light brown, tipped fair here and there by the heat of a foreign sun.

Marcus stared off in to middle distance, deliberating on his answer. For some reason he was reluctant to tell anybody, even his closest friend—especially his closest friend—that he was again pursuing Jemma Bailey.

'Well, I know you've not been with your fiancée,' Randolph mused sourly. 'Deborah tells me she's not seen or heard from you since you returned from Surrey.'

A half-smile tilted Marcus's mouth. 'Whereas she's seen and heard from you quite a lot, I gather?'

The two men clashed eyes. Randolph looked away. 'She doesn't deserve the way you treat her.'

'Has she complained to you about the way I treat her?' Marcus asked equably. Now they were getting to the crux of the matter, and not before time. It was a conversation long overdue. He would have preferred that they sit somewhere comfortable, perhaps with something alcoholic at hand, but he'd sooner get it done than postpone for the right setting.

'It's not a month since you proposed and already you're neglecting her,' Randolph said bluntly.

'Has she said as much?'

'She seems to avoid mentioning you.'

'Ah…whereas I recall she always has quite a lot to say about you. All good, too,' Marcus added mildly.

Randolph's hazel eyes narrowed and a muscle leapt in his jaw. 'Her parents aren't deaf or blind; neither are the old besoms who keep the rumour mill grinding,' he said. 'Aren't you concerned that Deborah's likely to be ridiculed over your neglect and preference for Lady Vaux?'

'You just said that you're aware I've been avoiding Pauline,' Marcus reminded him with a mirthless laugh. 'You can hardly accuse me of choosing my mistress over my fiancée.'

'And what about the Bailey chit?' Randolph interrogated. 'Cornwallis spotted you having some sort of tête-à-tête in the street with her on the day the Earl died. How many women do you want at one time?'

'And that coming from a man who I know for a fact kept a mistress north, south, east and west of Mayfair,' Marcus acidly drawled.

Randolph had the grace to grimace defeat at that reminder of his profligacy. 'A misspent youth, as you know, as you were there,' he said drolly. 'I think you're trying to avoid answering the question about Jemma Bailey. Something to hide?' he probed.

Marcus kept his hooded gaze on his carriage, still hemmed in by carts, as he responded mildly, 'We met by chance that day when I went to Hanover Square to have it out with Wyndham about those damn impertinent letters of his.'

'You'd certainly need to be a chump to be still interested in her after what she put you through.'

Randolph could remember well enough how smitten by Jemma Bailey his friend had been when courting her years ago. The immediate rapport that had sprung up between the couple had given rise to a good deal of sly chatter at the time. Most of it had arisen from the fact that Jemma was just turned seventeen whilst the man chasing her was almost a decade older. Randolph had been as astonished as everybody else when she'd rejected Marcus's inevitable marriage proposal. The spurned suitor had been equally bewildered; of course he'd had pride enough to conceal it, and had refrained from making accusations that the little tease had led him on. But once it leaked out that she'd all along been planning to marry her country lover, his friends and, more damningly for her, some of the *ton*'s top hostesses had liberally aired their views, and none of it had been complimentary to the scheming minx.

'It seemed to me that you took Wyndham's letter very seriously, very seriously indeed,' Randolph worried at his prey. 'You were the only one who did too. The other fellows had the sense to treat the matter with the contempt it deserved. Philip Duncan fed the fire with his note.'

'I think you'll find Crabbe took it a deal more to heart than I did. He's ready to marry her,' Marcus returned tersely.

'Is he now?' Randolph drawled in surprise. 'And how do you know that? Had it from the horse's mouth, have you?' he chivvied for an answer. 'Never took you and Crabbe for bosom chums. In fact, I recall you once gave him a dig when he got too close to Jemma at the Cranleighs' ball.'

Marcus pursed his lips and inwardly berated himself for a fool for letting slip that information.

'Who told you? Wyndham?' Randolph stared shrewdly at the chiselled profile turned towards him until Marcus showed him the back of his raven head instead. 'So, Miss Bailey confided in you, did she?'

'You're starting to irritate me, Ran,' Marcus warned.

'If you hadn't already proposed to Deborah, what would have been your answer to Wyndham's letter?'

'It would have been no different,' Marcus snapped, stuffing his hands into his pockets and turning on his friend a stony stare.

'Would it not?' Randolph deliberately taunted.

Marcus swore beneath his breath. In a fluid movement he gripped Randolph by a shoulder and spun him towards him. 'It's my business, not yours,' he gritted out. 'There's no need for you to concern yourself with any of it. Mistress, fiancée, Miss Bailey—I'll deal with them all.'

Randolph shrugged himself free of the brutal fingers digging into his arm. There followed a combative clash between two pairs of eyes, one silver, one hazel. 'You do that,' Randolph ejected through his teeth. 'But don't expect me to dance attendance on your fiancée while you're off whoring.'

'I didn't realise it was that much of an ordeal for you,' Marcus returned silkily. Without another word he pivoted on his heel and, dodging vehicles, caught up with his carriage, some way ahead now.

Once again settled in his transport, he jammed his head back against the squabs and closed his eyes. His teeth ground in frustrated anger. Nothing had been achieved by his meeting with Randolph. No reasonable conversation had taken place between them to try to eliminate the hostility that was creeping into their relationship and would eventually destroy it. Marcus dropped his face in to his hands and pinched at the tension between his eyes. Even now he couldn't prevent his mind from returning to again pick over his conversation with Jemma, and what he pondered on the longest was whether she had chosen to remain a spinster because Robert Burnham still held her heart captive— her body, too, perhaps.

In the beginning Marcus had despised Burnham for having cravenly aborted the jaunt to Gretna with the woman he was supposed to adore. Later he had a more cynically mellow outlook on life. He'd understood the fellow's predicament so would not again judge him harshly for doing his duty. Robert Burnham had acted rationally and married with his head, not his heart. Marcus had proposed to Deborah with that attitude. For the landed gentry marriage was usually a pragmatic affair, a commercial venture based on a merging of money and pedigree. Passion and affection were routinely sought elsewhere by both parties once legitimate heirs were in the nursery.

Until his mid-twenties the romanticism of love matches had appealed to him. He'd pursued Jemma Bailey because he'd fallen in love with her. He'd wanted a marriage that would provide both husband and wife with every human comfort. Thus their mutual passion would make the taking of mistresses and paramours superfluous.

Her rebuff had been the more humiliating for being so immediate. At twenty-six-years old he'd been crushed to the core by a girl who'd delighted in learning from him about sensuality, then had returned home in the hope of eloping with her teenage swain. Once Marcus had sufficiently recovered his ego and equilibrium he'd decided that acting the sentimental fool once in a lifetime was enough for any man. Henceforth the sensible solution would be to stick to the tried-and-tested method used by generations of gentlemen of his class. His Uncle Solomon's relationship with Mrs Paulson provided a prime example of how such an arrangement could work very well. They might not have married, but Victoria had for three decades been his wife in all but name. Thus Marcus no longer had any illusions about love and marriage being inextricable.

By separating his domestic arrangements and keeping two households, he'd gain a suitable bride for whom he had an adequate fondness and respect, and who was worthy of mothering future Gresham heirs, and a mistress who was a sensually compatible companion.

Marcus slowly dropped his head into his hands. Just a short while ago, when he had proposed to Deborah, and been ignorant of Wyndham scratching out his blasted begging notes, that theory had seemed so valid—so right. Now he was questioning it.

Chapter Eight

'Oh, it's you. What are you doing here?'

'I've come to see Maura. Is she at home?'

Theo Wyndham had been descending the stairs of his house to order a very late breakfast when Manwell opened the door and admitted his cousin Jemma at past two o'clock in the afternoon. His curt, unmannerly greeting had sprung from his irritation at having his nemesis materialise unexpectedly in front of him.

Immediately on rising he had again found the question of getting his infuriating ward wed nagging at his mind. A throbbing head from a night of imbibing had not prevented his painful concentration. His desperation to get his hands on the Bailey money was becoming more urgent by the day. Already this week he'd had the duns out the front and had only just avoided them by slipping out the back in a groom's garb. At the time he'd felt elated to have won the game—but a game it was no longer. Graham Quick had refused him another loan, and Theo had been relying on that cash, despite the fact the miser charged a rate of interest that would make a usurer blush. In fact, Quick was becoming threatening about overdue payments on IOUs that had been cluttering Theo's desk for more than a year. Theo knew he now needed another Peter to rob if he was to pay Paul and avoid a lengthy stay in the Fleet.

'Is Maura at home?' Jemma repeated as her guardian continued silently scowling at her. 'Is she in her chamber?'

'Umm, yes, she is, Miss Bailey,' Manwell interjected having realised that his master was not about to give his cousin the courtesy of a reply. 'I shall tell her you are here.'

'Oh, please don't worry…. I shall go up as usual,' Jemma said and, with a smile for the old retainer and a dainty raise of her eyebrows for her sullen cousin, she swept past to the stairs and lightly ascended the treads. In her eagerness to put space between her and Theo she'd been only partially aware that Manwell had stepped forwards with an animated expression as though to add something to his offer to announce her arrival.

Having watched Jemma step on to the landing, Theo stomped off towards the kitchens, still brooding on how to thwart her defiance. He had called on Jemma several days ago to show her Stephen Crabbe's letter. The ingrate's response had been to barely cast an eye over her suitor's nicely worded note. Baldly she'd declared that if the fellow came courting, she would tell him his advances were as unwelcome now as they had been five years ago.

Theo had known the graceless chit would do it, too! He thus had had to quickly get a message to Stephen, ordering him to await his instruction before making his initial approach. A sweet bashfulness in her character was the excuse given to Crabbe for the delay. A sour titter scraped at his throat. He hoped the fellow didn't too readily recall the saucy hussy who'd led Marcus Speer a merry dance! Theo's expression darkened. He still had a fading bruise on his windpipe courtesy of the new Earl of Gresham and every time he caught a glimpse of it a simmering desire for retribution overcame him. In his opinion his wilful cousin and the Earl of Gresham deserved one another. It would have been reward enough for damage done him by both if he'd managed to bring the insufferable pair together to claim his inheritance! Pondering on the pity of it, he kicked open the baize door and descended the stairs, bawling for his breakfast.

'Oh, I'm sorry, I didn't realise you had company.' Jemma and Maura had never stood on ceremony when paying visits to each other. Thus Jemma had knocked, then immediately entered Maura's bedchamber, as was customary. Now she flushed faintly, for the first person she'd clapped eyes on within the room was Deborah Cleveland. The Earl of Gresham's fiancée had been inspecting one of her cousin's gowns. The sherbet-lemon lawn trimmed with lace was hanging on the side of the clothes press and had obviously been the subject of debate between the two young ladies. Now they'd both turned to stare at her in surprise.

'Did Manwell not tell you that Deborah was here too?' Maura asked with a hint of vexation. She swung a doubtful glance between her two visitors to spot any sign of prickliness. She knew that Marcus Speer was a cause of possible hostility between them. Taking her lead from Deborah, who had regained equilibrium following the interruption, and was smiling warmly at the newcomer, Maura welcomed Jemma into the room with an outstretched hand. 'Deborah has kindly come to help me choose a gown to wear at the Clevelands' ball. It is only a few weeks away, you know,' she added excitedly. 'Deborah is having a wonderful new gown made by Madame Thierry, but my miserly brother won't buy me one, not even from a cheap *modiste*—'

'I think Manwell was about to tell me something,' Jemma interrupted her cousin's complaints. She didn't want the elderly servant in trouble on her account. 'But I hurried past and came straight up to avoid your brother. Theo seems more grumpy than usual this afternoon.'

Maura grimaced her understanding on hearing that comment. She hadn't seen Jemma since she'd taken the note from Theo's desk to warn her that Mr Crabbe had serious intentions towards her. She'd managed to replace it undetected and was sure that her brother remained ignorant of what she'd done. He'd have hauled her over the coals else. From his increased surliness over the past few days Maura had guessed that a meeting had taken place between Theo and Jemma, and obviously Jemma had exasperated her brother by declaring that she wouldn't have Mr Crabbe.

'I've always thought that colour suited you very well,' Jemma burst out conversationally. On spotting Deborah, Jemma had felt her stomach lurch, and her heart had started thumping with a mix of awkwardness and guilt. The awkwardness was to be expected considering she'd just thrust herself into the company of Marcus's future bride. The lustful brute had only days ago asked her to be his mistress. Yet she had no reason to feel guilty, she impressed on herself as she twitched the hem of the gown and studied the fine lacework that decorated it. She had done nothing to encourage Deborah's fiancé to kiss her, or proposition her! Her fingers rubbed back and forth on fabric as a niggling truth rotated in her mind. You did little to stop him, you wanton! *You kissed him back. And, fool that you are, you hoped he might marry you instead. You can't deny it. You would have accepted a proper proposal and selfishly broken this young woman's heart.*

'I'm of the same opinion.' Deborah's sweet tone penetrated Jemma's miserable introspection. 'I think you should choose this dress, Maura. The material is light and cool, so if the evening is humid you won't swoon from the heat.'

'I might like to swoon and make a handsome gallant take me to the terrace for some air,' Maura said saucily. A vision of the wicked Mr Quick entered her mind, making a shiver ripple on her skin.

'I expect every young lady would like to have a handsome gallant do so for her,' Deborah echoed with a conspiratorial chuckle. 'Perhaps we ought to pick winter outfits with romance in mind.'

Jemma joined in the knowing laughter although she felt the biggest fraud. No doubt Deborah was anticipating her fiancé would take her for an exciting interlude on the terrace on the night of her ball. Five years ago she had been the one being passionately seduced by Marcus Speer under the spell of a midsummer moon, yet she'd had no intention of accepting his proposal when it eventually came. She couldn't. She'd already accepted Robert's proposal and in lieu of a proper engagement ring slept with his gold signet ring on a chain around her neck. Today, as soon as Maura had talked of handsome gallants, a gentleman's image had leaped into her mind. She doubted Deborah would act so amiable towards her if she knew of the fellow's identity!

'Did you come to see me for a particular reason?' Maura blurted out rather gauchely. A little dent had appeared between her eyebrows. She was pleased to see her cousin, yet felt rather miffed too that she had to share her illustrious friend with anyone else this afternoon. It had been an unexpected and delightful honour when Deborah had offered to come to Hanover Square and help her select her outfit for the ball.

Also she'd recalled that, when she'd left her cousin alone with Deborah's fiancé, the two of them had looked as though they'd welcomed her absence. Had another argument ensued? Had Jemma come to tell her more trouble was afoot? Of course Maura had thought it best to say nothing to Deborah about the Earl's visit to Pereville Parade, despite knowing that the Viscount's daughter did not have a jealous bone in her body. When Deborah had found out that her fiancé had received one of Maura's brother's impertinent letters, asking for marriage proposals for Jemma, Deborah had simply shrugged and smiled whimsically.

'It was nothing important that brought me here.' Jemma had sensed Maura's change in mood, and her need to know that nothing unpleasant had prompted her visit. 'I was passing on my way to the Sheridans and just popped in to tell you that later in the week Mrs Sheridan and her daughter Susan will be coming to my house to dine. Susan is only thirteen, but has a very sweet voice.

We hope she will sing for us, but if she is too shy on the night then no doubt we shall all have a game of cards. Would you like to come too, Maura?' Jemma stepped towards the door with a casual little shrug to convey her apologies for the interruption. It seemed an inappropriate time to have issued an invitation to her modest little at home when they had just been discussing the most important social event in the summer calendar.

'That sounds rather nice,' Deborah said with genuine enthusiasm. 'You shall enjoy it, Maura,' she persuaded with a smile.

'Would you like to come, too?' Maura blurted out, making Jemma swivel to face them, her expression frozen in alarm.

'I think it must be for Miss Bailey to invite me or I shall feel unwelcome.' An appealing smile had accompanied Deborah's demurral. Jemma sensed that behind her diplomacy was a real desire to have an invitation.

'Well, of course, should you like to come?' Jemma stuttered.

'I should like it very much, if you are sure you don't mind an unexpected guest.'

'I would very much like you to come.' As soon as Jemma had said it she accepted it was the truth. Instinctively she knew that, but for the shadow of Marcus Speer wedged between them, she might become friends with Miss Deborah Cleveland.

Jemma had warmed to Deborah before when exchanging a few words, and thought her fortunate to be blessed with a trio of traits to make any young woman green with envy. A sweet nature, a natural vivacity and an ethereal pale beauty were all hers and made her scintillate amongst her peers. In addition to her personal charms she had a pedigree and a portion that would attract attention from even the most distinguished plutocrat, yet she appeared unspoiled by vanity or hauteur and quite deserving of the popularity she had.

'Of course, it goes without saying that I should like to come,' Maura piped up. 'Shall we ask some others? Lucy Duncan and—?'

'No!' Jemma chided in mock alarm. 'You will bankrupt me, Maura! I have my housekeeping accounts to think of, you know. I must have some dinner on other days in the week.'

'You should stop being so generous to those ruffians you support,' Maura declared, not wholly jokingly. 'Then you could hold parties more often.'

'I have started to read scripture to the children at St Peter's Sunday School,' Deborah said, immediately drawing Jemma's surprised glance. 'I'm not sure my parents approve of me "fraternising with the lower orders",' she quoted their terminology with a wry smile, 'but I rather enjoy doing it. Reverend Wells is a good chap.'

'I know Reverend Wells,' Jemma informed. 'He often comes to the meeting hall where the abolitionists give talks.'

'And he slum visits around the East End of London,' Deborah added in a tone that conveyed her awe at his valour in penetrating such unknown territory.

'I have often thought of helping the unfortunate,' Maura interjected, not liking to be left out of the discussion, even if to gain inclusion meant fibbing.

Her comment drew a wry smile from Jemma. It was certainly news to her that Maura felt that way. Usually her cousin listened with wrinkled nose and brow if Jemma described the conditions in tenement houses that some poor unfortunate souls must endure.

A light tap at the door halted their conversation and a maid entered when Maura bid her to do so.

'Mr Wyndham would like to see Miss Bailey in his study before she leaves the house,' the girl whispered shyly, her eyes flitting adoringly to the exquisitely dressed Viscount's daughter.

'It is time I left,' Jemma said, judging the interruption to be a tactful time to depart. 'I must call in and see the Sheridans and then on to Baldwin's for some odds and ends. I shall look forward to seeing you both on Wednesday at about six o'clock.'

Descending the stairs, Jemma wondered whether to simply ignore her guardian's summons to his study and go on her way. She knew that there was only one reason why Theo would want to speak to her: to again try to browbeat her in to allowing Stephen Crabbe to start his courtship. She decided she had no wish for a quarrel with Theo today. He'd looked as miserable as sin just a short while ago, and she didn't imagine his mood had much improved in the interim.

As she approached the foot of the stairs a noise attracted her attention, and she peered over the banister. She glimpsed Theo's sparse thatch over the curve of mahogany. He was loitering, pacing back and forth parallel to the stairs. A rueful smiled tipped her full rosy lips. Obviously he wasn't to be easily thwarted. He'd guessed she might simply slip off disobediently and was prowling in readiness to waylay her before she had a chance to do so.

'Ah, Jemma,' Theo called, forcing warmth to honey his voice, as he noticed her heading towards the exit. 'Don't hurry off. There are things we must discuss, my dear.'

'If it concerns Mr Crabbe, there is nothing to discuss,' Jemma calmly countered and continued walking, pulling on her gloves. 'There is no more to be said on the subject.'

Theo sped behind her slender figure, his studied, mild expression already darkening in frustration. His teeth were grinding on edge, but he managed to coo, 'Won't you at least give the chap ten minutes of your time? Will you do that for me, my dear? As a courtesy?'

With a sigh Jemma spun about, making her pursuer skitter back to avoid bumping in to her. 'I am being courteous to Mr Crabbe in not giving him hope where there is none to be had,' she said firmly. 'I will not be so cruel as to lead a gentleman on.'

'I recall a time when you did,' Theo sneered, forgetting to act nicely. 'I got the impression from Speer when he came here that he'd not forgotten either how you'd flirted with him like a little trollop.' He instinctively stretched his neck at the memory of that painful encounter.

'Well, as my guardian I'm sure you applaud my intention of never again acting so vulgarly.' Anger and shame at the spiteful reminder of how badly she'd once behaved made Jemma blush, then blanch. She knew what Marcus thought of her; he'd made that quite clear when he'd propositioned her as though she indeed were a trollop. Still, Theo's reminder had the power to wound her. With a jerky nod for Manwell, who was discreetly hovering in readiness to open the door, Jemma went out of the house and quickly down the steps.

Before she had even got out of the Square an ominous feeling washed over Jemma. So hot and bothered had she been made by Theo's attempt to antagonize her over her past sins that she had forgotten something silly she'd done far more recently. What had she been thinking of inviting Marcus's fiancée to her home? Of course he would find out about the invitation, and she imagined his immediate reaction would be to think she had done so intending to cause trouble. He would think that jealousy or spite had prompted her to try to sneak close to his fiancée in order that she might drip poison about him in Deborah's ears. *It's not the done thing, sweetheart, for a gentleman to worry his future wife over his mistress.* She recalled his awful words and how they'd shattered any illusion she'd cherished that his interest in her was honourable. He would think that *she* was prepared to worry his future wife by telling her of his planned infidelity and lechery.

Jemma came to a sudden halt and gazed, frowning, back the way she had come as though she might dash back and tell the two young ladies, happily planning their outfits for the Clevelands' ball, that she had made a mistake about her little party and she must cancel the whole thing. After a few deep breaths, and having tilted her chin skywards, she decided she would do no such craven thing! Again she had done nothing wrong. She had simply visited her cousin to issue a social invitation and then included Deborah in the invitation when to refuse to do so would have been impolite. Deborah was welcome to come to her home, and she was also welcome to him! Jemma inwardly asserted as she again marched on in the direction of Marylebone to see her friends. She was not obliged to explain a solitary thing to him. She was her own mistress—not his. And never would she be his!

Chapter Nine

The Palm House Gentlemen's Club was unusual in that on most evenings, within its doors and through a smoky fog, a startling sight could be glimpsed of high-price harlots plying their trade amongst its distinguished members. Although irregular in that respect, the Palm House could boast a clientele to rival the most staid establishment on St James's. An odd ambience of decadent cosiness, mixed with the warm aromas of wine and women, held an undeniable allure and the premises were always packed, after dark, from basement to rafters with affluent gamblers and philanderers.

On this occasion neither diversion had brought Marcus here. He evaded a petite curly-headed blonde who had attempted to accost him as soon as he'd entered and headed towards the faro tables in search of Randolph.

For the past week, during the daytime he'd been busy with Aaron Walters in his office in Cheapside, sorting out his late uncle's estate matters. Once business was done for the day he'd set off for Randolph's home to speak to him. On each occasion he'd been informed he was again out. The manner in which Randolph's man-servant had eloquently elevated his eyebrows this evening, whilst conveying that Mr Chadwicke was away from home, had told Marcus all he needed to know about his friend's physical and mental state. Randolph was lately roistering too hard and was in his cups deeper than was wise. Marcus had a feeling he knew why Randolph was attempting to drown his sorrows. He too wanted to liberate his mind from constantly brooding on their unfinished business.

Having squinted through smoke at the faces around the table, Marcus was disappointed in not finding Randolph's amongst them. He returned murmured greetings to those fellows who hailed him and casually watched for a while as cards swished over baize and the chink of coins and the clink of decanters created a comforting hum in the atmosphere. The blonde was more persistent than he'd expected. As he turned away he saw she'd followed him. She again slipped a white hand on his dark sleeve, but he removed it and continued on to another table. There was no sign of Randolph seated there either, but another fellow did engage his attention.

Stephen Crabbe was lounging on the back of a chair occupied by Philip Duncan. Duncan had his cards drooping in one hand and his forehead propped in the other, a sure sign that he was losing heavily.

Having sensed he was being watched, Stephen turned about. He acknowledged the Earl of Gresham with a wonky smile, then a moment later was weaving his way around the circumference of the card table towards him.

'I 'spect you've heard,' he slurred, swaying to a stop next to Marcus.

'Heard what?' Marcus asked with specious softness.

'No hard feelings this time, eh?' Stephen added on a slack-jawed beam that sent intoxicating fumes to bathe Marcus's face. 'After all, you've got the sweetest filly imaginable so why would you still want Miss Bailey?'

'Why, indeed?' Marcus drawled with such little volume that Stephen slanted an ear closer to listen.

A muscle started to pulse close to Marcus's mouth. He'd wondered how many people knew about Stephen Crabbe's intentions towards Jemma. He now guessed the answer to that must be…too many.

As though to put paid to that theory Crabbe put a finger to his lips to mime secrecy. 'Shh…' he hiccupped. 'Still a bit of a secret, y'see. Wyndham says she's gone all shy on me 'cos she's a li'l bit ashamed of what happened before. I said to Wyndham—tell her not to worry about before when she was a li'l gel. S'long as she's all grown up now.' He dropped Marcus a lewd wink and seemed oblivious to the fact that his words and his attitude were causing Marcus's fists to tighten at his sides.

Marcus began to turn, balancing lightly on his feet. He never usually would let any drunk annoy him, but…

''Course, Wyndham's got to come up with some blunt for her dowry, but he says 's'not a problem,' Stephen continued, oblivious to impending damage.

'You'd best get an IOU signed quickly then, Wyndham's out of credit.' Randolph's ironic advice came from somewhere behind. An instant later he'd pulled Marcus to one side.

'I thought you were about to hit him.' It was Randolph's way of apologising for rough-handling his friend.

'Why would I do that?' Marcus snarled. 'She can marry anybody she damn well wants.'

'It's who you damn well want that's the problem,' Randolph gritted in an underbreath. 'Cleveland collared me at White's this afternoon. He's starting to ask damn awkward questions about you.'

'Such as?'

'Such as, are you avoiding him or his daughter? Such as, are you intending to put in an appearance at their summer ball? Such as, have I any idea why Deborah has suddenly become friendly with Jemma Bailey?'

A ferocious silver gaze darted to Randolph. 'I don't think they're any more than nodding acquaintances.'

'Think again,' Randolph sourly suggested. 'Against her mother's advice Deborah has gone to Pereville Parade this evening to dine with Jemma and some other ladies.'

'Are you sure?' Marcus looked comically disbelieving.

Randolph nodded. 'Deborah has gone with Wyndham's sister in his carriage. She refused to travel in one of her father's. Probably she imagined he'd return in person to collect her and create an atmosphere.'

'I imagine Viscount Cleveland rolling up in a dress coach on Pereville Parade might cause some excitement,' Marcus observed drily.

'I thought so too. It'd be just like that time, not long ago, when the Earl of Gresham rolled up in his fancy phaeton and caused a stir amongst the neighbours.'

Marcus's lips twitched at his friend's sarcastic tone. 'Have you been checking up on me?'

'Not me…but you should know by now that the Earl of Gresham is under observation wherever he goes. Pereville Parade might be a bit of a backwater, but gossip still gets around and eventually the Mayfair tabbies will get their claws into it.'

'So it seems,' Marcus concurred and started for the exit.

'Where are you off to now?' Randolph went after his friend, fending off the blonde who'd given up her pursuit of the Earl.

Marcus pulled open the door and once they were both standing beneath a gaslight on the pavement he turned to answer Randolph. 'I'm going to do what you're always telling me I should do: I'm going to dance attendance upon my fiancée, then escort her home.'

'No, you're not,' Randolph gritted and gripped his friend by one shoulder, swinging him about. 'You're only going there as an excuse to see Jemma. You'll not insult Deborah by using her in such a despicable way.'

Very slowly and significantly Marcus lowered his eyes to the vicious fingers digging into his arm. Randolph removed his hand and thrust that and the other in his pockets. He might have stopped Marcus taking a swing at Stephen Crabbe, but he knew his friend was still impassioned and volatile. For a moment a leaden silence settled on the two men. It continued whilst a couple of merry revellers came out of the club with their doxies and swayed on their way.

'If you'd spoken up sooner we wouldn't all be in such an unholy mess,' Marcus bit out as the drunks disappeared around the corner. 'What do you want me to do, Ran?' His voice was coarsened by hopelessness. 'You know if I jilt Deborah it'll be far worse for her than if I keep a discreet mistress. But it's what you want, isn't it?'

Randolph turned a savage profile towards his friend. A muscle contracted rhythmically in his cheek whilst he considered his reply. 'I want what's best for Deborah, and as you're her future husband that's what you should want too. You'd better start to show her the respect and affection due to her and spend some time with her or I'll…'

'What will you do, Ran?' Marcus taunted deliberately. 'Will you find the courage to approach her yourself now it's too late? Why in damnation did you go off abroad for so long? Why didn't you tell me how you felt about her before you went? We've been friends for two decades. Why didn't you tell me?'

'Because I didn't know!' Randolph barked back in angry frustration. 'I wasn't sure,' he amended with some control. He shoved a hand through his hair. 'Anyhow, what's the point?'

'You should have said something,' Marcus stressed savagely.

Randolph turned on his friend a pair of biting dark eyes set in an anguished countenance. 'Say what?' he spat in a voice shaking with scorn. 'She's an heiress and a Viscount's daughter. I'm the second son of a baron with no prospects and too many cupboards rattling with skeletons.'

'Why didn't you say something to *me*?' Marcus gritted. 'If you'd been here in town when I went wife-hunting at Almack's…' He paused. 'Why, in God's name, did she accept me if she's in love with you?'

'She's not,' Randolph replied bitterly. 'I think she considers me a friend, because I'm your friend.' He grunted a harsh laugh. 'I imagine she accepted you because she knew it was what her parents wanted and she's a dutiful daughter. Or perhaps it's you she loves…'

'No,' Marcus reassured swiftly. 'She's told me it's no

love match on her part. She has *great respect and an adequate fondness for me.*' He'd paraphrased Deborah's acceptance speech to reassure Randolph. 'I was glad to have her honesty and relieved by it too. Unrequited love can be hell,' he muttered with a faraway look, unaware of his friend's eyes narrowing shrewdly on him. 'I told Deborah I felt the same way about her. And I do. Despite what you think I have the utmost respect and a good deal of fondness for her and nothing will change that.'

'Did you set out to find a wife as soon as you knew your uncle was dying?'

Marcus nodded and a hand went to massage his nape.

'Did Solomon say he wanted you to marry the Clevelands' daughter?'

'No!' Marcus gave a hoarse laugh. 'I chose her. I thought she'd be very suitable as the mother of future Gresham heirs. I wanted to make him proud.'

'And wasn't he?' Randolph sounded about to leap to Deborah's defence.

Again a mirthless laugh scratched at Marcus's throat. 'I don't know. He said the woman with whom I spent my life was my business. Of course he liked her, held nothing against her, she's a lovely young woman—God, what a mess!' Marcus groaned, finally lost for words.

'Are you going to carry on with this farce?'

'What else can I do?' Marcus swung on his friend a vicious look. 'I've just said I'd never intentionally hurt Deborah. Revoking the marriage contract would not only be humiliating for her, but for her parents too. Her reputation would suffer, as would mine; not that I give a toss for what the *ton* thinks of me. But I'd hate the Clevelands to suffer.' He took a pace away, returned immediately to snap, 'The Viscountess has started making plans for a blasted wedding. There would be financial losses to consider, but I'd be happy to cover all of their expenses…' Marcus's voice faded and he withdrew into his turbulent thoughts whilst glaring off into the night.

For a short while he'd sensed a weight lifting from his shoulders whilst the essential, soul-searing conversation between the two of them had taken place. But now the burden was creeping back and weighing more heavily than before. The idea of taking to bed, to use as a brood mare, the woman his best friend, a man who was like a brother to him, was in love with, made him feel sick.

'I suppose I'd sooner…it's better it's you than a stranger,' Randolph muttered.

'No, it's not, you fool!' Marcus ground out through closed teeth. 'It's worse; can't you see that?' He strode away towards his carriage, which was pulled up at the kerb.

'Where are you off to?'

'I'm going home, then I'm going to see the Clevelands, then I'm going to Pereville Parade. I need to speak to Deborah.'

'No!' Randolph caught up with his friend in two strides. 'I've nothing to offer her at present. It could take me a couple of years to get enough around me to approach her father.'

'I can help—' Marcus stressed desperately.

'No! I want the respect she's given you!' Randolph blasted back. 'I want respect and an adequate fondness. Do you think I'll go to her with borrowed money? *Your money?* How would that look?'

Marcus knew too well how it would look. It would

seem that he was determined to get rid of his fiancée and would pay another man to take her off his hands. To his shame he knew he would consider doing that to gain his liberty. 'Nobody need know the source of the loan.' The words were uttered, but he knew how futile they were.

'I'd know,' Randolph returned with grim quietness.

Marcus nodded defeat, then without another word he climbed into his coach. Randolph watched him for a moment before turning and going back in to the Palm House.

'Well, this is a capital surprise!'

Lord and Lady Cleveland were sitting opposite one another, ensconced in fireside chairs in the green salon, when the arrival of their future son-in-law was announced. Having enthusiastically welcomed their visitor, the Viscount threw aside his hunting journal. His wife let her novel fall into her satin lap

'Oh…Marcus! Of all days to call on Deborah!' Julia snatched up her fan to cool the heat of her disappointment. 'Debbie has gone out with her friend this evening. She will be so disappointed to have missed you.' She slanted a look at her husband as though unsure whether to divulge further details about their daughter's whereabouts.

Only an hour or so ago a rather one-sided conversation had taken place between husband and wife. Finally a consensus of opinion had been reached that Miss Jemma Bailey was not quite up to scratch as a suitable companion for their daughter. There was the business of her scandalous parents for a start; then the bizarre matter of her guardian begging for fellows to wed her had added to her notoriety. Julia had impressed those facts on her husband whilst he continued furtively glancing at the journal open on his knees rather than attending to her arguments. But eventually he had muttered vague agreement on spotting one of her dainty slippers beginning to tap in annoyance against the rug.

Julia frowned at her husband now whilst hoping he might give a hint as to whether they should reveal where Deborah had gone. It would be nice to delay the Earl's departure until after she returned so the young couple might spend some time together.

The Viscount was unaware his wife required assistance; he was still beaming at their very welcome visitor whilst struggling to lever his portly frame from his chair.

'A little musical recital, with Maura Wyndham, soon be home…' Julia had made a decision and mumbled a minimum of information from behind whizzing ivory sticks.

'How charming,' Marcus said, having just caught the gist of Julia's whispers. He proceeded further into the room, quite slowly, so the Viscount, hampered by an uneven gait, could be at his side.

'We indeed hope it is charming,' the Viscount declared. 'Debbie's gone to Miss Jemma Bailey's for dinner and music. Julia thinks that Deborah shouldn't fraternise with Miss Bailey as she's a bit…you know.' His eyebrows jiggled expressively. 'I say it's nice for these gels to have lots of friends to visit.' He looked at the clock on the wall to check the time, oblivious to his wife flushing fierily behind her fan.

Whilst the Viscount continued to amble across the rug his wife reminded herself of her valid reasons for being sceptical about their daughter fraternising with such a person.

When a whisper had reached Julia's ears that Wyndham had had the brass neck to send a letter to her future son-in-law she'd been in high dudgeon, and a little worried too. She could recall how Marcus had courted the girl some years ago. She'd wanted to shield Deborah from the news that her fiancé had been invited to renew his proposal to a woman he'd once courted. But her daughter had airily admitted she'd heard the rumours. Julia could only marvel at Deborah's unaffected serenity. But, of course, her exquisite daughter had every right to her confidence and self-esteem. Deborah was widely hailed as the most scintillating débutante to have graced Almack's in a long time, whereas Jemma Bailey was the wrong side of twenty and not quite *haute ton*.

Never the less, Julia had realised on that day in Baldwin's fabric emporium, when Lucy Duncan told them of the letters, that a tarnished reputation and the passing of a few more years could not detract from the fact that Miss Bailey was still very attractive. Her luxuriant chestnut tresses and curvaceous figure had, when added to the enviable attributes of regular features and large green eyes, chafed at Julia. That day, as she'd listened to Lucy Duncan reporting that Miss Bailey seemed to be on the hunt for a husband, the quiet, graceful young woman, who once had beguiled her future son-in-law, had seemed a monstrous threat and Julia had begun to feel uneasy.

Since then she'd calmed down for she'd heard the welcome news that Mr Crabbe was about to renew his proposal to Jemma. The Viscountess was of the happy opinion—and the ladies in her circle agreed with her— that Miss Bailey would be a fool not to take him this time. She was not old, exactly, but neither was she young. The pair had a social status that was similar. If she was fairer of face than was he her misdemeanours moderated her appeal, so overall, the match was deemed to be fitting.

'I asked your friend Chadwicke about Miss Bailey.' Gregory had reached his chair and now gratefully sank back into it. 'I recalled you once all were friends. He seemed to think her a nice enough young lady.' The Viscount placed his walking stick close by. 'God's teeth, but he has a heathenish colour on him.' He rumbled a chuckle that shook his chair and unsettled his stick. 'What the deuce has the fellow been doing out in foreign parts for so long?'

'I believe he was visiting people there,' Marcus informed neutrally whilst replacing the Viscount's cane upright and within his reach.

'Debbie might be back soon.' Gregory was again studying the clock. 'We said she must be home by ten-thirty. But you know what these young people are like when enjoying themselves.' He stared intently at the gilt hands that pointed at ten to eight.

'It is still very early,' Marcus said, nudging a foot against the fender. He gave every appearance of being but mildly interested in their discourse about their daughter's whereabouts. In fact, he was attending closely to every word. Randolph had given a hint that this couple was disapproving of Deborah becoming friendly with Jemma. He knew now that Julia especially was unhappy about it.

Oddly, Marcus wasn't sure how he felt about his future wife becoming close to the woman he was determined he would take as his mistress. He wondered if subconsciously he'd accepted that the betrothal was doomed and the marriage would never take place. That at some time he would make love to Jemma was not, however, in doubt.

'I should have insisted on sending Gibbons to get her.' The Viscount was clearly fretting about his only child on whom he unashamedly doted.

Marcus politely sat down as Julia wagged a finger to indicate he do so.

'I suppose we must accept that she's quite an independent young lady now,' Julia remarked on a sigh. 'She's soon to be a wife.' The ruggedly hewn features of her future son-in-law drew Julia's admiring eyes. 'She does not want her papa dogging her footsteps as though she is still a child. Soon she might have a child of her own.'

'She is not yet nineteen,' her husband reminded her, startled.

Julia then sought to remind him of something. She nodded significantly at the decanter on the table by his side.

The silver-stoppered glassware was immediately offered, but drew from Marcus a polite declination.

'I say,' the Viscount suddenly blurted, putting down the decanter rather heavily, 'I've had a capital idea. Why don't you fetch her home, Marcus?' He beamed at his wife, elated by his brainwave. 'As she's not seen you for weeks I'll wager she'll like that. So would the other ladies. They'll swoon to have the Earl of Gresham turn up at their little get together.'

Julia had immediately beamed at her husband's wisdom; it would kill two birds with one stone. She had been fretting about the engaged couple seeing too little of one another; also it would be sensible if Deborah spent a minimum of time at Pereville Parade. Julia's smile was fading as she recalled the identity of the hostess at that address. Of course Deborah could outshine any young lady; but there was no sense in putting Miss Bailey in Marcus's way if it could be avoided. 'But…' she started. It was too late. Marcus was again on his feet and strolling towards the door.

'Of course, I'd be happy to oblige. I know I haven't been as attentive recently as I ought—'

'Oh, understandable,' the Viscount interrupted, flapping a dismissing hand. 'Bad time for you. Your uncle and so on…much to do, understand.' He struggled up again from his chair despite Marcus politely insisting he should not. But the Viscount was too pleased to be deterred from showing his appreciation, and got up with the aid of his cane.

'You should not have meddled,' his wife hissed as the door closed on Marcus's departing figure.

'Eh?' the Viscount responded in bemusement as he once more sank down into his chair.

'Have you forgot where Deborah has gone this evening?'

'To Miss Bailey's singsong.'

'Yes, indeed! And once he wanted to marry *her*,' his huffy wife reminded him.

'But he doesn't any more,' Gregory grunted, putting down his stick. 'He's going to marry Deborah…isn't he?'

Chapter Ten

A gentleman was preparing to knock on Jemma's door when a startling sight made his hand drop back to his side. The Earl of Gresham's carriage had turned the corner into Pereville Parade and was now smoothly drawing to a halt at the kerb in front of him.

Unbeknown to Bert Sheridan, the coach's occupant was on a similar errand to the one that had brought him to Miss Bailey's home. Bert had come to collect his wife and eldest daughter to take them safely home to Marylebone.

Twilight was now approaching, but even so Bert could clearly see the splendid, crested coach parked close to his gig, and making it seem decidedly shabby in comparison. The Earl's two pairs of matched greys were impeccably behaved. They tossed their silken heads in unison, causing Bert's grumpy mare to snort suspiciously. Atop the magnificent equipage the coachmen were clothed in black and, but for the wink of silver buttons on their livery, they might have merged with the shadows so still were they.

A moment later, a lithe figure had descended from the vehicle. Had the Gresham crest not hinted at the occupant's identity Bert would in any case have recognised him. Yet he was still astonished to be confronted with the Earl of Gresham in such an unfashionable quarter of town.

Bert had never acquired the seniority needed to deal with the affairs of a client as important as Marcus Speer. But the fellow was a friendly gentleman who found it unnecessary to boost his ego by impressing his status on lesser mortals. His uncle, Solomon, had had the same sort of gracious spirit and would stop and chat when time permitted.

As the Earl strolled in his direction Bert was relieved to see that his lordship appeared quite casual. Probably due to the warmth of the evening he had at some time removed his jacket and carried it pegged over his shoulder on a thumb. His linen-clad torso looked dispiritingly muscular to Bert, who was of slight build and advanced years. He was glad when the Earl shrugged back in to the garment before any female managed to take a swooning gape at the breadth of his chest.

'I hope the ladies have enjoyed their entertainment,' Bert greeted him.

'I'm sure they have,' Marcus replied cordially. He shot snow-white cuffs free of his sleeves, then extended his hand.

Bert's wife had excitedly told him that this man's fiancée was attending Jemma's little at home, but not for one moment had Bert imagined that the Earl would arrive in person to collect her from such a modest gathering. The upper classes had all manner of lackeys to carry out such tasks for them. A romantic notion occurred to Bert that made him inwardly smile: upperclass members, even those fellows renowned for ruthless business dealings, were not immune to falling in love or wanting to find an excuse to see their beloved.

'I'm here to collect my wife and daughter.' Bert offered the information in case the Earl was wondering what had brought *him* here.

Marcus nodded in understanding. He then gestured that the older man should go before him back up the steps to knock on the door.

When Jemma's young housemaid continued to stare at him Marcus gave her what he hoped to be a disarming smile. He was used to being stared at by women. Usually they blushed and preened beneath his attention. Polly looked increasingly miserable to have his kind regard.

Once Mr Sheridan had stepped over the threshold Polly put her petite figure in front of the Earl's powerful body, blocking his way. She wasn't likely to forget this fellow upsetting her mistress, or that Miss Bailey had given her instructions on what to do should he come back.

'Miss…Miss Bailey's indisposed,' she stuttered and tried to close the door in the Earl's face.

At that moment the unmistakable note of Jemma's musical chuckle could be heard wafting from the parlour. A moment later more jovial females were heard joining in the laughter.

'It seems Miss Bailey has made a remarkable recovery,' Marcus said, staying the door with a firm hand and voice. So Jemma had banned him from her presence, had she? Obviously he was not yet forgiven…

or forgotten. 'Perhaps you would let Miss Cleveland know that I am here to take her home,' Marcus added dulcetly as Polly stood her ground.

Polly went as red as the tulips adorning the table by her side. She mumbled something unintelligible and scurried away without closing the door. Marcus performed the office and turned to see Bert gaping at him.

'It sounds as though the ladies are having good fun,' Bert blurted, valiantly trying to disguise his astonishment at having beheld a slip of a girl being insolent to the Earl of Gresham.

'Indeed it does,' Marcus replied easily and stuffed his hands in his pockets. As the laughter and chatter continued he looked about. When it abruptly ceased he knew his arrival had been announced. He smiled and remarked, 'I think we might be a little premature.' In fact, Marcus had guessed he'd arrived early to collect Deborah. He understood his fiancée's character well enough to expect her to tell him so.

A moment later a young lady of about thirteen had skipped into the hallway. She giggled at the sight of the two gentlemen and hared off with her pretty rosebud skirts swaying in her fingers. It was barely moments later that the wide passage was crowded with females of differing ages and appearances. The majority of those ladies were beaming happily, but two looked less pleased to see the new arrivals.

A short while ago when Polly had scurried up to Jemma and hissed in her ear that she'd had to let in that gentleman who was not allowed in because he'd come for Miss Cleveland, Jemma had simply continued happily smiling. A moment later the garbled message had untangled in her mind and she'd frowned in puzzlement. When young Susan had breathlessly blurted that a big handsome man was with her papa in the hall the awful truth had become apparent. Jemma had shot out of her chair. It was not too noticeable a reaction to knowing that Marcus Speer was close by. Most of the other ladies had also abandoned their game of charades and jumped to their feet on digesting Susan's exciting news.

With her heart drumming wildly, Jemma had followed the others to the hallway and halted at the back of the group. Being slightly taller than any of her guests, she could see over a cluster of light and dark coiffures and straight in to the Earl of Gresham's eyes. Steadily he stared back and with such intense impassivity that Mrs Sheridan and Maura Wyndham turned to locate the target of those boring silver eyes. They knew it wasn't Deborah, for she was at one side of the group and surely would draw a more affectionate look from her future husband?

The ladies were distracted from further inner debate on the matter as Deborah gave her illustrious fiancé a public ticking off.

'Oh, Marcus! Really! It is a nice surprise to see you, and very good of you to come to take me home, but you are here far too soon. I think I might send you away again.'

'I think you should reconsider doing so, my dear.'

His reply seemed cool and casual, but Jemma had recognised a threat in his drawling tone even if Deborah had not.

'It doesn't matter that the gentlemen are a little early,' Jemma attempted to soothe the situation, if rather shrilly. As the shock of seeing him receded a little, she tugged together the shreds of her composure and attempted to act the competent hostess. Her sharp little chin elevated; a smile hovered on her full lips and when she next spoke her voice had regained a well-modulated tone. 'Please…why do you not all come in to the parlour? Unless, of course, anyone would like to depart straight away?' A heavy hint accented her last few words and her eyes flitted, lingered pleadingly on Marcus. A familiar sardonic light in his languid gaze answered her tacit request that he go away. The message was clear; he had no intention of letting her get off lightly, or of taking Deborah immediately home. Her heart was hammering uncomfortably beneath her ribs, yet even before her eyes had skittered away from his she forlornly knew that despite everything—her futile prohibition, and the presence of his future wife—she was stupidly pleased to see him.

Butterflies were dancing in her stomach just as they had the last time he'd turned up unexpectedly. On that occasion he'd kissed her, branded her flesh through her clothes, then sought to expose her breasts to his artful touch. A glancing together of their eyes told her he understood what was in her mind, for he was thinking about it too. Heat seeped in to Jemma's face as sultry, seductive memories refused to be ejected from her head. Defiant images whirled behind her eyes, weakening her limbs, dulling her senses to the movements and conversations of her guests grouped around her. It was the sound of his fiancée's voice that finally hauled Jemma out of her sensual daze and back to an awful reality.

'Miss Bailey has provided us with some wonderful

fun this evening.' Deborah had linked arms with Marcus and now drew him towards her hostess.

Immediately Jemma moved away with a gesture that invited the company to join her in the front parlour. Behind the leading couple the other guests fell into step, still chatting, and obviously not yet ready to leave.

'We have had a very good supper and some amusing charades; also I partnered Miss Bailey at piquet, and we won two of the card games,' Deborah continued regaling Marcus with the details of their lively entertainment. 'Susan has sung for us; perhaps she might do so again so you might enjoy her fine voice.' Deborah gave the young songstress an enquiring smile. But Susan had become shy and was blushing and fidgeting behind her mother's back. Deborah gave the girl a nod of reassurance and changed the subject.

'Miss Bailey promised that before the end of the evening we could all visit her conservatory and enjoy the perfumed blooms.'

'Dusk is falling now, I fear,' Jemma interjected quickly. 'There will not be much light by which to see and the show is quite small.' She did not want any delays in the departure of her guests.

'Oh, but the scent of the jasmine will be wonderful in the evening air,' Deborah enthused. 'Might I still have a quick tour and a little sprig of it?'

The fact that the Clevelands had several greenhouses stocked with exotic species, both in town and in country, seemed to have escaped Miss Cleveland's memory. It had not, however, eluded Marcus. He knew the minx could enjoy bouquets of scented stuff at home, if she really wanted to. He gave Deborah a thoughtful look.

'Of course…if you would like to see the plants…*if you have time to*,' Jemma amended quickly, stressfully. She hoped Marcus would heed the hint that she wanted him to immediately take Deborah home. But, of course, he'd known she wished him to go from the moment their eyes had clashed in the hallway.

The situation for her was excruciating. This she had not anticipated! Of course she had realised the instant the invitation had been issued to Deborah that trouble might ensue when he found out. But not so soon! Not before the evening—and it had been such a good evening!—had properly come to a close. Deborah had obviously not expected, or wanted, him to escort her home. Why had he come? Was it simply to torment her with his presence and watch her squirm?

Deborah had been the perfect guest. She was charming, witty and so very amiable to everyone. Her only hint at ill humour had been when Marcus had turned up. How would Deborah react to knowing that recently her betrothed had been in this very room, offering to her those intimacies that soon he would vow to bestow only on his bride? Any fiancée must be distraught to know that her future husband was preparing to take a new mistress before he'd even taken her down the aisle. Jemma knew that if their positions were reversed she would be furious and mortified to be so insulted. Indeed, he had offended her already by offering to handsomely pay her for his pleasure.

A carte blanche…anything her heart or body desired he'd promised her…

She'd shown him too well what her body wanted, but what her heart yearned for… Jemma feared she knew the answer to that too. But it was too late to mourn for what might have been. Marcus Speer wanted Deborah for his wife, and he wanted Jemma to quench his lust. In return he assumed she would be satisfied with his ridiculous generosity. She imagined his *carte blanche* was intended to supply her with any amount of trinkets and gowns. A soulless arrangement, to be sure, but to her bitter shame she realised that still she longed to be with him; still she could not banish the thought that when one was hungry crumbs were better than nothing at all.

'I adore the scent of jasmine and lilies.'

Maura had interrupted Jemma's wistful thoughts with a bright observation.

'Lilies! Are there lilies? How wonderful! Do you know the way to the conservatory?' Deborah asked her fellow enthusiast.

Maura nodded. 'I know there is an orchid in bloom too.'

'Would you mind if Maura quickly gave me a little tour, Miss Bailey? I would not want you to abandon your other guests to indulge me. Unless…would anyone else like to come too?' Deborah asked, with an encompassing smile. 'I know Marcus has no interest in such things,' she added with a dismissive cluck of the tongue and a toss of her blonde curls.

'May I come with you?' Susan asked.

In reply Deborah put an arm about her shoulders and ushered her towards the door with her.

'Of course…do take a look…if you wish to…' Jemma murmured rather breathily.

As the little party trooped out only Bert and Yvette Sheridan remained in the room with Jemma and Marcus. The couple had distanced themselves and seemed to be engaged in a quiet, intimate conversation. From a stray word that floated to her side of the room, punctuating a tense silence, Jemma realised that they were discussing Mr Sheridan's mother who had been in poor health. Not wanting to seem to eavesdrop, Jemma struck the set of cushions on the sofa into shape whilst scouring her mind to find a neutral topic to discuss with the sardonic gentleman whose eyes she studiously sought to avoid.

She could feel a silver stare searing the top of her head. She sensed too that if she looked up at him she would glimpse a familiar mockery concealed behind his lashes. He was waiting to see if her nerve would crumble and she would cravenly flee his company and join the ladies in the conservatory. She realised an explanation was due from her as to why his fiancée was a guest in her house. She knew too that he was impatient to have it. There had been no malice or duplicity involved in issuing Deborah with an invitation yet, despite her innocence, she presently felt unequal to the task of defending herself.

But neither was she prepared to let him stampede her into cowardice or rudeness. It would be ill-mannered to deny him the offer of a chair and a little refreshment while he waited for his fiancée to indulge her whim to look at the plants. Indeed, the suggestion that he might like to join the party in the conservatory should be made even if Deborah had seemed reluctant to have his company.

'Would you like to see the orchids, my lord?' Jemma asked hoarsely.

'I think I'd like a drink,' Marcus murmured drily. 'Do you have some wine to offer me?'

'Yes, of course,' Jemma said with a slight smile. She was glad to have a task to perform that took her a little away from his overpowering presence. 'I'll get Polly to bring a carafe. Mr Sheridan might like some, too.'

'Will Polly pour me a glass or throw it over me?'

Jemma choked back a spontaneous giggle. 'I hope she was not rude to you?'

'Unwelcoming is, I think, a good description.'

'Good,' Jemma breathed, her voice pitched so only he could hear, her jade eyes challenging a steady silver gaze. 'It is nice to know one's servant follows instructions exactly.'

'Why am I unwelcome?'

'I think you know the answer to that,' Jemma immediately replied in the same low tone. She turned swiftly away and went to the door to summon Polly to bring the wine.

'We shall also take a stroll to the greenhouse, if we may.'

Jemma was startled to find Bert and Yvette waiting to exit the room as she twisted about.

'Umm…of course,' Jemma said, forcing a smile and trying not to let her alarm show. As a last resort to make the couple stay in the parlour, she blurted to Bert Sheridan, 'Would you not like to have a glass of wine? Polly has gone to fetch some.'

'Thank you, but no,' Bert replied but with a grateful smile for the offer. 'I should like to see an orchid,' he added. 'I've an ambition to grow an exotic species.'

The couple's footsteps could be heard echoing on the hallway flags. The hum of their conversation finally died away, and the silence in the room seemed to last for an eternity. The space between them was a few yards, yet it seemed to widen to a chasm. Finally Jemma found a voice, albeit one that was husky and stilted. In rapid bursts she said what she must, conscious that soon Polly or her guests would be back to interrupt them. And Lord only knew she did not want to be overheard.

'I should like to make it clear that I have not said a word to your fiancée about your disgusting offer to me. Neither is it my intention to do so. I am not trying to become her friend or your enemy. I invited her here this evening because not to do so would have been bad manners. I wished dearly at first to rescind the invitation…but only at first.' Her mutinous jade eyes swept away from the wall she'd been studying whilst speaking and clashed with a deceptively lazy gaze. 'Now I'm glad I did not.' She moistened her arid lips.

From beneath screening lashes Marcus's silver eyes followed the movement of Jemma's small pink tongue-tip trailing on her soft rosy mouth.

'Deborah is a delightful young woman,' Jemma resumed hoarsely. 'I like her, and regret that at some time she is sure to be distraught to discover that you were never worthy to be her husband.'

'And have you yet decided if I am worthy to be your lover?'

Jemma blushed to the roots of her glossy locks. She immediately glanced at the door to check that they were alone despite the fact that his insufferable amusement had been so quiet she'd barely heard the words. 'How dare you speak to me so when your future wife is under the same roof…under *my* roof!'

'I've said that my wife need not concern you.'

'It seems she need not concern you either!' Jemma countered in a reproachful hiss. 'You are to become Deborah's husband, yet still you will not curb your lechery even at such an inappropriate time as this. You are despicable.'

'And you are naïve, Jemma,' he countered softly, 'if you believe that marriage and passion must go hand in hand. I would have imagined that you'd learned at your mother's knee that they do not. If that were not lesson enough for you, then Burnham's betrayal must have convinced you love matches are a fantasy.'

His attitude had changed, hardened. No hint of indolent humour now honeyed his voice, although his easy stance made him appear relaxed.

For a moment Jemma was too stunned to think of anything sensible to say. She had not expected that he might use her parents' disastrous marriage as a tool against her, or that he would brutally remind her of Robert's detection. He'd sounded scornfully surprised that her experiences as a child had not shaped her attitude to love and made her as contemptuous of it as he seemed to be.

He didn't know, nor, she imagined, would he care to be told, that her parents' violent arguments and mutual despising had conversely instilled deep in her being a need to be loved and cherished as a wife. Equally, she yearned to return that devotion to the man she married. It was the reason she had clung tenaciously to her affection for Robert and had felt thoroughly ashamed of her attraction to Marcus. She could not deny that she'd thought of jilting Robert because of her growing attachment to Marcus, but her conscience had not allowed her to do it. Never would she want to cause another human being the pain she'd witnessed her parents endure because of their lack of loyalty and fidelity. Of course she'd heard the whispers that her father was equally to blame for the parlous state of his marriage. It wasn't just her mother's fault. She knew, too, that her father had discreetly kept a mistress until just before his death. But Jemma had sadly observed how the bitter humiliation of being abandoned by his wife had consumed her father up until the end of his life.

Tears of frustration and anger sprang to blur Jemma's vision. She would dearly have loved to blast at Marcus her opinion of his cynicism. She itched to tell him that long ago she'd decided she would sooner live her life as a spinster than submit to the sort of sham of a marriage he preferred. With her guests close by she could do nothing but glare at him through the glitter in her eyes.

'If you're still not convinced and need a different example you need only cast your mind back to what happened between us.' Marcus took a step closer to her. One of his hands moved as though he would comfort her as the sheen in her eyes crystallised on her lashes.

'How is that an example of a love match? It was nothing…a pointless flirtation.' Jemma noticed his fingers hover, then clench before returning to his side.

'Nothing? A pointless flirtation?' he echoed in a silky voice. 'Is that what it was? Thank you for finally enlightening me.' He braced a hand against the mantelpiece and the knuckles showed as white as the marble beneath them.

'What was it then, if not infatuation?' A jeering edge had entered her tone. 'You asked me to marry you, but you never once spoke of love.'

'And rightly so,' Marcus replied, 'as it turned out…'

'You never spoke of our future together either…or of family…or of children. You said nothing much at all…' she added, unable to stop now that festering questions, which had been buried too long and too deep, were finally unearthed. 'Why did you propose? What was it you wanted with me?'

'To get you into bed…what else?' he growled impenitently.

Jemma stared at him, her complexion alternating between pink and white. 'You would have married me just for that?' she whispered. 'Even though you have just said you can easily separate marriage and carnality?'

'Of course. I know you think me a debauched rake, Jemma, but even I'd baulk at taking a seventeen-year-old débutante as my mistress.'

'But…was that all?'

A chuckle grazed his throat that sounded low and lewd and filled with bitter meaning 'Believe me, when I was twenty-six and pathetically romantic, it was enough.'

Chapter Eleven

'I don't understand you.'

'You don't need to.' An idle gesture dismissed his brusque levity. 'All you need to know, Jemma, is that I want you and I know you want me, too. Why deny it?' He turned so his back was against the high marble shelf. Long, patrician fingers swept back his black jacket from his waist to plant themselves on his hips. A ruthless silver stare captured her restless glance. 'Why deny it, Jemma?' he repeated with mesmerising softness.

Even though separated by a space she felt overpowered by his presence, so very aware of the scent of sandalwood that clung to his clothes and skin. She knew if he came even one step closer she might succumb to the need to have him touch her, or to touch him. He looked quite magnificent, as usual. Again he wore clothes of sombre elegance, obviously expensive, and tailored by an expert so snugly did they sit on his athletic shape. His countenance was heartbreakingly handsome, his jaw contoured by dusky stubble that highlighted his cheeks' concavity. Her hands began to tremor as she recalled how she'd once, years ago, run her palms over that scratchy skin. She would giggle when his bruising kisses would abrade her cheeks as well as her lips.

She didn't understand or trust him, for his persuasion was full of sophistry and contradictions, but she was beginning to know obsession and how it might make someone who thought herself in love, and immune to temptation, act in a shameful way with another man. Conversely, it might make a wealthy philanderer act chivalrously and curb his lust for a silly willing girl. Obsession had made Marcus Speer ready to pledge his future to a child bride when all he'd truly desired was her virgin body in his bed. She'd glimpsed his predicament before her reason and her anger veiled it.

'Are you going to answer me, Jemma?' His voice was gentle and seemed to come from a long way off, but it had the power to penetrate her soulfulness.

'You may have your answer,' she finally said. 'I'll deny it because I have a conscience and I hope enough decency not to want to break another woman's heart by having what is not rightfully mine.'

'If Deborah were to have her heart broken, I assure you it wouldn't be my doing.'

There was an ironic significance in his voice that made Jemma's stomach lurch. Was he insinuating that an affair between them would be so discreet and meaningless that it would have no power to hurt Deborah? Or was it more his intention to emphasise his heartless opinion on marriage? He'd hinted that he was not in love with his future bride.

'I still don't understand you. But perhaps confusing me is your intention…' She waited, but gained nothing from him except an impassive stare that locked together their eyes. 'Must I now press you for a reply, my lord?'

He smiled, but she sensed it was because he found the way she'd addressed him amusing rather than the subject under discussion.

'Are you saying that Deborah shares your mercenary view on marriage?' Still Jemma found his expression inscrutable and he seemed unwilling to share his thoughts. 'I must conclude then that I am insignificant and you imagine your future wife won't be bothered to know that you want to sleep with me.' She tore her eyes from the steely gaze and turned away.

'And I conclude that you want my reassurance that you mean something to me. Do you?'

She had spoken rashly, as an enslaved woman would when she felt vulnerable and in need of sweet words from a man who intended to use her as a vessel for his lust. 'I want nothing from you,' Jemma croaked, spinning back towards him in a swish of skirts.

'I think you know that's not true, Jemma,' he contradicted quietly. 'I think you want as much from me as I want from you. And perhaps more than I've offered…'

He watched blood seep beneath her complexion as he insinuated at the passion they'd shared that day, and something else.

That same evening he had retrieved their conversation from where it whirred constantly at the back of his mind. Odd phrases Jemma had murmured, whilst languid in his embrace, about Deborah and a jilting, had finally made sense once his mind was free of numbing lust. She'd capitulated, revealed to him her need, and so thought he'd do the honourable thing and alter his proposition to a proper proposal. Despite her recent protestations to the contrary, Jemma still wanted him, and with as much fervour as when she'd been seventeen. The difference was that now Burnham had defected she was prepared to have him as the fellow's substitute. Never in his life had Marcus settled for second place, and he didn't intend to start now.

'The last time I was here I recall we were engaged in a similar conversation, before we were distracted and found something more pleasurable to do.'

Jemma turned her back on him to display her disdain, and conceal her burning cheeks. From the moment he'd arrived she'd hoped he might be gentleman enough not to mention her wanton behaviour on that occasion. His next words had her again pivoting back towards him in dismay.

'You said something that day that intrigued me. You asked if I'd spoken to Deborah and whether she would jilt me. You gave the impression that you believed I might gallantly allow Deborah to end our betrothal because I wanted to marry you instead.' He strolled a little closer. 'Were you worried about breaking another woman's heart then?'

He'd pinpointed an awful, shameful truth. Jemma's complexion turned chalky. She moistened her parched lips, desperately trying to conceal her guilt and think of a way to deny his allegation. 'You're wrong; I've already said I'd sooner marry Mr Crabbe than you. But I understand that a man of your arrogance would find ways of manipulating words to boost his conceit.'

'What did you mean when you said it?'

'I…I said I thought you should speak to Deborah because…it's only fair she knows you will be an incorrigible adulterer. She should jilt you and find a husband who will cherish her rather than humiliate her.'

'Have you been talking to my good friend Randolph?' Marcus muttered mordantly.

'I barely know your friend Mr Chadwicke,' she returned, frowning. 'I can assure you I haven't spoken to him in years.'

'It was a private joke, Jemma,' he gently explained. 'Forget about that. Tell me what you want.'

'*What I want?*' The words were ejected in suffocated outrage. 'Do you *care* what I want?' She allowed no time for him to answer before plunging on, 'Very well, I shall tell you what I dearly would like. I'd like to be free of my guardian's influence so I might never again be prey to a brute like you.' Jemma sucked in a breath that tautened the buttons on her bodice. Straining emerald silk drew eyes like silver stars to a shimmering outline of ripe round breasts. As though Jemma remembered that his plundering fingers had once before demolished her modesty, and her neat attire, her hand instinctively fluttered to protect her bodice fastenings. 'But presently what I want is that you go from here and never return,' she whispered.

'I've brought the wine, m'm.' Polly's mumbled announcement seemed a clamour in a terrible silence and made Jemma jerk about. The maid needed no more than her mistress's nervous reaction as an indication that the two of them were at odds again. Her eyes immediately glared blame at the Earl as she stepped into the room and slid a tray holding a carafe of red wine and several glasses on to polished mahogany. For some time Polly had hovered in the hallway, not wanting to eavesdrop, to be sure, but interpreting the intense bursts of hushed dialogue as a sign that an argument was taking place. As soon as a silence had allowed she had plunged into the room. Now Polly's eyes remained on the rug as she awaited her dismissal.

'Thank you.' Jemma rewarded her servant with a wavering smile, but Polly was already on her way out again. Jemma blinked rapidly, making dew drop from her lashes to her cheeks. Quickly she dashed it away, hoping that her maid had not noticed her upset.

Marcus swore beneath his breath. A gesture and grimace at the ceiling acknowledged his defeat; he'd noticed her small pearly teeth sinking in to her lower lip to still its wobble. He felt the brute she'd called him for having upset her, when what he wanted to do was haul her into his arms and kiss her.

Jemma splashed some wine into a glass. Instead of carrying it to him she left it on the tray and went instead to the door to go and hurry her guests' departure. 'Your wine, my lord,' she murmured from the threshold. In a voice that thrummed with emotion she added, 'I hope it chokes you.'

'Please say you will come!'

'Of course, we would all be greatly honoured to attend.' Yvette Sheridan sounded as pleased as punch, but also incredulous to have secured an invitation to the Clevelands' ball.

'Miss Bailey? You will come, won't you?' Deborah asked, turning to Jemma.

'I…umm…I…'

'But, of course, you must come, Jemma,' Maura interrupted her cousin's dithering response.

'I have very much enjoyed your party; I should like to return you an invitation. Please do come,' Deborah appealed with a winning smile for Jemma.

'Of course, I should be delighted to have an invitation,' Jemma replied, carefully avoiding indicating her acceptance.

They had all returned to the parlour to say their goodbyes when Deborah had stunned the company by declaring she would like everyone to attend her ball. Of course, she knew that Susan, at thirteen, and several years away from coming out, would not be able to attend. But she had soothed Susan's sulks by saying that she must instead come to her home to take tea.

While the lively chatter continued, Jemma kept her attention concentrated on her guests despite being very aware of a tall saturnine gentleman who was still lounging against the chimneypiece where she'd left him. It seemed there was no need to worry about avoiding his eyes; Marcus seemed equally keen now to ignore her. But, as she looked at the decanter and saw it was very depleted, she fleetingly peeked his way. He was toying with the stem of his glass, his eyes following the movement of his restless fingers. But his mouth quirked, as though he knew she'd glanced at him and that she was thinking that he'd not choked, as she'd hoped, but he might instead be drunk to spite her.

A moment later he spoke, and it was obvious he was in perfect control of all his faculties.

'I know you are enjoying yourself, Deborah, but I think it is time we left, my dear. Your parents want you home by ten-thirty.' He looked and sounded charm and elegance incarnate as he strolled away from the fireplace.

This time there was no excuse made to linger a while. His dutiful fiancée began to take her leave of the little assembly and within a very short while Polly had shown out the couple.

Half an hour later, having just waved on their way her other guests, Jemma was alone in her parlour and looking about at the debris of her party. Playing cards and counters were still scattered on two small baize tables. Teacups and saucers and smatterings of their buffet supper littered the sideboard. Some song sheets had also been discarded there by young Susan. Her jade eyes swerved towards the mantelpiece and found a goblet left on the shelf. It had a small amount of ruby wine left in it.

Jemma picked up the glass by its stem and rocked the liquid back and forth for a moment before sipping at it. She felt light-headed with nervous exhaustion, and her thick lashes drooped in an inky web over eyes that felt heavy. She swayed on her feet as she finished every drop. Dreamily, her small tongue tasted her sticky sweet lips as she replaced the glass and turned away to go to bed.

Across town another woman was savouring the claret on her palate whilst brooding on the same gentleman who was keeping Jemma's mind and body from sinking comfortably into slumber.

Finally Jemma dozed off, but Pauline Vaux was not interested in getting off to sleep. She was waiting impatiently for Marcus's arrival, yet drowning her sorrows, too, for she feared she was waiting in vain.

Having grown tired of sending him notes summoning him to visit her at her Ransome Street home, Pauline had that afternoon tried to snare him at his mansion. Of course she knew that in going there she would break every code and give the gossips something to tattle over.

She was the widow of a baronet, rightfully a Lady, but her husband had gone to meet his maker leaving her heavily in debt and languishing in the shadow of his unpopularity. Knowing the risks, still she had gone to Beaufort Place, fired with recklessness. She had sensed for some time that she was losing Marcus and must urgently recapture his interest.

Marcus had not been at home when she'd arrived; had he been in, Pauline imagined he would not have received her. But she had made her point. Or so she'd thought. If he tried to ignore her, she would force him to take notice of her. And he had. She had barely been home an hour before a note arrived informing her in one terse sentence that he would call on her tonight. She had felt jubilant to receive it.

Now as the minutes ticked by, and still no sign of him, she felt increasingly dejected. Pauline rolled on to her rounded belly and looked at the little clock above her head on the wall. It was just ten minutes past twelve, yet it seemed an age since she'd heard the chimes for midnight. She reached for the depleted bottle of claret and upended it. She let the empty vessel drop to the floor and gulped from her glass while resentful reminders of her rival circled in her mind.

Since Marcus had started to court Deborah Cleveland, his attitude towards her had seemed to change. Pauline had realised that at some point he would marry to continue his line. He had never denied that he wanted a legitimate heir. The match was generally regarded to be perfect, and so it appeared. But Pauline had been sure that Marcus had not fallen in love with Deborah.

It was galling to think that she might be mistaken and a milksop miss, who probably didn't even know how to properly kiss him, might have ousted her from the Earl of Gresham's life. Pauline knew that she'd never warm Marcus's heart sufficiently to prise a proposal from him, yet she'd been confident of her skill in warming his bed. Lately Marcus had been under siege from a particularly persistent opera dancer. In retaliation Pauline had deliberately made a show of encouraging one of the gallants in her circle in the hope of making him jealous. But none of those young bucks could match Marcus's bed skills. Sly-eyed women might constantly put themselves in his way, and he might succumb to one or two, but she was the woman known as Marcus Speer's mistress. Now he was the Earl of Gresham, and she intended enjoying the benefits the enhanced status would afford her.

The long-anticipated scrape of a key in a lock eluded her drink-dulled senses, but the sound of his boots hitting the stairs was unmistakable. With a guttural mew of triumph Pauline squirmed on to her back in a jumble of limbs that took her nightdress up high on her thighs. Quickly her flaxen tresses were artfully arranged on plumped-up pillows. The froth of lace at her bosom was tugged lower, allowing rosy buds to peep over the top.

Marcus braced a hand on the doorjamb and looked dispassionately at the seductive scene. The perfumed room was theatrically lit with candles, strategically placed to highlight Pauline's pale, plump flesh. She arched up to tempt him closer with thrusting cleavage and parted, wine-stained lips.

Alluring as she looked, Marcus realised the invitation to join her in bed would not be hard to resist. Pauline's absurd attempt to coerce him into dancing to her tune had completely quashed any lingering desire he felt for her. Despite the unrelieved throb in his groin that Jemma had started earlier that evening, his dearest need was to get this over with and go home to sleep alone. The evening had turned out to be an unexpected dilemma; it had taken its toll and he felt shattered.

He knew that Pauline had sensed he was cooling towards her. It was not just that tedium had set in on his part. This wasn't the only occasion that he'd turned up to find her rather too tipsy. Also he imagined she was flaunting her lovers intentionally in an attempt to provoke him. Instead of feeling jealous, he'd hoped one of those fellows might offer to take her off his hands.

Throughout their relationship he'd enjoyed the company of other women. Marcus was not selfish, or a hypocrite. But it was a tacit requirement of his mistress to act with self-respect and discretion. For some weeks Pauline had been lacking in both. This afternoon she'd compounded her faults by being brazen about it. It seemed she was sinking naturally into the role of common trollop. An indolent look flowed over her, noting the glaze of inebriation in her eyes. The glass was back at her lips, and she sipped whilst her fingers fumbled loose her bodice laces, exposing her breasts to his gaze.

'Are you going to stand and stare all night?' Pauline slurred. His expression appeared a little odd, but she never the less felt confident of making him stay. She twirled a blonde curl about a finger while shifting apart her thighs on silk sheets. 'Why don't you come here, Marcus, and let me show you how much I've missed you?' she purred.

A hard smile tilted Marcus's mouth. 'First I think it's only fair I tell you something,' he said.

Chapter Twelve

⤜⟷⤛

Theo was also out after midnight in the environs of Cheapside. As his carriage passed the top of Ransome Street at half past midnight, he twitched the blind at the window at an opportune moment to observe the Earl of Gresham descending the steps of Lady Vaux's residence. His features twisted into a study of leering resentfulness. Just as with everything else in his damnably charmed life, it seemed Speer was blessed when it came to women. His future wife was an angel bearing riches, his mistress a luscious, lusty blonde.

He glanced back at the Earl of Gresham's coach to see it just turning the corner in the direction of Mayfair. No doubt the bastard was heading home sated; Theo doubted he would be so lucky in half an hour's time.

Theo was en route to see his paramour. Becky Wright was in every way Pauline Vaux's inferior, and the comparison was deflating. Becky liked to tell her friends that she lived in a lodging house. A more correct term for the property would be a brothel. Theo realised that even affording the niggardly relief Becky provided would soon be beyond his means, unless he could quickly find a solution to his financial difficulties. Musing on his money worries brought his accursed cousin, Jemma, to mind, and his scowl became blacker. If the chit weren't so damned proud and obstinate, and put her mind to getting a husband like every other female of her age and class, he'd have no problems to speak of.

As Theo's carriage halted in Old Street he plunged out on to the pavement, feeling in a foul mood. Many times he had been here, yet always he hesitated to take a disdainful peer about at his seedy surroundings. A far smarter vehicle than his own, parked a few yards along the street, arrested his stabbing eyes as they penetrated the dusk. As the owner of the vehicle alighted, and a gas lamp glinted on flaxen curls, Theo cursed—he'd recognised the fellow. But it was too late to hop back in his carriage and escape. He'd been spotted.

'I hope you're not going to tell me again you're out of funds, Wyndham.' Graham Quick approached with a purposeful stride that clacked boot leather on cobbles. 'If you can afford to pay for sweet Becky tonight, you can pay me something from what you owe.'

'I hadn't realised you were desperate for half a guinea,' Theo sneered.

'Half a guinea?' Graham crowed. 'Is that what the jade charges you? She lets me have it for a crown.'

Theo knew that he was deliberately being baited. With his back teeth grinding he shrugged and forced a careless smile. He made to saunter past, but Graham dug vicious fingers into his shoulder to halt him. 'I'm done with asking nicely for my money back, Wyndham,' he menaced dulcetly. 'I'm damned sure you must have something to sell to raise a little capital. What about that mouse of a sister of yours? Not to everyone's taste, I'll own. But a man with his pockets to let and an itch that needs scratching wouldn't say no. And you've nigh on emptied mine, Wyndham…'

Alarm tautened Theo's features into a shocked mask. A trembling finger threatened Graham. 'You've never been introduced to my sister. How do you know my sister?' he demanded to know in a panic.

Graham smiled with sinister satisfaction. He'd found a weak spot and intended applying pressure to it. 'A joke, dear fellow,' he soothed and clapped a hand on Theo's shoulder. 'I'm only jesting. I caught the chit spying on me through the banisters when I came to your house not so long ago. Homely, ain't she?'

'Don't ever come to Hanover Square again,' Theo spluttered through quivering lips. He knew it had been a mistake receiving such a notorious blackguard at home.

'Once you've paid up I won't need to come looking for you, will I?'

Theo pushed past Graham and got into his carriage; his interest in visiting Becky had wilted.

Graham watched Theo's vehicle turn the corner with a savage light in his eyes. He knew soon he would be in dire straits if he didn't draw in cash from somewhere. Yet he wouldn't need to deny himself much at all if Wyndham were simply to hand over what he owed. He'd see Theo in hell before he'd end in the Fleet with his pockets stuffed with IOUs.

'I hope I am not interrupting your reading?'

Jemma scrambled to her feet from where she'd been

sitting with her feet curled under her on the sofa, a journal open on her lap.

'No, of course not, how nice to see you…' she lied, forcing a smile to her lips for her unexpected visitor.

Deborah was not fooled by Jemma's pleasant welcome. 'I think you are wishing your maid had announced me so you might have arranged to be indisposed.' She gave a wry chuckle. 'Please don't scold her. It's my fault; I asked her not to.' Deborah's little grimace was wryly apologetic. 'You see, I imagined you might make an excuse not to receive me.'

Jemma flushed faintly. Indeed, she would have done exactly that, and she made no attempt to deny it. Instead she enquired, 'Are you alone?' She tilted her head to see past Deborah. It was mid-afternoon, an appropriate visiting hour, yet it would be unusual for a young lady of such high status and tender age to be out unchaperoned. Jemma hoped Deborah's mother, the Viscountess, had not been left waiting outside in a carriage.

'I often go out on my own, or just with Pam, my maid,' Deborah declared. 'My mother doesn't like it, of course. Pam is sitting on a chair in your vestibule, so I am not completely flouting the rules today.' Deborah dimpled mischievously. 'I was going to ask Maura to come with me to visit you. I thought you'd be bound to welcome her in. But then it wouldn't really have helped to have her company because we wouldn't have been able to have a private chat. And that is why I've come.'

Jemma felt her heart skip a beat. Was Deborah subtly hinting that she knew that Marcus had propositioned her? Was she here to warn her off, or start a catfight over her fiancé? She certainly did not seem argumentative. Jemma ran a female eye over her visitor's beautifully stylish appearance. Deborah not only looked immaculately clothed and coiffed, but at her ease, too. If indeed she were here to do battle, Jemma realised she must be a débutante of some considerable maturity. Although younger, and at a disadvantage as she was on her rival's territory, Deborah gave the appearance of being disturbingly composed. Jemma's wry inner smile acknowledged that it was possible Deborah felt she had nothing to fret over. If she had guessed about Marcus's lechery, and where it was presently directed, she might have deemed it no threat to her position as his future wife. If that were so, how well matched the two of them were! Had it been presumptuous of her to berate Marcus for humiliating his future wife? She had no proof that Deborah objected to his lifestyle, or the way he treated her.

'I told Mama I was going to Bond Street to shop. I don't like to tell a lie, so I was hoping that later, once we've had a chat, you might like to come for a drive with me in the landau to Bond Street. Then we can go to the Park and—'

'It is kind of you, Miss Cleveland, but I don't think so,' Jemma quickly interrupted. Despite Deborah's conspiratorial mood and friendly attitude, Jemma was still aware that too much remained uncertain between them.

'Oh, enough of this Miss Cleveland. I should be pleased if you would call me Deborah…or Debbie. And might I call you Jemma if you have no objection?'

'Yes, of course…no objection,' Jemma replied rather disjointedly. 'But—'

'Might I sit down and have a cup of tea?'

'Yes, please do sit down, Miss Cleve…Debbie…' Jemma stuttered.

Gracefully Deborah settled on to the sofa, immediately removing her pretty pansy-trimmed bonnet and lace gloves while Jemma gave an order to Polly to fetch refreshment.

'You must think me the rudest creature to boldly invite myself here, then ask you to offer me this and that.'

'No…' Jemma began. She hesitated on seeing Deborah's rueful smile. 'Oh, very well; I admit I am surprised you've called on me, especially without a companion. But I approve of confidence and pluck.'

'You have both of those qualities,' Deborah said with wistful admiration.

'I would like to think so,' Jemma returned in a sour accent. It was sweet of Deborah to be complimentary, but she couldn't judge her character if they barely knew one another.

'Oh, but surely you *must* know it,' Deborah emphasised with an arch look slanting up from beneath her brunette brows. 'You managed to put Marcus in his place when you were younger than me. Thwarting Marcus is something I've not yet achieved. I couldn't even manage to send him away when he turned up far too early to take me home from your party. But perhaps I must very quickly learn to do it.'

'What *do* you want, Miss Cleveland?' Jemma asked frigidly. So! It seemed Deborah's visit had been prompted after all by a need to bring up the thorny subject of the three of them. Now Deborah had settled herself in cosily on the sofa she had made her opening gambit. It had been an unmistakable, if oblique, reference to Jemma having acted the tease with Marcus when she made her début.

'Oh, don't go vinegary on me,' Deborah implored. 'I'd like us to become friends.' She gave Jemma an appealing look. 'Let us first talk of something other than annoying gentlemen. I meant to say straight away how much I enjoyed your party earlier this week. I know you didn't intend to invite me, but were cornered into it by Maura and your good manners.'

'I'm glad you came,' Jemma said honestly. 'I enjoyed your company.'

Deborah smiled in pleasure. 'I must return to you that compliment. And it was nice to meet the Sheridans.' Deborah's mouth curved mischievously. 'You really *did* enjoy my company?'

'Yes, I did.'

'Then you will surely want to come to my ball and enjoy some more of it!'

Jemma's soft lips parted in a gasp of dismay. The little minx had easily trapped her into either accepting the invitation or seeming a fraud. And Deborah thought herself incapable of thwarting Marcus! Jemma believed this shrewd young lady could do anything she wished to do. She knew too that she would dearly love to dress up in her finery—her best summer dress had had very little airing—and go to such a glittering occasion. But she could not. It would be excruciating hypocrisy to celebrate the forthcoming nuptials of the Clevelands' daughter when privately she knew the bridegroom's attitude to marriage and fidelity—and how it might involve her should she allow it to. 'I…I'm sorry, but I cannot yet say for sure whether I will come.' It was a mealy-mouthed excuse and Jemma regretted having uttered it.

'I *want* you to come,' Deborah said with an intransigence that bordered on temper.

'I don't know if it would be right for any of us if I attend. In particular, I think your parents might object to my presence.' Jemma looked directly into her visitor's lucid blue eyes. 'You haven't told them that you've asked me to go, have you?'

'I *have* told them,' Deborah avowed. She opened her reticule. 'They know that I have had a card made for you and for your friends too. Here it is.' She placed the gilt-edged invitation on the tea table that stood on spindly legs on a rug spread between their chairs.

Jemma looked at the elegantly scripted parchment, unsure for a moment how to proceed. It seemed there was no other way forwards but to grasp the least injurious nettle in the thicket. 'You have already mentioned Marcus,' Jemma began carefully. 'And from what you have said I gather you know that several years ago he proposed marriage to me and I turned him down.' She paused. 'I was not very kind to him. We had become quite…close…and he had every right to expect I would accept him.' Jemma swallowed, unable for a moment to continue. 'I feel ashamed still of my behaviour,' she resumed huskily. 'There are some people…quite a few, I expect,' she added with a twist of a smile, 'who would gladly recall that time and think it very inappropriate of me to attend your ball as you are to marry him.'

'Fiddlesticks! Who cares what stuffy people think?'

'Your parents might,' Jemma began.

Deborah simply shook her blonde curls until they

danced in denial about her enchanting face. 'I know you are brave enough to face down the gossips. I know you risked ostracism when you flirted with Marcus, then resisted him and went home with the intention of marrying the man who'd already claimed your heart. That is true courage, and displayed for the finest of reasons…love.'

A welcome interruption came in the shape of Polly bearing the tea tray. Polly had gleaned the gist of the ladies' intimate discussion whilst quietly hovering goggle-eyed on the threshold. Now she made all due haste in depositing the refreshment on the table before she attempted to immediately exit the room.

'Would you pour, please, Polly?' Jemma asked faintly. 'And we will have some of your cinnamon biscuits, too. Would you bring some?' Jemma was keen to keep her servant in the room whilst she concealed her astonishment at what Deborah had just said and attempted to compose in her mind a suitable reply. Deborah obviously harboured an idyll of romantic love. Her forthcoming marriage to Marcus—a self-confessed cynic on the subject—could only be a disaster.

Finally the tea was poured, the cups distributed and the door closed behind Polly's bustling figure as she hurried off to fetch the biscuits.

'I had no idea you knew so much about my history. Did Marcus tell you?'

'No!' Deborah smiled. 'He makes no comment about you. He doesn't need to. We've not long been engaged, but I know him well enough to understand what he's thinking when he looks at you.'

Jemma's cup and saucer found the table in a clatter

of crockery, and she covered her lips to stifle a choking sound. 'And what is he thinking?' she finally gasped very hoarsely.

'I think Marcus is still regretting that you turned him down and also that he didn't pursue you again when that scoundrel Robert Burnham reneged on his proposal to you.'

Whilst watching the young lady opposite, who was dreamily gazing into space, Jemma slowly remarked, 'It's a romantic idea and I think incorrect.' She paused. 'But if it were true…would you not very much mind?'

'No, not really…' Deborah murmured, her frown deepening as though she were still troubled by some inner debate. 'I would understand if Marcus wanted to marry you. I know Marcus doesn't love me and I don't love him. But we were truthful about it all from the start.' She sank back against the cushions and propped her chin in a hand. 'We like one another well enough,' she resumed. 'He is everything a young lady wants in a husband: rich and funny and so very tall and handsome. I have to admit that if things were different I'd adore having him as my husband because I'm certain eventually I would fall in love with him. But I know now that I can't carry on with it.' She suddenly shifted forwards to perch on the very edge of the sofa and fixed on Jemma a pair of earnest blue eyes. 'I'd be much obliged, Jemma, if you would tell him you've changed your mind and you will have him after all.'

Chapter Thirteen

'But...but I can't do that!' Jemma finally blurted out, having conquered a daze that had rendered her speechless for several seconds. She scanned Deborah's expression for a sign of humour. But Deborah was not joking; her azure eyes seemed to float in tears.

'Why on earth did you agree to the betrothal?' Jemma asked, gently exasperated. 'Oh, I know you have said you like Marcus, and think you could eventually fall in love with him, but...' She hesitated as a reason occurred to her. 'Did your parents command you to marry him?'

Deborah fiercely shook her head. 'They would never do that. I knew of course that they were keen for me to accept him. They like Marcus too. Everybody adores Marcus,' Deborah remarked wryly. 'I could have had my eyes scratched out by a dozen or more jealous girls who came out this Season.' She slumped back against the sofa. 'It was my decision; *I* said yes to him.'

'But...' Jemma put a hand to her brow as she tried to soothe her confusion. She hadn't known Deborah very long, but what she had learned very quickly was that this young lady was not dimwitted or a victim. 'Surely if you weren't convinced it was the right thing to do, you should have said no. You must have given such an important decision a great deal of thought.'

'I did,' Deborah confirmed miserably. 'Marcus said to me that I must consider his offer carefully. He said I was young and inexperienced and all those other wise things that older people say. So I thought and thought about it. Still I agreed to marry him. I had a crafty motive, you see. To my shame…' Deborah hung her head and choked back a sob. 'I intended to make another gentleman jealous. I hadn't seen him for some while, and when I did I told him straight away that I'd accepted Marcus's offer.' Deborah blinked rapidly to clear the film in her blue eyes. 'I told him it was no love match and the pity was I'd sooner have a man who adored me. I thought he would guess I had fallen for him and declare that I had his heart.' A whirling hand illustrated that the dullard had divined no such sign from her. 'The betrothal hadn't been formally announced so it could all have been called off at that point and no harm done. But do you know what he said?' She jerked up her head and gave Jemma a speaking look, her small mouth pursed in to a tight, angry knot. 'He said, "*I'll be groomsman, I expect*".' Deborah's accent indicated she'd found her beloved intensely dense that day; her blistering blue gaze betrayed that she wished she'd told him so at the time. 'I could have hit him! I thought he would immediately declare his devotion when he found out he might lose me to someone else.' Deborah covered her eyes with her quivering fingers. 'But it didn't work.'

After a moment she sat straight, sniffed back tears

and folded her hands in her lap. 'So I thought, *I'll show him*, and the betrothal was gazetted, and it all went on from there. It was a dreadful, selfish thing to do.' Her show of composure had again crumbled. Her shoulders had slumped in remorse and dejection. 'Either I must go ahead and marry Marcus or jilt him. At least you didn't humiliate him like that. You turned him down *before* the engagement had been announced.' Whitish curls trembled as she jerkily swayed her head in despair. 'All the preparations are underway. I feel I am trapped by it all and no way out. The bridesmaids have been chosen. Mama has been visiting *modistes* to order wedding finery and not heeding a word I say about not yet setting a date.' She looked up at Jemma. 'I have no proper excuse to give to delay any longer. Mama says it is just wedding jitters and I will get over it.' Deborah jumped to her feet and paced back and forth, small gestures describing emotions she was unable to articulate. 'How will I get over marrying the wrong man? Even were I to eventually fall in love with Marcus, I know he never would love me back. It's you he wants and always will.'

Jemma made as though to protest, but Deborah was too lost in her inner turmoil to pay heed. She carried on traversing the rug, little grimaces at the ceiling betraying her warring emotions. 'Mama's keen to have the wedding this year and assures me Marcus doesn't mind when it is. She's told the gardeners that we must have plenty of flowers for Michaelmas. Michaelmas! It is far too soon!' Fresh brine on her lashes was smeared away with her fingers.

'Have you not asked Marcus directly if you can delay

until you sort it all out?' Jemma ventured firmly and quietly, although she felt far from calm. Never would she have imagined what this day held in store for her!

'I tried to engage him in conversation when he took me home from your party. It was the first occasion we'd had to be private for some time.' Deborah paused, took a steadying breath. 'I understand now that it was foolish not to make use of the opportunity. I *tried* to talk about calling it all off, but he seemed... too forbidding...to disturb when he was so deep in thought.' She pulled a little face. 'I do find Marcus quite daunting at times. I know you don't think he is, Jemma, but you know how to handle him and keep him tame.'

Jemma's sighing laugh met that. *If only you knew how dangerous I think him, how passionately we clash*, was the response that ran through her mind, but she cautiously prevented it spilling from her lips.

'I guessed it was you he was brooding about on that journey, and that was why he looked so stern,' Deborah carried on, oblivious to Jemma's acerbic expression. 'As soon as we turned in to Upper Brook Street I decided I'd try to make him loiter with me in the hallway so we would be unheard when I told him how I felt. But...he didn't even come in. He did his duty, of course. He saw me inside, then quickly set off again as though he had an appointment to keep.' She stopped marching back and forth to frown at Jemma. 'I'm sure now he is again interested in you, he would like to jilt me, but is too well-mannered to do so.' She suddenly slumped back on to the sofa and dropped her head in to her hands. 'It is all such a mess! And it is *my* fault!'

A wailing sob from Deborah had Jemma on her feet. In an instant she'd rushed to her visitor's side.

Polly hovered in the doorway, plate of biscuits in hand. A moment later she'd tottered about and disappeared, muttering.

'Hush…hush…' Jemma soothed, taking one of Deborah's quivering hands in to her own and patting at it. 'It *is* a pickle…' In recognition of her grievous understatement a sigh escaped her soft lips and gently ruffled the top of Deborah's bowed fair head.

'I think Marcus only came to get me from your party because he wanted to see you,' Deborah gurgled. She knuckled wet from her eyes. 'I could tell he wanted to be alone with you, that's why I took myself and the others off to the conservatory.'

Jemma continued to look at a crown of fair hair while she digested that. She also reflected that she had been vindicated in thinking this young lady wily beyond her years.

'Did it work?' Deborah suddenly looked up at her through misty eyes. 'Did you make up? I had my doubts; had you done so he would have been in a better mood on the journey home.'

'We argued again,' Jemma said huskily while far back in her mind she questioned why she was revealing secrets to a young woman she hardly knew at all. A bond of friendship seemed to have been forging during their meeting today, and Jemma sensed that no gentleman would ever sever it.

Deborah sighed and sank her chin again on to her chest. 'What an idiot I've been.'

'We do foolish things in our youth. Heaven only knows I did my fair share.' Jemma paused, and as

Deborah again looked up they spontaneously smiled in ruefulness. 'Better to do them early rather than late, I suppose,' was Jemma's wise conclusion.

After snuffling into the handkerchief, swiped from her reticule, Deborah scrubbed the lacy scrap over her eyes to remove tearstains. With a final steadying breath she calmly stuffed the hanky again out of sight. 'I can't marry Marcus. It wouldn't be right,' she announced flatly. 'Will you help me, please?'

Jemma sank back on to her heels next to Deborah's chair. She rolled jade eyes upwards as though searching for an answer. She found none. 'I don't see what I can do to help.'

'You could speak to Marcus. It's you he wants, I'm sure of it.'

Jemma closed her eyes. *Oh, yes*, she thought. *It's me he wants, but not as a wife, not as your replacement by his side, at his table, in his drawing room. But he'll have me in his bed...*

'You're wrong, Debbie,' Jemma said quietly. 'He doesn't want to marry me now. He's told me so.' Slowly Jemma pushed upright and went back to her chair to sit down. She met a pair of melancholy blue eyes that were watching her intently. 'I'm sure you remember the incident in the fabric warehouse when Lucy Duncan said—and it was quite untrue—I'd sent a letter to her brother asking him to renew his proposal to me. I expect you later heard a fuller version of events. Anyway...' she sighed '...the truth is that my interfering cousin—who is also my guardian and will continue in that role until I wed, or until my twenty-ninth birthday, whichever comes sooner—has been trying to get me a husband behind my back.' She paused, fiddling with the cup and saucer on the table. 'Theodore Wyndham had the outrageous cheek to send letters to four gentlemen who had proposed marriage to me during the Season I made my début. I'd turned them all down, Marcus included, as you know.' She could tell from Deborah's stillness that she was attending avidly to her tale. 'Marcus was very, very angry to receive that note. His anger was not only directed at Theo, but at me, too, for he suspected, at first, that I'd had a hand in it all and was trying to trap him in to having me as his wife. In case I had not guessed from his reaction, he plainly told me that he had no intention of ever renewing his proposal to me.' She looked at Deborah, who was still listening closely. 'I said that it was just as well, as if he did I would reject him for a second time.' A small mirthless laugh escaped Jemma. 'So you see, there is little hope of us becoming friends, let alone more than that.'

'Did you say you'd not have him because of wounded pride?'

A reflexive denial withered on Jemma's tongue. It seemed wrong to fib when already they'd confided many truths. 'Probably,' she murmured, her expression telling although her answer sounded doubtful.

'Are you going to accept Mr Crabbe?'

'You've heard gossip about that, too, have you?' Jemma said. 'I've no intention of marrying anyone at present. I want a husband to love or no one at all. Unfortunately my cousin Theo has other ideas.'

'Your guardian sounds very bossy,' Deborah said darkly. She appeared again quite composed as she listened to Jemma's woes.

'He *is* very bossy and very grasping. When I marry, Theo will inherit everything I presently own.'

Deborah's eyes had widened in shock. 'That I didn't know! How vile of him to try to marry you off so he might get his hands on your money!'

'He insists he's doing it simply for my own good.'

'I fear he's doing it for *his* own good,' Deborah said pithily. She picked up her teacup and took a sip. 'Oh, it's cold,' she said bluntly and grimaced as she replaced the cup. 'Shall we have some fresh made? And some of those biscuits?'

Jemma chuckled. 'You *are* ordering me to do this and that, aren't you, Miss Cleveland?'

'I'm sorry,' Deborah said with an impish, impenitent smile. 'But I think a nice cup of tea and a cinnamon biscuit might assist us in understanding the ways of vexing gentlemen.'

'Well, you may have your tea if in return I may know the identity of your vexing gentleman,' Jemma gave a wry smile. 'It seems only fair as you've guessed the identity of mine.'

As the landau headed smartly along Pall Mall on its way towards Hyde Park several people stopped in their tracks to peer at it. The sight of two ladies, who might have been expected to keep a distance, sitting chatting amiably beneath a parasol protecting them from the sun, was indeed noteworthy.

Unusually, Theo was out with his sister shopping in Pall Mall. Maura had grown impatient of asking her tight-fisted brother to hand over her allowance. That morning at breakfast she had insisted, as she had no credit anywhere, and not a sixpence to her name either, that he accompany her to the shops, for she was not going about a day longer in stockings with darns in them. Theo had recognised that if need be he must certainly go to the shops with the wasteful chit. At least that way he could haggle for a discount with the merchants.

Now he stood slack-jawed outside the drapery as the landau sailed past in a flash of sleek chestnut horseflesh and glossy bottle-green coachwork. A moment later Maura ceased peering in to the package holding her meagre purchases and looked up to see what had caused her brother to quit moaning about the cost of silly fripperies.

'That's the Clevelands' landau. It looks as though Jemma and Deborah are in it,' Maura exclaimed excitedly.

The landau had slowed down behind a cart a little way along the street. Immediately Maura set off at a very unladylike pace to seize the chance to speak to her friend and her cousin. She had not known that the two women had become close friends. In fact, she had thought Jemma acted rather reserved with Deborah. She was keen to discover what had brought about such a change.

Jemma had been enjoying their drive. Deborah's maid, Pam, a spinster in her mid-thirties, was happy enough to be left to her own devices while the young ladies chatted. Pam sat opposite her charge and happily stitched embroidery on to a handkerchief, apparently unruffled when ruts in the road caused her needle to plunge awry and her to unpick a petal. Now, as the landau became hemmed in by traffic, Jemma was first to glance idly about and spy Maura haring along the pavement towards them, her little parcel of shopping swinging in her fist. A sigh escaped Jemma as she glimpsed her cousin Theo striding purposefully along in Maura's wake.

'Oh, no,' Jemma muttered, making Deborah turn to look enquiringly at her. 'I'm afraid my cousin Theo is heading this way. I apologise in advance for him; he is sure to say something crude.'

The coachman took immediate heed of his young mistress and negotiated a path towards the kerb where he expertly drew the horses to a halt. Thereafter Jemma didn't have to wait long to be proved right about her cousin's boorishness.

'I had no idea that you and Miss Cleveland were friends, Jemma,' Theo puffed out breathlessly. He was quite a portly fellow and the exertion of covering quite a distance in a short time had made him wheeze and perspire. He planted a supporting hand on the vehicle's burnished bodywork and gave Deborah a servile bow. 'Did Marcus introduce you?' An oily smirk had accompanied the remark.

Jemma returned Theo a poisonous glower; Deborah looked at him as though he might recently have emerged from under one of the cobbles she was about to delicately step upon. Having told Jemma she would be but a moment, she alighted from the landau and went to a nearby shop window to look at something that Maura seemed keen to point out.

Theo watched his mousy sister with the Viscount's daughter, thinking she looked even more insipid than usual next to such a vivacious beauty. He regretted having allowed malice to get the better of him. His goading had been directed at Jemma because she annoyed him so. He certainly didn't want to upset

Deborah when the Clevelands' ball was approaching. His sister was wont to twitter on about the fabulous affair all the time. He'd hoped that as Maura knew Deborah she might be able to wangle him an invitation. It was sure to be a magnificent event and everybody who was anybody would be there. It was just the sort of occasion—peopled by wealthy fellows—that might turn up a solution to his financial woes.

Many a time in the past Theo had managed to secure a loan from a deep-pocketed fellow who was deep in his cups. He slanted a glance at Jemma as another sly thought occurred to him. If his cousin were to attend— and it seemed highly likely she would as she and Deborah appeared to be bosom chums—what a splendid opportunity it would be to whisper in a few bachelors' ears about his ward's wifely qualities. He could kill two birds with one stone by attending, and feast at someone else's expense too.

Jemma was not to his taste; Theo preferred buxom wenches of placid temperament to skinny shrews who were almost as tall as he was. But Theo had to admit that his cousin Jemma brushed up well, and it seemed some fellows had found her engaging. She'd attracted her fair share of male attention when a débutante.

'Have you no urgent matters to attend to?' Jemma hissed when Theo seemed determined to loiter by her in brooding silence.

'I'm accompanying my sister shopping this afternoon,' Theo sighed out piously. His eyes settled on Deborah. 'I see you've ingratiated yourself with Speer's fiancée. I applaud your strategy. But it won't work. He won't have you. He's made that clear enough.'

'And I have made clear,' Jemma fumed in a low breath, 'that I do not want a husband; I especially will not have one that you have chosen for me.' She wondered how her guardian might react to knowing that indeed Marcus would have her…illicitly. Far from being outraged, she would not put it past Theo to encourage a liaison if he thought he might wangle a financial benefit from it.

'Stephen Crabbe is still keen to pay his respects to you,' Theo carried on as though he'd not heard his ward's stricture. In fact, he suspected that Stephen had lost interest in pursuing Jemma. Since Crabbe had got wind of the fact that Jemma's dowry was in question he'd seemed to avoid Theo. Had Theo known sooner that the fellow was a fortune hunter on his uppers he'd not have bothered to send him a letter.

A pair of beady eyes hovered on Miss Cleveland's graceful back view while Theo's crafty brain coddled ideas. If he could secure an invitation to the ball he might do very much better than Crabbe. He might find a fellow—perhaps a well-to-do widower keen to get a mother for his brood and a partner for his bed—who'd take her without a penny to her name. The Clevelands were peculiarly liberal aristocrats and socialised with all and sundry. Their ballroom was sure to be jammed full of rich cits.

'Why is that woman glaring at us?' Jemma sent another discreet glance to the opposite side of the road where a fancy barouche was stationed. Two women were in it; one was speaking to an acquaintance on the pavement. The other was definitely observing them. 'Do you know her? Have you upset her?' Jemma watched as the woman drew her blonde head behind the shelter of the hood folded back on her vehicle. She was obviously keen not to be seen as she continued glowering sideways at them. Jemma judged her to be young and pretty and well-to-do. The vehicle looked new and the pale-grey upholstery was a dazzling contrast with the ebony-coloured coachwork. But despite being surrounded by the trappings of wealth and gentility Jemma had detected a hint of bitterness distorting her features.

Theo surfaced from his calculations to register Jemma's question. He turned to look and a leer lifted his top lip. 'I doubt she's staring at *us*,' he sneered. 'That sour face of hers is for her rival, Miss Cleveland.' Theo nodded at the two ladies still engrossed in the shop-window display a few feet away.

'Rival?' Jemma murmured hoarsely, a knot of suspicion squeezing her stomach.

'Lady Pauline Vaux is Marcus Speer's…' Theo hesitated. He might not like his cousin, but he hesitated to act too vulgar in the presence of any well-bred young woman. '…dear friend,' he finished, but his sneer was telling. 'Not quite a Lady Wednesday night, I'll warrant…' He chortled at the private joke under his breath. Theo's attention was soon elsewhere, and he missed Jemma's quizzical look. With an impatient tut he took out his watch. 'What is Maura about?' he muttered. 'She knows I have a pressing appointment this afternoon.' His fingers rapped rhythmically on the landau, and he seemed quite oblivious to the fact that Jemma had gone very quiet and very pale.

Jemma raised her eyes from her fingers, threaded together in her lap. This time she paid more attention to the woman who, although unaware of it, had her as a rival, not Deborah. From beneath a concealing bonnet brim she studied Marcus's mistress.

She was nothing like her in looks. Perhaps Marcus had no particular preference in the women he slept with—blondes, brunettes, all were welcomed into his bed. Jemma felt anger consuming her, subduing the shock and hurt that had initially wrenched at her heart. When he'd first propositioned her he'd known that he would be betraying not only his future wife, but his mistress too. Just days ago, at her party, he had again tried to persuade her to sleep with him—then he'd gone to Lady Vaux's bed.

Theo had let slip he knew how the Earl of Gresham had finished his evening on Wednesday. Jemma had no reason to doubt the veracity of his sniggering hints, especially as he hadn't intended she hear or understand them. He'd simply been amusing himself with what he knew. Marcus had hurriedly left Deborah at her door that evening because he had a visit to make, a visit that was so urgent he'd not even had the manners to say a proper goodnight to his future wife and her parents. How could he let lechery make him so brutish?

Another sideways glance and Jemma could distinguish anguish on Pauline Vaux's profile despite the fact that she remained half-hidden by the hood. The woman was obviously unwilling to share her lover with his wife. How deeply wounded she must be to discover that Marcus was recruiting for an additional paramour, too.

'Oh, thank goodness he is gone. He is unpleasant, isn't he?'

Jemma was startled from her painful reflection by the

sound of Deborah's voice. A footman was helping her back into the landau and she settled with a sigh into the supple hide squabs. Jemma managed a distracted smile and looked about for her cousins. Theo had hold of one of Maura's elbows and appeared to be propelling her along the street. He was obviously keen to get his sister home so he might get to his pressing appointment.

'Has your guardian said something to upset you?' Deborah had sensed something was amiss.

'Theo was no more obnoxious than usual.' Jemma forced a smile. Her mind and body seemed to fizz with enervating emotion. *I hate him*, was the indelible phrase rotating in her mind as she dwelled on Marcus. Concentrating on making conversation with Deborah seemed beyond her. Never the less, Jemma knew that Deborah should be protected from knowing that Marcus's mistress was a mere stone's throw away and looking daggers at her. 'Shall we carry on now to Hyde Park? It is a glorious afternoon for a drive.'

Deborah's darting eyes returned to a certain spot. 'Do you know Pauline Vaux? She's just over there in a black barouche, with her friend. She seems to be staring at us.'

'Do *you* know her?' Jemma demanded in astonishment.

'I know she is Marcus's *chère amie*,' Deborah returned lightly. 'The woman with Lady Vaux is Cressida Forbes. She has a daughter, Maude, who is a débutante. She made a point of dropping hints about Pauline's *fondness* for Marcus in my hearing. It must have been galling for her when I did not seem too upset.' Her eyes narrowed on the black barouche. 'Oh, she is turning away. She probably knows she's been spotted and is embarrassed to have been caught gaping at us.' Deborah settled back. 'I expect she feels insecure. Perhaps she is in love with him,' she ventured.

'If she is, I feel sorry for her.' Jemma's voice throbbed with harsh emotion.

'So do I,' Deborah concurred. 'I think Marcus gave his heart away a long while ago.'

'I'm not sure he has ever had a heart to give,' Jemma returned rawly and, closing her eyes, turned her cold face up to be warmed by the sun.

Chapter Fourteen

'If I were in your shoes, I might find the next few minutes extremely tricky. In fact, if I were you, I think I might make a dash for it.'

Intrigued by his friend's odd tone of voice, Marcus turned a quizzical look on Randolph. A moment later his mercurial eyes had followed the direction of his friend's narrowed gaze, and he muttered an oath, and then another that was loud enough to draw a disapproving frown from a promenading matron.

The two men were on horseback and had been about to trot abreast through an entrance to Hyde Park when Randolph had made his dry observation. As Marcus's grip became unusually tight on the reins of his stallion the horse displayed his resentment and reared. Marcus soothed him with a hand and a word, but his eyes remained elsewhere as he brought the spirited beast skilfully under control.

The bottle-green landau he'd recognised straight away. Unsurprisingly, as he'd paid for it just a few months ago. He also knew to whom the black barouche belonged. Pauline was slightly behind Deborah on the road. For any man, the appearance of a fiancée and a mistress, with just yards separating them as they bore down on him, was undoubtedly a daunting spectacle. But it was the presence of the woman as yet unconnected to him that drew Marcus's grim attention as the carriages came inexorably closer.

'Look! There's Randolph and Marcus! They're going into the park, too.' Following her announcement Deborah whooped happily, but it was hearing Marcus's name, rather than Deborah's excitement, that had startled Jemma to wakefulness.

For some time they had enjoyed the drive in amicable silence. But however outwardly serene Jemma might have looked, with her eyes closed and her face turned up towards golden radiance, inwardly her mind had been seething. Theo had provided a catalyst to her mental turmoil; now her feline eyes pounced upon the gentleman who was the source of it.

Sitting astride the beautiful pale beast, his powerful torso clothed in a dark riding jacket, his black locks swept back from his bronzed face by the breeze, Marcus looked every inch the noble hero. It was a sham! The only honour he had was that bestowed by birth, Jemma inwardly fumed as her eyes continued to fire angry sparks at him. He was ruled by lust and she hoped—though doubted—that he might be thoroughly embarrassed by the situation in which he found himself. She could tell from the hard set of his features that he was displeased and she could guess why. A small tilt of her head confirmed that indeed Pauline was still on the road, a smidgeon behind them, and heading towards the park too.

A flash of enlightenment parted Jemma's soft lips in a gasp of soundless censure. Perhaps it was no coincidence that Marcus and his mistress were converging on the park gates at the same time. If a rendezvous had been planned, Deborah's untimely arrival was undoubtedly about to ruin it. It would certainly explain why Pauline had seemed keen to observe them earlier, and why Marcus was looking so frustrated now. Jemma's conjecture was abruptly curtailed by Deborah's urgent hiss.

'It is an ideal opportunity for me to speak to Marcus about ending our betrothal.' She took a deep breath and clasped together her hands in her lap as though strengthening her resolve. 'I must do it whilst I'm feeling brave,' she muttered. 'Would you be kind enough to keep Randolph occupied if Marcus and I take a walk? We might be a while.'

Deborah instructed the coachman to pull up close to the entrance to the park. Fully immersing herself in preparation for the daunting task ahead, she barely noticed how hesitant was Jemma's murmur of agreement. She then swivelled on the seat and waved at her fiancé and the gentleman with him...whom she hoped to marry.

A moment later Marcus brusquely acknowledged Pauline with a dip of his head; it seemed she was determined to make him notice her as she passed by slowly in the barouche. He was too well-mannered to snub a former lover who, just days ago, had clung to him, sobbing, because he'd given her a generous pension. When his erstwhile mistress stopped just a little way into the park, as though to lure him to her side, Marcus's tolerance evaporated. He turned his mount's head in the opposite direction, indicating that he'd meant what he'd said, and she might as well move on.

Marcus gave his fiancée a smile and Jemma an enigmatic look that caused her to tilt her head and flash hard emerald eyes at him.

Deborah immediately held out her fingers to Marcus as the two riders dismounted by the landau. After an infinitesimal hesitation he took them and courteously lifted them to his lips.

'I want you to help me get down, please,' Deborah nervously said. 'I should like to stretch my legs. We have been in the carriage some time.' She glanced at her maid. 'Will you mind to be left a while, Pam, if we take a stroll around the park?'

Pam shook her head, then her embroidery, to indicate she would be well occupied.

For a moment Jemma was sure Marcus would refuse to go with Deborah. It seemed with some reluctance he eventually offered his fiancée his arm and they set off, the stallion clip-clopping docilely at his master's heels. Only once did Deborah look back at them, and Jemma knew that soulful-eyed stare was not directed at her. A glance at Randolph was enough to satisfy Jemma that Deborah had gained his attention. After a moment he busied himself with winding his mount's reins about his palm in a thoughtful manner.

'Would you like to take a walk in the park, Miss Bailey?' he coolly enquired.

'Yes, thank you, I would,' Jemma replied quickly, although she'd sensed Randolph's frostiness. This gentleman might like Deborah very much, but she feared he did not like her at all. Never the less, she was pleased that she'd not had to prompt him to ask her to take a stroll. She placed her hand in the one he'd outstretched, and a short while later they'd started to promenade in their friends' wake.

Soon, Jemma realised, Marcus and Deborah would draw level with his mistress's carriage. The barouche was still stationary at the side of the drive. Would Lady Vaux try to catch his eye? How would he respond? As they got within a yard of the vehicle it suddenly pulled off. Jemma felt annoyed that he'd not been tested over it, but had got off too lightly. A fleeting study of Marcus's profile told her he was talking fluently to Deborah, and there was nothing in his expression that showed he'd noticed his mistress had been in close proximity.

He *deserved* to be discomfited, yet still Jemma felt ashamed of wishing it. He brought out the worst side of her character, she realised. She must not allow him to make her spiteful or vulgarly inquisitive. Still she remained curious as to what was being said. How would he react to knowing that his fiancée had decided she must have a husband to love and a marriage that was more than a shell of convenience and respectability? Perhaps he would be simply annoyed that he must renew his search for a suitable mate.

Abruptly she turned her attention to the gentleman strolling at her side. 'I have not seen you for some time, Mr Chadwicke,' she rattled off cordially. 'Have you been keeping well since last we spoke?'

'I have, thank you,' he replied in the same remote tone. 'And I hope you have been well, too, Miss Bailey.'

Jemma inclined her head to indicate that she had

been in fine fettle. 'Indeed, I ought to have guessed
your answer for myself,' Jemma persevered amiably,
hoping to make him thaw just a little. Her eyes travelled
on his suntanned skin. 'You look a picture of health.
Have you lately been somewhere very hot?'

'I have been in the Indies,' Randolph told her.

Jemma looked up interestedly at him. She knew, of
course, that exotic goods such as silks and spices were
imported from the Indies. 'Were you there for reasons
of commerce?'

'In part...' Randolph hesitated. 'And for family
reasons too.'

Jemma was about to ask him more about that
faraway land, keen to have a topic of conversation to
keep her thoughts from Marcus. But she got the impression Randolph had said all he wanted to on the subject
of his time abroad. A moment later that suspicion was
confirmed when he abruptly changed the subject.

'I wasn't aware that you and Miss Cleveland knew
each other well, Miss Bailey.'

'It is only recently we have become friends. Maura
Wyndham is a mutual acquaintance and recently circumstances have drawn us together to socialise.'

'Ah, I remember your cousin Maura. She made her
début the same year as you did.'

'Yes, she did,' Jemma answered, more subdued. She
knew at once that Randolph was recalling the occasion
when he'd created a diversion and thus helped Marcus
lead her, with clandestine speed, into one of the secluded
walkways at Vauxhall Pleasure Gardens. Once
Randolph had helped his friend to woo her; now that
same friend was engaged to a woman who wanted

Randolph as her husband. It was a dreadful tangle! Jemma would have expected that the two men might have fallen out over the eternal triangle, but they seemed amiable enough. Jemma frowned. Was she wrong in suspecting Randolph returned Deborah's affection? He'd definitely been returning her stare a while ago, but that didn't signify much. Jemma decided a little probing conversation might help her find out.

'I'm glad I have come to know Deborah better.'

'Is your cousin now a married woman?'

They had spoken simultaneously and fell quiet together too.

Randolph gestured she should go first.

'I was just saying that now I know Miss Cleveland better I think her very pleasant and charming.'

'She is a fine young woman,' Randolph endorsed with a throb to his voice.

Contentment twitched Jemma's lips. He was definitely *not* indifferent to Miss Cleveland. 'I believe you were enquiring if Maura has yet found a husband?'

Randolph nodded.

'She has not. I think she worries of the risk to her brother's health should she encourage a suitor.'

A quizzing look from Randolph demanded she clarify her enigmatic response.

'The idea of providing Maura's dowry is sure to send Theo into a decline.'

'She may need a lure, too,' Randolph ventured drily. A moment later he coughed, loosened his cravat from his neck. He had not meant to be nasty about Miss Wyndham's plain looks.

'Maura seems content to remain single,' Jemma said

lightly, hoping to ease his embarrassment. She knew he had simply joined in the banter that she had started, and had not intended to be malicious. But it seemed already Randolph was withdrawing from her behind a reserved demeanour.

Jemma gave a sigh. 'I fear you do not like me, Mr Chadwicke.'

'Is there a reason you can think of why I would not?' he asked curtly.

'I think you know there is,' Jemma replied quietly. 'Believe me, sir, there is much about my past behaviour I regret—'

'And so you should,' Randolph cut over her words, 'for it had repercussions that were not pleasant.'

'What do you mean by that, sir?' Jemma frowned up at him. 'It was not pleasant certainly for me to be shunned and called names because I was foolhardy at seventeen. We are all allowed just one shameful episode in our youth, surely?' Moments ago she'd felt rather defensive, but no longer. She might have been wrong five years ago to flirt outrageously with his sophisticated friend before rebuffing him, but, by all accounts, Marcus had soon forgotten about her. She aired that view and in response got a sour snort of laughter.

'Are you implying that he did not soon forget me and plunge into all manner of licentious behaviour?'

'You're half-right, Miss Bailey,' Randolph advised. 'He didn't forget you, no matter how hard he tried to protect his pride by plunging into all manner of licentious behaviour.'

The sound of thundering hooves became louder and drew Jemma's attention from Randolph's set profile.

She squinted into the distance. A group of men on horse-back were approaching over the grass. It was obviously a race between them, but one fellow, in front by a head, suddenly reined back and wheeled about before canter-ing in their direction.

Jemma's eyes widened in disbelief. She had recog-nised the approaching gentleman despite not having seen or spoken to him in many years. And he had obvi-ously recognised her too.

Robert Burnham doffed his hat to them both; after a long moment, in which it seemed he struggled and failed to find something to say, he saluted them again then kicked his mount into action. The beast leaped forwards and soon Robert was in hot pursuit of his friends.

'Would you like to return to the carriage?'

Jemma had hoped her shock had not been too apparent. A glance at Randolph told her he had recognised her distress and understood its cause. Oddly his solicitousness brought a surge of brine to sting her eyes, yet she was annoyed, too, that an impromptu meeting with Robert had unsettled her. He was a married man and the father of two small children; she'd had the report from her sister Monica last time she'd visited town. She knew that Robert kept a town house in Mayfair, but rarely used it. He and his family spent most of their time in Berkshire, in a manor house that had come to him as part of his wife's wedding dowry. There had not been a single occasion when they had bumped into one another in London.

At some time in the intervening years Jemma had ac-knowledged that she'd had a lucky escape. She might have married Robert and been saddled with a man she did not know very well. When fond of him in her youth

she had believed him to be courageous and committed
to her as strongly as she was to him. Robert had proved
himself to be fickle and venal enough to go back on his
word to acquire wealth and property. But he had not
changed much in looks. He still resembled the teenage
sweetheart who had sat beside her in meadow grass in
Thaxham and planned with her their elopement to
Gretna Green.

Jemma slowly became aware that she was standing
stock-still, gazing after Robert, and that Randolph was
patiently awaiting her reply. With an inspiriting breath
she looked for Deborah and Marcus, but they were lost
to sight now. The vital nature of their conversation might
occupy them for some while yet. She felt a sudden
yearning to be alone to pull apart the clutter in her mind
so she might slot her thoughts sensibly back together.

'I think I should be getting along home,' she said
with husky brightness. 'My servant, Polly, will wonder
what has become of me. I said I would not be out more
than an hour or two.' She squinted at the low sun, then
at Randolph. 'Have you the time, sir?'

A slanting golden beam glinted on the watch
Randolph extracted from a pocket. 'It is almost half
past five.'

'Indeed, I must be going,' Jemma said firmly. She
knew that Polly, and Mrs Lewis who came in to cook for
her, would be wondering whether she wanted any dinner.
'I will make my apologies to Deborah another time.'

They turned and started back the way they had come.
As they approached the park gates Jemma slipped her
hand from Randolph's arm and skipped to the kerb to
hail a passing cab.

'You must allow me to escort you home, Miss Bailey,' Randolph insisted. 'I can leave my horse tethered to the landau. The coachmen will watch…' Randolph began to protest.

'No…indeed you must not,' Jemma declined his offer, but with gratitude accenting her tone. 'I am quite used to travelling on such transport,' she added truthfully. 'Might I ask you to convey my farewells to Deborah?' With no more ado Jemma climbed aboard, with Randolph's assistance. She even managed a little wave for her gallant before the jarvey set the nag to a brisk trot.

Randolph watched the cab disappear around the corner. He felt rather mean now to have been so abrupt with her. Jemma had seemed genuinely shocked to hear his hint that Marcus had been heartbroken to lose her. But then his friend had done his utmost at the time to make his careless attitude seem genuine. Randolph had known him too well to be fooled…. He still knew him too well to be fooled. If Marcus ever found out what he'd told Jemma, he'd be in for a tongue-lashing, and no mistake. But Randolph sensed that it was a time for plain speaking between all four of them. It was obvious that Marcus wanted to spend his life with Jemma just as *he* wanted Deborah by his side in the future.

The day had been filled with staggering surprises, yet it seemed fate had another waiting to send Jemma's pulse again racing.

She had asked the jarvey to drop her at the top of Pereville Parade; despite all the excitement of the day, she had remembered a mundane task she must perform. The grocer who supplied her with provisions had been patiently waiting for his bill to be settled. Having done her duty and signed the chitty he was to take to her bank, she was out of the shop and walking home when she spotted, at a distance, Robert Burnham mounting her steps.

Jemma drew back against a shielding shrub overhanging a neighbour's wall. Her heart was hammering in apprehension, yet she felt thoroughly annoyed, too, that he had come so boldly to visit her. Not once in the past five years had he made any attempt to contact her in person. The most she'd had from him was a brief letter in which he'd apologised for the necessity to break their unofficial engagement. Now, twice in one day, he was putting himself in her way! She could only assume that following his failure to articulate a greeting earlier in the park he thought to come to her home to explain himself.

It was far too late for that! He had no right to turn up uninvited. It was well past a reasonable visiting hour, something that was bound to be of note to her neighbours. She had no intention of going up to him and either asking him in, or conducting a conversation with him in the street. With a huff of exasperation Jemma realised she would have to take a walk about until he had gone. Carefully hugging the wall so he did not spot her, she retraced her steps, heading towards a little square of greenery on Parson's Row. She decided she would loiter in the garden there to allow him time to take himself off.

Having chosen a small wooden bench to sit upon, Jemma boldly met the eyes of a promenading gentleman. She gracefully inclined her dark head, settled back and folded her arms over her middle, as though sitting there at such a time was a ritual she was wont to observe. Her confident display drew a startled nod from him and he carried on towards the exit.

Jemma began impatiently tapping her feet against the cobbles beneath them. It had been a glorious day, but now the air was getting chilly and the purple nimbus hunched in the sky threatened rain was on its way. She rubbed her palms against her upper arms to warm them, cursing Robert. Despite the fact he still looked boyishly attractive, and had found a sudden eagerness to see her, she realised she had no desire to be in his company. So sunk in reflection was she that she hadn't noticed that a sleek coach had passed, juddered to a halt, then returned to draw up by the railings, or that a tall, dark figure had emerged from it and was now strolling the path towards her.

'What are you doing, Jemma?'

Jemma jumped to her feet. 'I…I'm sitting having a rest.' She'd garbled the first words that entered her mind.

'Would it not be wiser and more comfortable to do so at home?' Marcus ventured ironically.

'I dare say it would,' Jemma breathlessly agreed. Her heart had commenced pounding again, but this time thrilling exhilaration rather than anger had caused it. Familiar cramps coiled in her stomach, a bittersweet pain encircled her heart. Her eyes clung to the impressive sight he made, all thought of Robert obliterated from her mind. A moment later she remembered when last she had seen him Deborah had been preparing to jilt him and his mistress had been hovering in the vicinity. Perhaps Lady Vaux was already aware Marcus was newly single and was confident of being upgraded to fill the vacancy. Jemma abruptly sat down again. 'If I choose to rest here a while, I don't see that it is any of your concern.'

Indolent amusement was barely perceptible between his close black lashes. 'I think you know, Jemma, that I consider you my concern,' he corrected, and made himself comfortable beside her.

'It's going to rain.'

'I believe it is,' he said with a glance at the sky.

'What do you want?'

'Nothing new,' he murmured with a private smile at his clasped hands.

'And I have nothing new to say on the matter, or any other, so you might as well go away,' she said with faux nonchalance.

'Oh, I think you have,' Marcus said on a grunt of laughter. He lounged back against the wooden slats and looked at her. 'I think you have a great deal to say to me. And none of it complimentary.'

'I admire your perception, my lord.'

'Well, that's a start, I suppose,' he returned, adopting her acerbic tone.

Glossy conker-coloured ringlets tumbled over her shoulders as Jemma tilted her head to a haughty angle.

'Did you arrange at your party in the week to go for a drive with Deborah today?'

'No…I…I was none the less pleased to see her this afternoon when she paid me a visit.'

'I am sure you were.'

'What's that supposed to mean?' Jemma swung a fierce frown towards him.

'It means that I'm sure my ears should have been burning for most of the afternoon.'

'I think it means that your conceit is undiminished by knowing that Deborah doesn't want to marry you.' Jemma bit her lip and swiftly looked away. She hadn't meant to disclose she knew that. She took a peek sideways and noticed the set of his features had subtly softened. The firm line of his lips had pursed in to what might have been a smile, but when he glanced at her his expression was again inscrutable.

'Is that what you were talking about? Did she tell you why she doesn't want to marry me?'

'I'd rather not say,' Jemma mumbled. He would know, of course, that her closed answer could be taken as an affirmative.

'Are you pleased?'

'Pleased?' Jemma echoed, raising her face.

'Are you pleased that Deborah doesn't want me?'

'It matters not a jot to me either way,' Jemma replied with a transparent lack of honesty.

'That's not what you said yesterday. Yesterday it mattered very much to you. You told me you thought Deborah deserved better, and that she should know I'll be an incorrigibly adulterous husband. Have you changed your mind about it?'

'No, I have not. And if you are about to accuse me of poisoning her mind against you, you are wrong. I think Deborah is wise enough to have formed her own opinion on your character.'

'Indeed, she's an intelligent girl,' he agreed with a rueful inflection. 'She said she finds me a perfect gentleman in every way.'

'There, you have your proof then that I have not meddled. She certainly could not have heard such rot from me,' Jemma muttered.

A deep chuckle met her sarcasm, and he slid an arm casually along the back of the bench. Jemma jumped to her feet, but a relentless hand brought her to sit down beside him again.

'Tell me why you think I'm no gentleman.'

A spontaneous, bitter laugh burst from Jemma, and she let it answer for her whilst studying the shrubbery to one side of her. After a moment curiosity got the better of her. 'Were you surprised to hear what Deborah had to say?' she asked.

'Not at all. She accepted my proposal too quickly. In truth, I anticipated she might air her misgivings a bit sooner.'

'Perhaps she tried to do so, but found you had no time to listen as you had to rush off elsewhere,' Jemma sniped. Thanks to Theo's snide remarks about Lady Vaux, Jemma had an inkling where and to whom Marcus had rushed after he took Deborah home from her party.

'To what are you referring?'

'Deborah said she tried to speak to you when you took her home from my house. She said you gave her scant chance to do so and rushed off. Did you?'

'Yes. I had something to attend to.'

Their eyes strained until Jemma's abruptly sprang away from his granite gaze. 'Well, it is done now and Deborah is free to find someone else,' she said with an air of finality.

'Do you want to know where I went?'

'It's none of my concern.'

'No, it isn't,' he concurred. 'Never the less it seems you're keen to have my movements.'

'You're wrong,' Jemma flashed, 'and unbelievably arrogant to say such a thing. I have no interest in where you go or who you see.'

'Deborah said nothing indelicate, but I got the impression from her that she knows I'm interested in you. Have you told her I want you as my mistress?'

'No!' Jemma squeaked. 'Of course not! I have said nothing of the sort to her.' She felt her face flaming in mortification. She would hate anyone to know the Earl of Gresham had treated her as though she were a common doxy. 'I pray she has not guessed you have insulted me in such a vile way. Thankfully I doubt she has; she knows you already have a mis—' Jemma clamped together her lips, regretting that he had provoked her in to saying too much. She could tell from the sardonic gleam at the back of his eyes that he'd intended to manoeuvre the conversation to this point.

'Ah…I collect you have been talking about my mistress. You know where I went after taking Deborah home, don't you.'

Jemma didn't deign to answer what was, in any case, given as a flat statement.

'Who told you?'

Again Jemma was on her feet. She started swiftly for the exit, but had taken no more than a few paces before a firm grip on a wrist halted her.

'Before you run away, enlighten me—who is presently my mistress?'

Jemma felt blood again toasting her cheeks. She was not about to be tricked into disclosing that Theo, and then Deborah, had alerted her to the role Lady Vaux had in his life.

'I am not running away,' Jemma enunciated. 'Neither am I prepared to be drawn into a vulgar discussion about your women. If you get confused remembering all their names, perhaps you should limit yourself to just one.' Jemma tried to fling off his fingers, but not only did they continue to grip they brought her unwillingly closer.

She could no longer pretend that her painful indignation at knowing he wanted to add her to his harem had been prompted by sympathy for his fiancée. She was hurt on her own account. She was jealous on her own account. Mostly she was mortified to think he might guess how she felt about him.

She was falling in love with him all over again. And she knew now that at a tender seventeen she'd had her first taste of that enslaving emotion…but not with Robert. With the wisdom of hindsight she realised that had been a fantasy that had evolved from their childish games played with dolls and soldiers in a tree-house home. Never had Robert kissed her in a way that made her feel as though honey flowed in her veins. Never had she felt the urge to simultaneously hit or hug Robert. Yet she knew she was teetering on the brink of unleashing one or other assault on Marcus.

'Who told you about Pauline Vaux?' he asked levelly.

Jemma moistened her lips. 'I don't remember— nobody—it's common knowledge. Release me at once,' she commanded in a quavering tone. She was unwilling to wrestle with him in public in an attempt to liberate her wrist.

'Are you jealous?'

Jemma snorted a scornful laugh, but a betraying flush was flooding her complexion, causing a dangerously satisfied smile to tug upwards a corner of his mouth.

'Did you think I'd wait five years and act the monk until you again let me kiss you?' he taunted softly.

'I've heard you found it impossible to wait one day after my rejection before finding solace elsewhere— everywhere,' she stormed. Immediately she regretted having sounded exactly what he thought her, jealous. But the idea of him roistering in town with a horde of petticoats before she had even reached Thaxham House with her papa had been tormenting her for half a decade. It niggled unbearably still, and she knew a moment or two more of his quiet mockery might make the sob, swelling in her chest, burst. In desperation to be free she swung her free fist up at his dark, sardonic face.

In response he ducked, so that her blow skimmed his shoulder; simultaneously he started to stride towards the exit, taking her, skipping to keep up, with him.

Reaching his carriage, she renewed her effort to liberate herself, for she guessed his intention was to make her go with him. She could tell by the unyielding set of his narrow mouth that he was not done with her yet. As if to act as his accomplice the heavy clouds let fall their burden and cold crystals of rain started to moisten her complexion and quivering eyelashes.

He flung open the door and ordered curtly, 'Get in.'

'Is this what it has come to, my lord?' she baited him bitterly. 'You cannot have your own way so you must use force. Will you kidnap me?'

'If needs be,' he growled. 'I've no intention of getting soaked to the skin, Jemma. Get in.'

Chapter Fifteen

❦

'I must tell Polly of my whereabouts. She will be worried.' The coach swayed away from the kerb, and Jemma felt confused as to why she'd submitted to his will so soon. He'd not needed to coerce, or kidnap her. Following a staring match through misty drizzle—she'd been conquered very quickly—he'd withdrawn his hands from his pockets and assisted her, unresisting, into the coach.

'I think Polly might guess you're sheltering from the rain. Or perhaps she might think you're with Burnham.'

After a stunned, silent moment when her mind raced to and fro, she blurted, 'You have been to Pereville Parade? When?' He was sitting opposite her, ruffling his dark locks to remove the raindrops from them.

'Oh, I would have waited until Burnham had quit your doorstep before I stood upon it, if you're worried for your reputation,' he drawled and shot a dark look at her.

'Yes, I am worried for my reputation,' Jemma announced tightly. 'A procession of gentlemen callers at my door in the early evening might stir gossip of the worst kind.'

'I watched Burnham get turned away by Polly from the comfort of my coach. I knew I'd fare no better with your sentinel, so I stayed where I was. But it seems you really were from home,' he added mordantly whilst a profoundly penetrating look captured her eyes. 'It was the sight of Burnham that made you bolt from Hyde Park, wasn't it? I imagine he's the reason you were idling on that bench too. Randolph told me he rode up and stopped by you this afternoon, looking lovelorn.'

'I would thank you not to say so!' Jemma choked in a suffocated voice. 'He is a husband and father now.'

'You once more seem naïve, Jemma.' Marcus sounded bored. 'If you think that acquiring for himself a family will deter Burnham from approaching you, I can assure you it will not.'

'You judge every man by your own immoral standards. I'm sure most gentlemen honour the sanctity of their marriage vows,' Jemma snapped.

'You must excuse me for not knowing any such paragons of virtue,' he returned exceedingly drily.

'Mayhap you need some better friends, then.' Jemma removed her bonnet and laid the damp hat on the plush seat. She bit her lip and remained frowning at passing scenery, her insides writhing because she knew his cynicism, and his opinion of her naïvety, were founded. Her own papa—allowably with no wife to cheat—had kept Mrs Brannigan for many years. Jemma had realised when the woman's name appeared in his will that her father sought to continue to care for the widow after his death.

'Did you encourage Burnham to call, then deliberately go out to avoid him? Are you trying to punish him?'

'No, I am not!' Jemma gasped angrily. 'I've not spoken to him in many years and nor do I want to.'

'It seems he doesn't share that sentiment.'

'Whether he does or doesn't is of no significance to me, and it is certainly none of your business.'

'You are my business, Jemma. You know I mean to protect you.'

'And you know that I have rejected your offer to do so,' Jemma retorted.

'Only in words.'

Jemma abruptly turned her head, hating him for reminding her so succinctly of how easily he could crumble her defences. She knew he was considering doing so now. Those long dark fingers resting deceptively idle could reach out and touch her at any moment. A tussle might ensue, but not for long. She knew how vulnerable was her pride when pitted against his sensual skill. Should he want to he could subdue her with one crafty kiss. Involuntarily her lips parted as though to welcome his mouth's pressure. Her breasts rose to meet a phantom caress trailing fire in its wake on her tender flesh.

A silence between them lengthened, vibrated with unbearable tension. 'Where are you taking me?' she burst out.

'Somewhere private where we can talk.'

'I've nothing to say to you.' Jemma struggled to sound composed as the rain started to beat heavily down on the roof of the carriage, making an involuntary shiver ripple through her. 'You may ask me the same question a million times, and a million times I will give you the same answer.'

'Why?'

'Why? *Why?*' Jemma cried. 'I'm not one of your

happy widows,' she snapped. 'I'm a spinster with a reputation to keep. Yet you want to degrade me, and you ask me why I will not allow it?'

'I want to make love to you, Jemma.'

'In this instance it is the same thing,' she muttered.

'I think you know it is not,' he said softly. 'I think you want me to make love to you.'

'And I think your arrogance has addled your wits.'

A flash of white in the gloomy interior of the coach told her he found that amusing. 'Something has addled my wits, I'll agree. Perhaps not my arrogance.'

'Indeed,' Jemma agreed sourly. 'Perhaps it's not your mind but a different part of your person you can't control.'

He burst out laughing. 'Which are you, Jemma? Saucy wench? Puritan maid? I'll take either…or both at the same time would be even better,' he murmured throatily. 'God's Teeth, you might frustrate the life out of me, but you'll never bore me.'

Immediately the vulgarity had escaped she'd regretted uttering it. She'd invited his lewd response, and the pitiless stare that was scorching one side of her face. She squinted out at rain-soaked scenery, trying to think of a comment to even the score and neutralise the charge in the atmosphere. 'I take it that Deborah jilting you has not caused you unbearable heartache?' she suggested acidly whilst scouring the grey heavens for a sign of light on the horizon. 'Oh, of course, you have said your heart was not in it,' she added in the same scathing tone. 'Your bank balance will no doubt suffer, but it seems not sufficiently to put you in a bad mood.'

'My bank balance continues to do very well, I assure

you,' he said, a smile still in his tone. 'Money was not a consideration when I asked Deborah to be my wife.'

'Well, what was?' Jemma burst out in exasperation. 'You already had all you needed; what moved you enough to make you decide to have someone else in your grand life at all?'

'The imminent death of my uncle,' he said mildly, no hint of humour now apparent. 'When alive he made no secret of the fact that he wanted the Gresham line to continue. He entrusted to me his lifetime's work and that of his ancestors. Everything I have, everything I am, I owe to him. The least I could give back to him was a grandchild.'

Their eyes merged through the murky interior of the coach. Although it was not yet dusk, the storm clouds had cast a darkling shadow over everything.

'I…I didn't know,' Jemma said with a hint of apology in her tone. She was taken aback by hearing such blunt personal information from him.

'Why would you? I've never before told you.'

'You loved him very much?'

'Yes—he was like a father to me.'

'I remember you telling me that your father had died from a war wound when you were young. Is your mother still alive?'

He nodded. 'She lives in Norfolk with my stepfather.'

'Does she visit you in town?'

'Not often—her delicate nerves can't withstand the strain of travelling far. I go there to visit about twice a year.'

'Is that all?' A delicate grimace displayed her surprise. 'Do you miss her?'

'I don't know her very well. After my father died my

mother was glad to hand over my rearing to her brother-in-law. From my infancy she found me too boisterous for her fragile constitution.' He paused, restlessly eased his muscular shoulders against the squabs. 'Even during school holidays she was glad, after a dutiful day or two, to pack me off back to stay with Solomon. I preferred being with him. I liked roaming Gresham Hall's thousands of acres.' He turned to stare out of the coach window, a nostalgic smile slanting his sensual mouth. 'Randolph would come to stay for months at a time and we'd ride, fish, tumble out of trees. They were good days,' he murmured, his eyes distant. 'So, no, I don't miss my mother. Up until I was eight I was mostly in the care of tutors or nursemaids; after that age I was at boarding school, or at Gresham Hall.' He paused. 'How long is it since you saw your mother?' he abruptly asked, turning his head to look at her.

Jemma started to attention. Her usual reaction to outsiders' questions about her parents, or their miserable marriage, was to bristle defensively and limit her reply to a curt word or two. Her mother had done wrong, and had acted shamefully with her French lover, but she was still her mama. In contrast to Marcus's attitude to his distant parent, Jemma missed her mother dreadfully and yearned to see her.

As a young girl Jemma had often wished she could make a trip to Paris to visit her mother. Of course, while her papa was alive she had realised it would never be. He would have considered her request a grievous insult, and would never have agreed to fund such a trip for her. But since he'd gone, and Jemma had her bequest to make the dream a reality, she had decided that she would go. In fact, a few months ago she'd decided that before the weather changed and the Channel became choppy she would set out for France this year. The mourning etiquette for her papa had been observed and, whilst she did not want to betray him, even after death, she had a gnawing need to make contact with the parent who remained to her. She would hate at some time to receive word that her mother too had gone to meet her maker and with her the opportunity to lay to rest some past hurts.

She was aware that Marcus had been quietly watching her whilst she brooded on her family. 'It is a long while since I saw my mother—about…eight years, I think,' she finally answered him. For some reason she knew, dangerous as he was, she no longer considered Marcus a stranger. A moment ago he had divulged information that was precious and private to him. It seemed fair to trust him equally with things about her kin that usually remained locked in a treasury in her mind. 'I expect you know my parents were divorced some years before then. But Mama returned from France to see her girls, as she called her three daughters. She came alone, without the Count, for obvious reasons, for Papa was still alive. She knew Patricia, who is the eldest, was due to make her come out. She brought gifts: French lace to trim some dresses, and some other pretty things.' Jemma's eyes again sought the sodden scenery. 'It was a meeting that had to be conducted away from home; Papa remained unyielding towards her up until his death.' A tiny, involuntary sigh escaped Jemma. 'It is such a long while since I saw her that sometimes I think I will forget what she looks like. But I have a painted likeness in a locket to remind me until

I see her again.' She glanced at him almost shyly. 'I am planning to take a trip to see her quite soon.' She forced brightness into her voice. 'It is nice to have family to visit. I have my sisters and brothers-in-law. I go to Nottingham in the autumn to stay with Monica, then on to Derby where Patricia lives. She has two boys. It is good to see my nephews and take their Christmas gifts.'

'Do you stay until the New Year?'

'No!' Jemma laughed. 'They are mischievous children and their mother is glad of a rest. After a week or two of taking charge I am quite worn out too and ready to come home. Besides, it is safer to travel before the January snows arrive.'

'Where is home at Christmas?'

'At Thaxham House usually. Only rarely do I remain in town during the winter. But if the weather is too bad to enjoy the countryside sometimes it is more sensible to do so.'

'Does Wyndham not ask you to spend the holiday with him?'

An extremely wry expression resulted from that question. 'What? You believe he might meet the cost of feeding me? I don't think Theo would willingly give me the scraps from his table. Especially not now I've defied him over…' She fell quiet. She had been about to say that her guardian disliked her more than ever now that she'd refused to marry and let him take her inheritance. 'I'm happy to avoid him when I can,' she resumed quickly. 'But Maura and I exchange gifts at Christmas.' She dropped her eyes from his steady silver gaze, feeling again quite bashful. They had been talking as good friends would: about mundane matters, and the trials and tribulations of family life. Even when he had been courting her he had volunteered little information about himself. But then a short while ago he'd honestly told her that only one thing about her interested him at that time: coupling with her. She knew nothing much had changed apart from his willingness to participate in a proper conversation. Jemma took a swift searching glance at his face, wondering if he would tolerate her prolonging this innocuous intimacy.

'You will be lonely this year at Christmas time without your uncle. Have you any half- or step-siblings?' Jemma knew he was the only child from his widowed mother's brief first marriage.

'No. But I won't be lonely,' he said with a boyish bravado that tweaked at Jemma's heart and drew from her a soft smile. She wanted to say he could come, if he liked, and dine at her table on Christmas Day before re-alising how absurd it would sound. Since she had lost her papa's companionship she had spent a solitary Christmas. Wistfully she knew she'd like to have a dinner guest, but the Earl of Gresham was unlikely to want to forgo his splendid house and luxurious fare, no doubt prepared by a battery of chefs, to share her small goose and plum pudding at Pereville Parade. She, of course, would be far lonelier than would he over the winter holiday. She felt foolish for letting this warm interlude between them make her forget that he had a mistress with whom he could share bed and board. No doubt Lady Vaux would welcome and lavishly entertain him, should he choose to spend Yuletide with her.

She sensed his eyes travelling over her, sensed him withdrawing his speech and offering something more sensually stimulating in its place. Beneath that scalding gaze she felt her limbs quake in anticipation. But she wasn't yet ready to surrender to him her pride.

'I expect your uncle would have been upset to know that Deborah has jilted you,' she rattled off.

'I don't think he would.'

Jemma's widening eyes begged an explanation. Everybody adored Deborah; she was sure the old Earl must have been smitten too. She gestured for him to enlighten her and ignored a look of exaggerated impatience that her demand elicited. He waited some moments before indulging her need to keep him at arm's length with conversation.

'He seemed to think I might have settled on Deborah too quickly, without giving the matter sufficient thought.'

'And was he right?' Jemma asked breathily.

'I know now our betrothal was a mistake. I did act impulsively. I'd held back on the tedious business of propping up pillars in Almack's assembly rooms to seek someone suitable. Then my uncle's physician told him to put his affairs in order. I wanted to reassure Solomon, while there was still time, that I had started the process of continuing his line.'

'You sound very cold, very calculating, however worthy your motive.'

'Shall I demonstrate that I'm not?' he smoothly suggested.

In the dim interior of the coach it was impossible to read his expression. But she'd understood from his suggestive tone that he'd finished talking to her. 'You may save your demonstrations for your mistress,' she returned in a whisper. 'Or perhaps you will marry Lady Vaux instead now you lack a bride.'

'Which surely would present me with another vacancy,' he coolly countered. 'For a person who had nothing to say to me, Jemma, you've said quite a lot. But I think that's enough.'

He didn't lunge for her as she'd expected and overpower her inhibitions with an erotic onslaught on her senses. He held out a hand in invitation, for just a few seconds, before it beckoned peremptorily. Jemma tapped it away with nervous fingers and shifted along the seat away from him. Her insolent rebuff caused him to ram his back against the seat and his hands into his pockets. One booted foot was raised and jammed against the seat opposite, while he stared sulkily up at the roof of the carriage. She knew then that, oddly, she wielded a power over him that had surprised them both. But she remained vigilant to his movements. She feared at any moment he might regret having allowed her to easily leash him.

'Your poor coachmen will be soaked through. You must take me home, then take yourself home too,' she blurted as she blinked at the rain bouncing off the cobbles.

'I've heard you're a philanthropist.'

'Is that a bad thing?'

'Indeed it isn't, Jemma.' He sighed theatrically. 'I'm counting on you soon taking pity on me.'

She'd understood the message in his drawling words and quickly asked, 'Who told you I'm philanthropic?'

'Wyndham let slip that you donate to good causes. On the day I visited him about that damned letter he sent he said you squander your money.'

'It *is* my money. And I will do as I please with it.'

'I'm not criticising. I have been known to support benevolent funds myself,' he returned placidly, and with great understatement. A year ago Marcus had donated half the cost of building a new wing to a hospital in the East End of London.

'Take me home now,' Jemma said hoarsely. 'Please....'

'Don't you want to talk to me any more?'

'No.'

'Why not?'

'Because...because talking to me isn't really what you want to do.'

'That's true,' he muttered, savagely sardonic.

'I'm glad you haven't tried to deny it.' She sounded as though she were rewarding a mischievous child for his honesty.

'Are you going to be as truthful? Are you going to tell me you don't want me to kiss you goodnight?'

'A goodnight kiss?' she scoffed. 'I doubt you will be satisfied with a goodnight kiss.'

'Will you?' he immediately taunted her.

A flush stole from her throat to her cheeks. He knew he had only to touch together their lips to inflame her senses and make her crave the balm of his touch on her naked skin.

'One goodnight kiss, Jemma, then I'll take you home, I promise.'

'No.'

'I'll stop when you say, I swear. When have I not?'

She could hear the amusement in his hateful, husky tone. He thought he had her bested. He thought he understood her weakness and could use it to his advantage. Then no doubt once he'd got his way he would despise her for capitulating.

'Stop the carriage, please, and let me out,' she gasped, and her fingers flew to the door as though she might jump down whilst the vehicle was moving if he refused to do as she asked.

A hand whipped out to manacle her wrist and jerk her on to his seat. She tipped against him, battling him with her free fist. 'Let me go! You're hurting me,' she shrieked as his hand twisted in her thick soft hair in an attempt to still her thrashing.

'Trust me, it'll hurt more if you're crushed under hooves and axles,' he gritted furiously, easily catching her swinging fist and subduing her so she lay panting against his chest. 'Be still,' he urged, before a vehement oath burst out from between his teeth. 'I thought you meant to try to get down.'

She could feel the thundering of his heart beneath her cheek and her eyes closed. He'd been genuinely afraid she meant to leap out to escape him. In fact, she felt quite a perilous, cosy contentment creeping over her, tempting her to stay where she was. She felt drugged simply by breathing in the warm closeness of him, the musky scent of sandalwood cologne that clung to his coat. She was piquantly aware of her frail resolve when this near to him. She gathered enough energy to whisper raggedly, 'Let me go.'

'I can't…' It emerged as a hoarse groan, tinged with wry humour.

The fingers curving on her scalp softened, moved to stroke against her nape with mesmerising gentleness.

'Believe me, I want to forget you. I've tried before and thought I'd succeeded. But I can't,' he repeated and tilted her chin, quite roughly, as though punishing her for making him admit to that. But his mouth when it touched hers was not cruel, but achingly tender as it tasted, then shaped her lips to fit against his.

Jemma recognised his desperation; heaven only knew she felt it too. His kiss was light, unthreatening, almost mutual comfort. She moulded against his solid torso, her fingers unclenching to clutch, then pull at his coat so she might elevate her face and assist him in sliding together their mouths. There was no harm in a goodnight kiss….

Immediately Marcus reacted to her tacit permission, and his tongue-tip touched, then teased at the line of her lips, persuasively petitioning for entry. As soon as she parted for him his tongue slipped in to explore and tantalise hers.

Jolts of familiar sapping sensation leached bone from Jemma's limbs and she melted against him, winding her arms about his neck. She kissed him back, in a way long ago he'd taught her, mimicking the flicks and nips that were teasing her to dizzy, breathless languor. His hot mouth slid to her cheek, then to her ear to nuzzle at the hollow behind the lobe. A blissful sigh escaped her lips, and she angled her head to allow his lips better access to the sensitive spot.

'One goodnight kiss,' he tormented her. 'There, it's done.'

A gasp of surprise, of loss, escaped her, and she tried to seduce his mouth back to hers by trailing her lips on his abrasive jaw. But he resisted and continued breathing warmth and words against skin that felt raw. 'Do you want more?' he murmured. 'You'll have to tell me.'

Her head moved so she could see his expression, and

she pleaded with her eyes, incapable of betraying herself
with speech.

'Show me then,' he demanded roughly.

He tasted her mouth again, sliding his lips silkily
back and forth with teasing skill that made her whimper.
Then his fingers caught at hers, took them to her bodice
so between them they unfastened a button. When his
hand moved away hers trembled, momentarily unmoving, before it continued to work, blindly fumbling
at hooks. Her mouth clung tenaciously, hungrily accepting the reward of a sweetly sensual kiss that caused
a sigh to tremble in her throat. When she was undone
to the waist, his hands went to her shoulders, and her
gown was slowly pushed back to expose delicate nude
shoulder bones and a ribbon-tied chemise. A single pull
loosened it, and then he trailed a finger up and down the
vertical expanse of creamy skin he'd exposed, making
her shiver excitedly. His mouth lowered, steaming heat
on tightening nubs through lawn. A moment later the
cotton was peeled aside, and his head lowered with savouring slowness to the satiny mounds of her bare rose-
tipped breasts.

Jemma moaned, pulling his head closer and arching
up to meet him as finally she felt him draw on her
nipples, lavishing attention equally until she shrieked
and squirmed and he roughly pulled her to straddle his
lap, laughing against her skin.

'Hush, sweet,' he growled, skimming his lips against
an ear. 'My coachmen might be getting pneumonia, but
they're not going deaf.' He covered her mouth with his
again, his tongue plunging between her lips in erotic
rhythm while he gathered her skirts in one hand and

deftly exposed her thighs. A knuckle rotated over the dewy curls, tempting her to tilt towards him. When she did he again tasted her breasts, putting pressure on pulsing flesh with practised skill until her head fell back and her eyes and mouth were screwed shut in ecstasy. Instinctively her thighs parted, allowing a finger to gently ease into her wet warmth.

Raging heat began to streak through Jemma's veins and she tried to wriggle away, alarmed by an untested, violent sensation that was building deep within, making her feel she must flee from its force. But ruthlessly he kept her pelvis against his fist and the driving thrust of his fingers was matched by his tongue's slow plunges into her mouth. In seconds she was again pliant and breathing in shallow pants as the coil of excitement tightened with teasing slowness, drawing her inexorably towards she knew not what. Her pent-up breath escaped in a stifled scream, wrenched from her lips, swallowed by his mouth, as the coach swayed side to side over a pothole and he held her hips hard against him while she writhed and moaned and tried to escape the explosive pleasure.

Finally she drooped, sapped of energy against him. Gentle hands moved the tumble of chestnut curls draping in disarray about her face.

'One goodnight kiss it is next time,' he said with fond amusement. 'Bates and Watts will think I've murdered you.'

Jemma buried her burning face in his coat. Oh, he hadn't murdered her, but she did feel as though she were slowly dying. A narcotic lassitude was already ebbing from her mind, shame filling the void. She'd showed him she was weak, his for the taking, and the noise she'd made! His servants would consider her no better than a coarse harlot.

Never had she imagined that such sensual bliss was possible. Oh, he had kissed her almost to insensibility when she was seventeen; he had exposed her breasts to be teased by his hands and mouth, but never had he introduced her to such overpowering intimacy. Now she felt unsure of herself. She was at a loss as to what to say, or how to find the brashness to meet his eyes. With quivering fingers she refastened her gaping bodice over breasts that felt heavy and bruised by the tender assault he'd inflicted. She swiftly sat upright, slid the seat out of his reach, then took her place opposite again. 'Take me home.'

'Now?'

'Yes, now! Why not?' she cried in muted anguish, too conscious of being overheard by Bates and Watts. 'You've got what you wanted, haven't you?'

'Hardly,' he returned softly.

There was such irony in the single word that Jemma felt a painful rush of blood make her feel light-headed, and she gripped either side of her, digging her fingernails into leather. Seconds later a dousing with cold water could not have brought her more thoroughly to her senses and to understanding his meaning. She might be sated, but he wasn't. He'd given her what she'd begged for with her body, if not with her words; now he expected her to fairly reciprocate and allow him his release.

In common with most spinster ladies of her station Jemma's knowledge of the physical act of union was limited. She knew that a state of undress and supine position were usually required for a gentleman to fully couple with a woman. Marcus had told her he wanted to get her into bed, and she knew that a wedding night saw the bride and groom retire to one together. But she guessed Marcus must know of a compromise to be had at a time like this when his lust wouldn't wait for refinements. No doubt Lady Vaux had a repertoire of skills that included a way of discreetly satisfying her lover in the confines of a coach.

'Not here!' she whispered, aghast, her eyes flying, pleadingly to his. Whatever it was he wanted to do, or wanted her to do, she desperately hoped he would not instruct her in it now. 'It would be…sordid.'

For a moment it seemed that the space between them thickened with tension. Jemma sat rigidly, primed for his next move. He smiled in a way that was perilously ambiguous, and she was not sure whether to relax or reach for the door handle. Suddenly he jammed a boot against the seat edge again, and with such force this time that she bounced.

'Do you think me an uncouth barbarian?' he eventually said. His mouth twisted; his eyes glittered sardonically. 'Perhaps it might be wise not to anger me with an honest answer, Jemma.'

'Please take me home,' she choked on a sound that was suspiciously like a sob.

In response he rapped on the roof of the coach and barked out her direction. The coach slowed down and was manoeuvred about.

'Thank you,' Jemma murmured, trying to inconspicuously remove dew from her eyes. She felt foolish, childish, to have made her lack of sophistication so glaringly obvious.

'I won't leap on you, sweet, and tumble you in a

coach, no matter how tempted I am to do so. After waiting so long, I think I'd sooner savour the moment.'

Unable to formulate a reply to that, she simply dipped her head in a way that could have been gratitude.

'My pleasure,' he muttered mordantly. It was the last thing he said before courteously helping her down in Pereville Parade and watching her run through the rain, without a backward glance, towards her door.

Chapter Sixteen

'I'm pleased to meet you, ma'am.'

Viscountess Cleveland graciously inclined her head as Jemma rose from her polite curtsy. Having made the introduction, Deborah stood back, happily smiling.

'Do come in then, my dear, and sit down,' the Viscountess invited briskly. 'Deborah has told me how very much she enjoyed your little *musicale*. She said the child who sang for you all was very talented. Do you think she might sing for us today?' An airy hand indicated in the direction of a pianoforte in the corner of the salon. It appeared Julia Cleveland was confident of not being disappointed in her request. The lid of the instrument was up and a pile of music was stacked neatly near by.

'I hope she will, ma'am,' Jemma politely said. 'She might need a little persuasion. Susan can be rather shy at times.'

'Whilst we wait for the other guests to arrive, I shall take Miss Bailey to my chamber and show her my new ballgown.' Deborah linked arms with Jemma and turned her about. 'It is the most beautiful thing: cream silk with a lace over-net embroidered with pink rosebuds and threaded gold ribbon.' Her hand wove to and fro to embellish the description.

'It sounds exquisite! I should love to see it,' Jemma truthfully said.

The Viscountess looked a trifle taken aback to be abandoned so soon. The other ladies were not due to arrive for twenty minutes more. She had been perplexed as to why Deborah had favoured Miss Bailey turning up earlier than the rest when she was such a new acquaintance. But Julia could tell that her daughter liked the young woman; since she had attended her party she had spoken warmly about her on several occasions. Julia believed it to be a genuine friendship and not one her wise daughter had fostered from an ethos of keeping one's enemies close. Julia had listened to Deborah praising her new friend and had decided she must put aside her misgivings and like her too. She only had to look at her distinguished future son-in-law to know that her only child was adept at forming worthy attachments. Julia gave Deborah's back view an indulgent smile as the young ladies proceeded towards the door of her opulent rose salon.

A few days ago Jemma had received a little note from Deborah inviting her to tea at the Clevelands' mansion in Upper Brook Street. Deborah had written that the Mrs Sheridan and Susan were also to be invited, as was Maura Wyndham and Lucy Duncan and her mother. Jemma had been pleased to receive it; she had been on the point of setting pen to paper to apologise to Deborah for having so suddenly left Hyde Park, and without a proper farewell.

Judging from the note's little postscript, which informed Jemma that Deborah had much to tell her, she'd imagined she would learn how Deborah had gone about jilting Marcus. Jemma knew she had an aching curiosity to hear it.

The silk-and-satin appointments of Deborah's vast bedchamber momentarily held Jemma awestruck, but Deborah would not indulge her friend in stopping a moment to admire her sumptuous surroundings. She hurriedly drew Jemma towards two blue velvet armchairs sited in the window embrasure.

'Have you seen Marcus since I called off our betrothal?' Deborah launched straight away into her questions once they were seated.

'Yes,' Jemma replied in a voice that was admirably neutral, considering her stomach had lurched at the mention of his name.

'I knew it!' Deborah squeaked triumphantly. 'He has visited you to ask you to marry him, hasn't he?'

Jemma shook her head, not trusting herself to give a steady reply this time.

Deborah frowned her disappointment. 'He was very good about it all when I told him I couldn't marry him. Of course I rather expected he would be. He was gallant, but I could tell it was what he wanted. If it is not *you* he intends to marry, who is it? He has someone in mind.'

'Did he say so?' Jemma asked hoarsely.

'No, it is just an impression I had from him. I noticed he could not keep his eyes from you in the park, and was vexed that he could not take you for a walk. I know he intends to soon marry to get an heir. I was convinced it was you he wanted.'

Jemma could not prevent a bitter little choke of laughter escaping on hearing that.

'It *is* you he wants,' Deborah breathed in dawning comprehension. 'Has he been…*bad* about it?' she asked, agog with naughty thoughts.

'Very bad,' Jemma said. 'But please don't ask me to divulge more, and I trust that you will not—'

'Of course I will not say anything!' Deborah interrupted. 'I know *you* will say nothing of what I've confided to you about my feelings for Randolph.'

'Do your parents know you have jilted the Earl?' Something had been niggling at Jemma since the moment she'd been introduced to the Viscountess. Julia Cleveland did not look or act like a woman who had recently had all her plans dashed.

'No!' Deborah mouthed urgently, as though anxious her mother might overhear the shocking news despite being downstairs. 'Marcus was very good about that too. I asked him if we could keep it our secret for a little while longer…until after the ball. I know Mama would be very upset to face all the guests after I have cried off marrying the Earl of Gresham.' A glum, guilty look preceded, 'Then there is the cost to consider. I know Papa has spent a small fortune on my début so far, plus the expense of wedding preparations—that I tried to tell Mama not to yet make,' she spiritedly added in her defence, then sighed. 'Mama might decide to cancel the ball rather than be discomposed on the night by constant whispers and sniggers.' Her lips thrust in to a belligerent knot at the thought of her mama's mortification. 'There will be a frenzy amongst the ladies when it is known Marcus is again available. Mama couldn't bear them all swooning over him in our house. I so much want her to enjoy the occasion.' She put her chin in her cupped hands and looked mournful. 'I wish I hadn't caused so much trouble.'

'The ball will be a wonderful affair, I'm sure.' Jemma could see that Deborah badly needed cheering up. As her friend's hands flopped to her lap she took one and gave it a reassuring squeeze. 'Your parents only want you to be happy, Debbie, I'm sure of that, too. I take it that they've no idea about your feelings for Randolph?'

Deborah sorrowfully shook her head. 'He has no title and no prospects, other than being the Earl of Gresham's best friend. I don't care that he has nothing, but I'm sure they will.'

'Perhaps they won't,' Jemma offered, a tad unconvincingly. She knew well enough that a young woman of Deborah's pedigree and beauty would be expected to marry a man of wealth and status. 'I'm sure they only have your best interests at heart.'

'You *will* come to the ball?'

Jemma nodded. 'I'm looking forward to it.' It was a simple truthful statement. She had already sorted through her gowns to select one to wear next week. After a moment she released her friend's hand. 'I must apologise to you for leaving the park so abruptly on that afternoon.'

'I know why you did,' Deborah declared. 'When we returned to the landau Randolph said that you had gone home because Robert Burnham charged up to you in the park.'

A slightly self-conscious smile tilted a corner of Jemma's mouth. 'I feel quite foolish now for letting him unsettle me to such a degree that I scampered away. It was just…a great shock to see him after so long. He has never before tried to contact me.'

'Do you think he will try again to see you?'

'He already has,' Jemma confided. 'When I reached home he was loitering on my doorstep.'

Deborah gasped her surprise. 'And what did he say? What did *you* say?'

'I gave him no chance to say anything,' Jemma ruefully admitted. 'By lucky chance I happened to see him before he spied me. I turned about and took myself off to wait for him to leave.' A frown preceded, 'I won't let him intimidate me. But I had no intention of inviting him in, and I was certainly not going to hold a conversation with him in the street while curtains twitched behind us. It is pointless to dredge up the past and pick it over.' She paused before saying with some feeling, 'Thankfully he has not returned since.' She gave Deborah a quizzical look. 'Have you told Randolph that you have jilted Marcus?'

Deborah shook her head. 'But I'm quite sure that Marcus has done so. Randolph is loyal to Marcus and conscious of proper etiquette. He won't mention anything about it until after the matter is broadcast or he will betray that Marcus has confided our secret to someone, just as I have.' Her eyes became distant. 'But he knows, I can tell by the way he looks at me. I can tell, too, that he's pleased about it.'

'I believe I heard a carriage stopping outside,' Jemma said, causing Deborah's misty vision to focus on the window.

In a moment Deborah was on her feet in a swish of

skirts and moving aside the blind. 'It is Maura and…
Oh, no! It is her brother, too! What does *he* want?'

It was soon quite clear to everybody what Theo
Wyndham wanted, and why he'd unnecessarily accompanied his sister to her afternoon tea at the Clevelands' house.

'Well, yes, Mr Wyndham, the preparations for the
ball *are* very well underway,' Julia Cleveland answered
him for the second time. Faint annoyance had puckered
her brow. Usually she limited her acknowledgement of
Maura's brother to a gracious nod. She had never harboured any desire to improve on that acquaintance; presently she wished he would hurry up and remove
himself from where he stoutly stood, chest puffed, ob-
scuring her elegant reflection in the gilt-framed over-
mantel mirror. Again Julia sent a significant look at
Maura as though simultaneously blaming her and appealing for her help in hurrying the departure of this
thick-skinned interloper. It seemed that Maura was too
greatly embarrassed by her brother's atrocious social
climbing to do much at all. She again shuffled at his side
and looked at her shoes. As Theo again launched into
fulsome praise of the room's appointments, and how
fitting a venue the mansion was for a grand début ball,
Maura slipped away, her cheeks glowing, and went to
stand with Jemma and Deborah by the pianoforte.

'I'm sorry,' she mumbled to Deborah. 'I wish now I
had stayed at home rather than endure this. The Viscountess looks very put out. I just couldn't shake him off.'

'Well, I can,' Deborah declared. 'He's here to
wheedle for an invitation to the ball, isn't he?'

Maura nodded miserably. 'He's been nagging at me

for ages to ask you if he might come. He has the cheek of the devil and hates being thwarted. It would please him enormously to have an invitation,' she added forlornly.

'Well, if pleasing him is the only way to be rid of him,' Deborah said, 'I shall do a good deed for the day. There are above two hundred guests who've accepted, so we will be able to avoid him in the crush.' She determinedly marched off to join her mama, who was more than happy to have her company.

Every step Julia had edged away, Theo had taken one to close the gap, so that now they had traversed the carpet and stood together by the French windows. A moment after her daughter was welcomed to her side, Julia was gazing at Deborah as though she'd taken leave of her senses. Her jaw sagged towards her swelling bosom as she realised that the upstart had just received a verbal invitation to their summer ball. A moment later Julia was reminded of how wily was her daughter. Having got what he wanted, Theo Wyndham took his leave and was soon strutting towards the door. A languid lift of the hand was his sister's only farewell.

After a reflective moment Julia hurried after him. It would not hurt to take a leaf out of her daughter's book and employ a little tactic of her own. Julia had been struck by how worryingly attractive Jemma Bailey was at close quarters. Although a little taller than the norm for a female, her figure was very womanly, with full bosom and hips accentuated by a slender waist. Her glossy locks flowed about a slender column of neck, tinted by strips of sunlight to the shade of sweet sherry. A neat nose and rosy mouth were set in a flawless heart-shaped face. But it was those eyes, large and lustrous as a bishop's emeralds, that were the focus of Julia's reluctant admiration. A friend of Deborah's she might be, but it would not do to tempt fate, or the Earl of Gresham…

'As you are to come to the ball, Mr Wyndham, perhaps you might like to bring along one of your cronies. I always think it is a good thing to have lots of dancing partners for the young ladies on such an occasion.'

'Of course. I should be charmed to oblige, ma'am. Have you a specific gentleman in mind?' Theo asked, his cheeks flushing, his chest puffing in pleasure.

'Mr Crabbe,' Julia said immediately. 'I understand he is a friend of yours, and I believe he is close to Miss Bailey, too?' An innocent look was flicked sideways at him. 'I shall arrange for formal invitations for you both.' With that she sailed away towards the young ladies to await the imminent arrival of the remaining guests.

A wondrous smile stretched Theo's lips as he settled back in to his carriage. As the vehicle pulled off he clasped his hands behind his head and hooted a laugh.

Stephen Crabbe should be very surprised, and humbly grateful, to him for what had occurred this afternoon. Theo had, with very little effort, just secured them both an invitation to the most prestigious party to be held during the whole of the Season. During the evening they would mix with people of wealth and influence. Any canny, ambitious fellow must surely gain from it an advantage. Theo intended to subtly canvas for some cash, and a husband for his cousin. However, if no better candidate than Crabbe presented himself, Theo would remind Stephen he was due some thanks and a proposal to his ward.

* * *

'For a fellow in love you look damned miserable.' Randolph's fingers continued to form an intricate pleat in his cravat as his eyes slid from his reflection to that of his friend.

Marcus was propped on one hand against the window frame. From his lounging position in his bedchamber he'd been moodily watching the bustle in the street below. Having digested Randolph's comment, he jerked upright and turned on him a savage frown.

'I'm not in love.'

Randolph raised his eyebrows, wordlessly contesting that, and continued faultlessly folding the snowy lawn at his throat.

'I'm not,' Marcus insisted in response to his friend's amused scepticism. 'What makes you think that I love her?'

'Well, I didn't need to mention a name for a start,' Randolph said with a glimmer of a smile. 'Then, of course, there's the way you were looking at her that day…'

'What? Which day?' Marcus snarled. 'How was I looking at her?'

'You were ravishing her with your eyes, which was probably a wise restraint as we were in Hyde Park at the time.' Randolph continued to reflect on his handiwork. 'If Deborah hadn't had the good sense to jilt you, she'd have every reason to feel jealous of Jemma Bailey.'

Marcus snatched up his whisky tumbler from the dressing chest and shot the fiery liquid to the back of his throat. He spun on his heel; once his broad back was presented to his chuckling friend, he closed his eyes. He hoped to God he hadn't made his lust for Jemma too obvious. Yet he feared he might have done so because wanting her never went away. She was in his thoughts every minute of every day. Every morning he woke angry and frustrated, not just because he was in a permanent state of unrelieved sexual arousal, but because he felt mired in uncertainty. He couldn't judge how Jemma really felt about him. Did she like him? Hate him? The only certainty he had was that she was no more indifferent to him than he was to her. He knew he could give her pleasure. But he'd known that some years ago when she'd wanted his lovemaking, yet refused him as her husband. Now when he drew cries of ecstasy from her he feared she loathed him for making her feel weak and wanton. And then he hated himself.

She'd found out about Pauline Vaux, no doubt from Wyndham; he'd seen his carriage on the road on the night he'd told Pauline they were finished. But he'd not told Jemma that Pauline was in his past because he'd sensed her jealousy. And it had pleased him. He wanted her to experience a similar feeling to the one that constantly gnawed at him. It wasn't the demented, draining emotion that had brought him to his knees years ago when she'd rejected him in favour of her country lover. None the less, when Randolph had told him that Burnham had approached her, a jealous rage had sent him straight away to Pereville Parade to find her. And find her he had, and Burnham too, loitering on her step.

The deterrent of a scandalous scene ensuing had kept him from jumping from his carriage and demanding an explanation from the fellow for his presence outside Jemma's home. Marcus speared five restless fingers though his dark hair as a grunt of mirthless laughter scraped his throat. She certainly wouldn't have thanked him for jeopardising what remained of the Bailey reputation by brawling in the gutter over her.

'I'd sooner stay away this evening than watch Deborah pretending she's still your fiancée. I'll be glad when this farce is over.'

Marcus swung about to see his friend was walking towards him, looking glum. 'Not nearly as glad as I'll be, I promise,' he gritted out. He consulted his watch and saw it was time to go.

The two elegantly attired gentlemen proceeded towards the door, each lost in private contemplation of the ordeal ahead of them.

Marcus hated pretence, yet he understood why Deborah wanted to protect her parents from spiteful people this evening. Their daughter's début ball should be a joyful occasion for the Clevelands. It was his duty, and the least he could do in appreciation of Deborah setting him free, to help her make the occasion a success. He knew that a day or two hence he would be closeted with her father, terminating a betrothal that neither of them had ever truly wanted.

Then he'd rally the courage to test Jemma's declaration that she'd sooner marry Stephen Crabbe than him.

Chapter Seventeen

'Accept Mr Crabbe's arm!'

Jemma ignored her guardian's sibilant command. She moved to stand on the other side of her cousin Maura as they waited in a queue of fashionable people for their turn to ascend the shallow stone steps to the Clevelands' gracious mansion.

Half an hour ago Jemma had been astonished to find that Stephen Crabbe was already seated in Theo's coach when it had called to collect her from Pereville Parade. Maura had been sitting opposite him looking uneasy. She had surreptitiously flashed at Jemma a look that declared her to be innocent of knowing about her brother's blatant strategy to force the two of them together. Having endured a few hundred yards of Mr Crabbe fidgeting and coughing beside her, Jemma had taken pity on the fellow. It had become obvious to her that Stephen Crabbe was no happier with the situation than was she, and that had given Jemma reason to hope that his interest in her had waned. She thus had started a bland conversation about the warm weather and how it might adversely affect guests crowded in a ballroom. Stephen had eagerly commenced stuttering his opinion on the necessity of cool drinks and cool air entering open doors and windows, and they had both successfully ignored Theo's triumphant smirk all the way to Upper Brook Street where they had just alighted.

Once on the pavement Jemma had noticed that Stephen had seemed friskier. A few times he had seemed on the point of jerking his elbow in her direction, but she'd managed to avoid rejecting him by engaging her attention elsewhere. She knew he was staring at her now, believing her unaware of his roving eyes admiring her gossamer-clad figure. She casually adjusted her silk shawl so her décolletage was more discreet.

Jemma knew, without conceit, she looked at her best. Indeed Polly had told her she looked beautiful a dozen times whilst circling her with the perfume spray and sending a flowery mist to moisten her skin. Polly was a competent lady's maid and a talented hairdresser. Having cleverly applied the tongs to create a sleek coiffure, she'd woven a rope of lustrous pearls through Jemma's conker-coloured curls, allowing a sinuous length of beads to sway free at her nape. Jemma's lashes needed no artifice, being naturally lush and dark, but she'd used a little carmine to accentuate the rose of her lips. The gown she'd chosen to wear was the newest she possessed. It had been made for Mr and Mrs Sheridan's tenth anniversary party almost a year ago. She'd not since worn the dress as the cut and cloth were suited to summer. The shade of the flimsy lawn was midway between green and blue, and Jemma knew that it intensified the jade flecks in her eyes.

'Take Mr Crabbe's arm!' was once more hissed at her across Maura's buttoned bodice.

'I will not,' Jemma this time calmly answered her guardian. 'I have no quarrel with Mr Crabbe, but if I hang on his arm it might give credence to the absurd gossip you started months ago that I am husband-hunting amongst past suitors.' A significant pause preceded, 'And nothing could be further from the truth.'

Theo's lips disappeared into a purple line. 'Your arrogant and selfish independence does you no favours, miss,' he snarled before so abruptly stomping up the two steps that had become vacant that his sister stumbled at his side.

'Wyndham is your kin, I know, but I have to say, Miss Bailey, that I think you deserve better than such as he to guard your interests.'

Stephen Crabbe had obviously overheard their heated exchange and was looking at Jemma with meek apology for his blurted opinion. With a tentative gesture he invited Jemma to move on to the bottom step before joining her on it.

'I…I didn't mean to be impertinent and neither was it my intention to…that is, I am not applying to take on the role of your protector—no, not a *protector*,' he hastily corrected himself. 'I only wanted to tell you I think you deserve a kinder guardian.' Having floundered in to a miserable quiet, he turned aside his florid face and grimaced.

'I understand,' Jemma said gently. 'Often it is hard to put it into words how unpleasant Theo can be.'

Stephen vigorously nodded then turned slightly to stare at a stone pillar. 'I hope you were not…too upset…by my travelling with you today. I wanted to use my own transport, but Wyndham insisted I share his. As he was good enough to secure me an invitation it seemed churlish to argue over something so trivial. Of course he did not mention that you…that is…I had not realised you might be in the coach too. I would have insisted on travelling separately rather than embarrass you with my presence.'

'I admit I was at first rather flustered to see you. But only because Theo has told me you want to renew your proposal to me.' Jemma had decided to take the bull by the horns and mention the disconcerting matter. She angled her head the better to see his crimson face. 'I think you have come to your senses and have changed your mind.' She tried to ease his hideous floridity with a little whispered levity.

Stephen wobbled his head up and down. 'I had no right to indicate I would again approach you, and am ashamed that I did,' he blurted gruffly. 'My affairs need to be far tidier before I contemplate taking on a wife. I was being stupid. Selfish.' He slid a look at the lovely young woman at his side and added wistfully, 'But if my financial situation *were* better, then I would not hesitate in—'

'Shh,' Jemma interrupted him and placed a gloved finger against her lips as they curved in to a winsome smile. 'We are dealing well together, sir, let's not spoil it.'

On hearing that Stephen relaxed so visibly he seemed to shrink back in to his shoes. 'I know Wyndham has been meddling in your life, and that you were innocent of knowing about his letters.' He diffidently peeked sideways at Jemma and her warm expression encouraged him to resume. 'I don't want to stir gossip about us, or upset you in any way.' He paused, garnered

courage to blurt, 'But would you do me the honour…?
He tentatively proffered an elbow.

Jemma looked at it, then at him. Already his quivering sleeve was lowering, his colour again heightening.
She placed an elegant hand firmly upon his arm,
drawing it up with slender, kid-gloved fingers.

Sedately and very proudly Mr Crabbe escorted Miss
Bailey up the steps behind Wyndham's bristling back.

The colonnaded ballroom was blindingly bright, gilt
and marble surfaces burnished by a succession of stupendous chandeliers strung high along its central length.
A current of balmy air from the terrace swayed crystal
drops and rainbow light dappled the room, rivalling the
fabulous jewels sparkling against pearly female skin. A
raised dais at one end of the stately apartment was home
to a small orchestra and the light melody they were
playing added to an air of gracefulness that pervaded the
environment.

'It's all very nice,' Mr Crabbe said with monumental
understatement as he gaped, thunder-struck, at their
opulent surroundings.

'It is indeed, sir, very nice,' Jemma wryly agreed,
but she got no further in her praise of the magnificent
setting for her friend's ball. The young lady herself was
bearing down on them, looking appealingly ethereal in
her pale ball gown.

Deborah clasped both of Jemma's hands in her own
in welcome.

'This is Mr Crabbe,' Jemma introduced her companion in case Deborah had not heard them announced.

If Deborah was shocked to know the identity of the
gentleman accompanying Jemma, she admirably con-

cealed her surprise. 'How do you do, sir?' she politely greeted him.

'Very well, thank you,' Stephen stuttered. He was aware that they were being watched, and envied, by loftier guests present who had not been singled out for such special treatment. Theo, in particular, was observing the scene with a very sour expression on his face.

'Would you mind, Mr Crabbe, if I take Miss Bailey from you so she might help me choose some livelier music to start the dancing?'

'Of course not,' Stephen said, all affability, his confidence mounting. 'You young ladies must go along and enjoy yourselves.' He coughed to halt them before they got too far. 'Might I beg a place on your dance card early on, Miss Bailey, before it is full?'

'Of course, sir. I shall try not to tread on your toes if we join a quadrille, if that suits you?'

He nodded, smiling happily.

Linking arms with her friend, Deborah headed off towards a quiet anteroom where crisply uniformed servants were spreading out a supper. Upon pristine cloths were being arranged silver platters and bowls brimming with delicious-looking sweet and savoury pastries. Having led Jemma to a private corner, Debbie launched into, 'I knew it was Mr Crabbe. I came straight away. I thought you might want to be rescued from him.'

'That's very good of you, Debbie,' Jemma said with a smile in her voice. 'But actually he is rather sweet; far nicer now than I remember him to be when he proposed to me. When younger he was rather flashy and forward. He says he is in straitened circumstances. Perhaps losing his money has improved him.'

Aghast, Deborah widened her eyes on her. 'You are not after all considering…?'

'No!' Jemma breathed on a laugh. 'And neither does he really want a wife. He told me he acted in haste, no doubt with Theo's considerable prodding. I think my guardian is to be very disappointed in Mr Crabbe. I feel rather chastened for having thought ill of him.' She paused before saying brightly, 'Enough of that! It is your very special evening and you look beautiful. Your gown is exquisite and the style and colour suits you so very well.' Jemma gently touched a pink satin rosebud with a finger. 'I never did get a glimpse of it on the afternoon of your tea party.'

'And you look stunning,' Deborah said, keen to return her friend a compliment. 'The colour of your gown matches your eyes.' Her smile suddenly faded as she tilted her head the better to see somebody in the ballroom. 'I'm so sorry, Jemma, but I think a gentleman you will want to avoid thinks you look ravishing and is itching to come and tell you so. He has been staring at you for some while.'

Jemma felt excitement ripple through her. From the moment she had entered the house her darting little glances had been seeking out a dark, distinguished figure. But she'd not caught a glimpse of Marcus. She might feel unbearably tense and excited when she knew he was near, but she couldn't deny that always she longed to see him. Already liquid fire seemed to streak in her veins in anticipation of soon doing so. 'Is Marcus watching us from the ballroom?' she asked huskily.

'I wish it *were* Marcus watching us,' Deborah said before nibbling at her lower lip. 'I'm so sorry,' she said with a regretful grimace. 'As soon as I clapped eyes on him I asked Mama how he came to be here. She says she did not actually *invite* him; he is simply filling a vacant place. My cousin Phyllis's husband is ailing and has stayed home. His friend…' she hesitated before naming the fellow '…Mr Burnham is escorting Phyllis in her husband's stead.'

Even before Deborah had concluded her explanation for Robert's presence, Jemma, with sinking heart, had guessed the worst. Never the less, having her fears confirmed made her cheeks prickle unpleasantly. In a moment she had rallied sufficiently to try to cheer up her friend. 'It doesn't matter, Debbie! Your mama and your cousin Phyllis have every right to choose what company they keep. We agreed, did we not, it should be simple in the crush to avoid people we'd sooner not speak to this evening.' Following that brave statement, Jemma half-turned so she might scan the available view of the guests beyond the open double doors of the supper room.

He must have stationed himself in a prime position to watch them, Jemma realised. Her wide green gaze had not needed to rove far to find a familiar, boyish face. It again began to emerge from behind a marble pillar directly opposite the supper-room doorway. She felt her heart increase tempo as her eyes clashed with Robert's. When he suddenly, urgently beckoned, whilst surreptitiously glancing about to check if he was under observation, she quickly looked away, flustered as to how to react. She was sorely tempted to gesture back at him her annoyance at being spied on.

'Oh, here is Randolph.' Deborah's tone betrayed her pleasure at seeing him.

Mr Chadwicke was approaching them with a suave smile, looking the epitome of polished civility in his formal evening clothes. Jemma had to acknowledge that it was the first time she had noticed just how attractive he was. Before, he had just been Marcus's friend to her. But now she saw him through Deborah's eyes, and appreciated his masculine appeal.

He executed a debonair bow for them both. Immediately Deborah took his arm as though it were the most natural thing in the world to partner him.

'Your mother is looking for you, Miss Cleveland. She is keen to start the dancing. I believe the first dance is quite sedate, and is promised to your father.'

'It is! We must prise him from his cronies and make him join in the fun. The second dance, or is it the third, is with Marcus,' Debbie said. 'I have not seen him since you both arrived. Where is he?'

Randolph's eyes collided with Jemma's before hers glided away. 'I believe he was with your father, trying to get him to abandon his game of chess with Lord Carlisle and join the party now most of the guests have arrived.' Lightly he asked, 'Have you saved a dance for me?'

'Of course,' Deborah said rather breathily. 'Did you think I would not?'

'I must go and find out if the Sheridans have yet arrived,' Jemma interjected brightly. Knowing what she did about this couple, she was beginning to feel a gooseberry. 'And I expect Maura is wondering what has become of me. I have not spoken a word to her since we arrived.' With a smile she signalled that she was quite happy to go alone and locate her friends and her cousin in the throng.

In truth, she was glad to be on her own. She needed to find a discreet way to impress on Robert that he must stop harassing her. She was aware of his continuing observation as she picked a path through the people on the perimeter of the dance floor. Casual glimpses told her that he was moving, too, keeping abreast of her on the opposite side of the room.

It was obvious he was determined to speak to her and was putting some effort into bringing it about. Beneath her ribs her heart was pounding painfully. A delicate lace fan was extracted from her reticule and, having snapped it open, she cooled her complexion. She glanced his way again, hoping her obvious disinclination to join him might have prompted him to take himself off. It had not, and as their eyes met, a crooked finger came up in a demand that she meet him behind a concealing column. Jemma felt increasingly angry. She had been looking forward to the ball and had intended to enjoy it. Robert Burnham had as much right to be here as she did. But she was not going to let him stalk her, or ruin her pleasure, and she intended telling him so. Plunging her fan into her reticule, she put up her chin and began to weave a swift yet graceful path through groups of chattering people.

As soon as Jemma came within a few feet of Robert he muttered, 'I have something of great import to say to you. We need to be alone, I think, outside.'

A throb of urgency and purpose in his voice was not lost on Jemma. A cold reproof had been about to trip off her tongue, but it slowly withered.

'It is nothing to do with…our history,' he blurted. 'What I have to say concerns a very recent event—' He broke off to nod and murmur a greeting to a couple sauntering past arm in arm. 'Perhaps it is not a good time to tell you after all,' he muttered, looking about. 'It is very crowded; someone might overhear.' Oddly, it was his sudden reluctance to proceed that brought Jemma a step closer to him. Instinctively she knew he was not about to embarrass her by dragging up their youthful romance, but had something different on his mind.

'I have seen your mother.' Robert launched immediately into his news in a whisper as she placed a hand on the arm he'd offered her. 'Please don't think me impertinent, Jemma. I only want to help you. In truth, I'm not sure if I'm doing right or wrong. I have turned it over in my mind and can only imagine that you *would* rather know now than be shocked in a few days time when she turns up on your doorstep.' A searching look was scanning her face as though he was unsure whether to divulge more. But it was the mingling of pity and regret at the back of his eyes that made her inwardly shiver in foreboding.

'Will you step upon the terrace for a moment?' Robert asked hoarsely. 'Trust me, it is better that nobody overhears what I have to say.'

The music had changed tempo. Lilting strings had been replaced by a stronger beat and the guests were being lured towards the far end of the ballroom where sets were forming on the polished parquet. But soon Jemma's eyes were again scouring Robert's face. She knew it would be sensible to move somewhere where they might talk discreetly.

'Is my mother in England?' Jemma asked hoarsely on the second attempt to eject the words. She'd felt a mix of joy and trepidation on hearing he wanted to speak about her mother. It seemed logical to assume he'd recently bumped in to her.

'She is,' Robert confirmed quickly. 'I had recently disembarked at Newhaven when I spotted her. I had been on a trip to France on a friend's yacht. She too had recently arrived from Paris. But the rest of it must wait till we are private.'

Jemma's large green eyes flitted from left to right. As she'd feared, they were coming under observation. Some of the people sliding peeks their way were sure to have long memories. They would remember she'd rejected Marcus Speer in favour of this man. They'd know, too, that Robert Burnham was now a husband and father, and had no business conducting a tête-à-tête with a former sweetheart. But he had news of her mother! She was desperately impatient to hear it. A single nod gave Robert permission to escort her outside.

Once on the paved terrace, they moved instinctively away from the ballroom doors and towards steps that led to the garden. Dusk was descending on a startling sunset in the west, but the romantic setting was lost on Jemma and, it seemed, on her companion too. Robert walked with his head bent, as though he were deep in thought. As soon as they were out of view of the ballroom and shaded by the overhanging branches of a mulberry tree, Jemma let go of his arm. 'Is the Count with my mother in Newhaven?' she demanded to know.

Robert shook his head. 'I think I must start at the beginning,' he said gravely. 'First I must apologise for my impulsive behaviour in Hyde Park. I saw you and immediately wanted to tell you what I know. Of course, it was not the right time to do so. I'm sorry I acted like an idiot. I could think of nothing sensible to say, so rode off rather than compound my mistake.'

'Is that why you came to my home later that same day? To tell me about having seen my mother in Newhaven?'

Robert shot an enquiring look at her, then grimaced a smile. 'Of course, your servant would have told you that I had called. Again, I did not want to thrust my presence on you unexpectedly. I thought of putting pen to paper, but decided that what I have to relate is best done in person, not by letter. Besides, I feared you might think me lying. I imagine you have no good opinion of me now. Nor do I deserve it,' he said bleakly. 'So I have been in a dilemma, unsure whether to seek you out and speak to you, or mind my own business. But I concluded that you wouldn't thank me for having kept quiet when I could have warned you. And I know I owe you a good turn.'

Jemma was obliquely aware that he was hinting at an apology for having abandoned her years ago. But all that seemed inconsequential now. She simply wanted a vital, terrifying question answered. 'Is my mother ill? Has she come back here alone to spend her final days near her daughters?'

'No! Indeed, no!' Robert clasped one of her hands to comfort her. 'It is nothing like that. She looked in fine fettle, although older. I did not at first recognise her as her hair is now streaked with white and her face rather lined.' He paused. 'She is not with the Count. But neither is she alone, Jemma. Your mother has a child with her; a boy of about seven years old, I should say. She told me he is her son.'

Chapter Eighteen

Jemma felt momentarily shocked into speechlessness. Slowly the significance of what he'd said penetrated her daze. Now she understood why Robert had been so desperate to keep his news from being overheard. Her mother had gone off with her French Count more than a decade ago, but as his mistress and with no prospect of becoming his wife. Pierre Devereux already had a wife, and as far as Jemma was aware her mother had never managed to oust her.

She had a brother! The knowledge filled her with a mingling of elation and anxiety. If her mother hadn't married the man who'd sired her son—she assumed it to be Pierre—she would be despised and ostracised if she tried to rejoin society with a bastard in tow. She had left these shores branded a scandalous hussy. Was she returning with the proof of her shameless behaviour? Why had she returned? Had Pierre tired of her, or she of him?

'Did you speak to her?' Jemma demanded to know. It would be wise not to jump to conclusions until she had the facts. Perhaps Pierre's wife *had* died and he'd finally made an honest woman of her mother.

'We had a brief conversation. She seemed rather disconcerted to be spotted so soon after landing on English soil.' He paused. 'I know she is sensitive to spite. But I made it clear that I bore her no ill will. In fact, I remember her as being kind to me. She always welcomed me into your home when we lived as neighbours in Essex.' He glanced at Jemma to read her reaction so far. Her searching gaze was roving his face, wordlessly begging more information from him. 'She asked how you were and said that it was her intention to travel to London to see you.' Robert shifted position. 'She is aware that you are the only one of her girls who remains unwed. She knew, too, that your father had passed away.'

'She would not be coming to London else,' Jemma remarked hoarsely. 'Never would she have returned to Pereville Parade if she thought Papa alive to castigate her and then eject her from his doorstep. What Papa would think of her bringing back her child, the Count's child…' She scanned Robert's features as though she could read in his face the answer to a question she dreaded to ask. 'Is…is my mother remarried?'

'She uses the name Mrs Bailey still,' he answered quietly. 'She was wearing mourning; it came out in conversation that Devereux had recently died. Although she did not say, I assumed that was why she had left France and returned to her homeland. She seemed to be a trifle embarrassed for funds. We stayed at the same inn, and I noticed she was carefully counting pennies. She did not want me to assist her in purchasing a meal for them both, but I insisted and gave over the cost to the landlord.'

Jemma felt her stomach lurch sickeningly. So, her mother's lover had died and left her with nothing but his child. Of course Robert was trying to be as diplomatic as he could, but she could tell that he knew the scale of the scandal that her mother's return would wreak. And, naturally, she and her sisters would once more be enveloped in her shame. Instead of being slightly sullied by past misdemeanours, all the Bailey women would once more be beyond the pale.

'I'm so very sorry to have to tell you this news, and at such an inopportune moment. It is a fine occasion, and we must try to enjoy ourselves. But time is of the essence. I thought you would sooner be prepared for your mother's, and your brother's, arrival. He rubbed at the bridge of his nose, shuffling uneasily. 'There is something else, but I'm not sure I should mention it to you in case it is too great an impertinence... Oh, I don't know!' he groaned as though battling some inner torment. 'Tell me, Jemma, *have* I interfered?' he interrupted himself to ask with a frown.

Jemma shook her head and gave him a faltering smile. 'I owe you my thanks, Robert,' she said huskily. 'Thank you firstly for kindly giving my mother assistance when at the inn. Indeed, I *would* sooner know about her return to England and her son. I'm sure that my sisters too would want to be apprised of it as quickly as possible. Although they are a distance from London gossip travels eventually. I pray it will not affect them too badly.' Jemma felt utterly relieved that her young nephews were far enough away not to immediately be blighted by the stigma of their prodigal grandmother returning to the fold with their uncle, who was not much older than they were.

A sudden noise from the ballroom made Jemma start. A laughing couple had stepped on to the terrace, but mercifully had turned in the opposite direction and strolled away arm in arm. It was enough of a reminder of her indecorous behaviour to make Jemma step away from Robert as though she would now return to the party. If they were spotted whispering together in the shadows, the tabbies would unsheathe their claws before the evening ended.

'Before we part I must tell you how sorry I am that I treated you badly.' Robert suddenly clasped one of Jemma's hands and gazed at her with a hangdog expression. 'I hope very much that you have come to see, as I have, that our parting was for the best. We were very young, and I know now I was silly and immature. I owe you my deepest apology for having ever put into your head that we could elope. It was my fault. I ruined things for you. I know you turned down the chance to marry very well because of loyalty to me. I hope you will find happiness as I have.' Having rattled all that off, he took a breath and frowned as though worried that last remark might have sounded smug.

'I can't say that I didn't hate you for a while, Robert,' Jemma answered huskily. 'Your abandonment was hard to bear. But it wouldn't have worked, would it? We *were* being silly. We were little more than children when we began our plans to elope.'

'Caroline told me a while ago that I should find an

opportunity to properly apologise to you. A letter, she said, was no good at all in such circumstances.'

'Caroline? Your wife?'

Robert nodded. 'I think you would approve of her. She is a plain speaker and happiest at home in Berkshire with our sons. But she is not at all the sort of woman to want me under her feet all the time. She allows me my friends and my hobbies, and I love her for it.'

Jemma gave him a small smile. 'I think you have a found a very good wife.'

'Better than I deserve,' he admitted immediately. 'She put up with my moods and sulks when first we were shackled together by our parents. But something fine has grown between us.'

'I'm glad,' Jemma said simply. To emphasise that she was pleased that they'd finally cleared the air, and that she wished him well, she clasped his hands and gave them a squeeze. 'Come,' she said briskly. 'You said there was something else to tell me about my mother's return home. I don't consider your concern an impertinence, so please carry on.'

'I don't want to interrupt a private moment, but you might like to know you've been missed, Miss Bailey.'

The couple had been so engrossed in their hushed conversation that they had not heard someone softly approaching over the stone flags. Robert snatched his hands from Jemma's as though they were scalding him, and took a hasty step back.

Even before she'd pivoted about to face him, Jemma knew who had spoken. Despite her startled daze a bittersweet feeling had washed over her at the sound of his voice. Her eyes swerved to lock with an icy stare.

As he came closer Marcus's powerful shoulders seemed to obliterate the mellow light flickering in the ballroom. The balmy evening seemed darker, cooler for his presence on the terrace. A slice of shadow had planed his face to hard angles beneath dangerously gleaming eyes. He covered the paving with an easy powerful pace, his muscular frame perfectly attired in black evening clothes. He looked ruthless sophistication incarnate and even before Jemma could clearly read his expression a shiver had rippled through her, for she'd sensed in him a dangerous fury.

'Mr Crabbe believes you've promised to partner him in the next set,' Marcus commented coolly, a vague question in the words as he continued his predatory approach.

'Is it a quadrille?' Jemma forced out in a croak. She knew how unbelievably bad it must look for her to be caught holding hands with a married man…a married man she once had professed to love. Obliquely she realised she must be thankful that it had been Marcus who had disturbed them.

'I believe it is,' Marcus drawled as eyes like silver bullets targeted Robert.

The lethal look made Robert visibly flinch. He knew it was his fault that Jemma had rebuffed Marcus Speer's proposal. He'd heard the gossip that she'd surprised everybody by turning down this man despite having flirted outrageously with him for many weeks during her début. Robert recognised the look of a fellow in the throes of a jealous rage. Obviously Speer was still smitten with Jemma, and from the soulful look in her eyes she was no more immune to him now he was a surly aristocrat than she'd been when once he'd been charming Mr Speer. Robert had no intention of again getting in their way, or of pondering too long on the fact that the belle of this evening's ball was the Earl's fiancée. Robert might have been unsure whether to interfere in the Baileys' affairs; on this he had no such qualms. He was definitely minding his own business. 'Servant, my lord,' he mumbled. He jerked a bow to Jemma and snapped his head in Marcus's direction before moving swiftly towards the terrace doors.

Jemma would have followed him, and not simply because she knew Robert had more to tell her about her mother's return. As Marcus took Robert's place beside her at the balustrade she could clearly see just how enraged he was. She'd managed a single pace before vice-like fingers imprisoned her wrist, halting her, forcing her inexorably back against cold iron.

'Let me go.' Considering her anxious and preoccupied state she sounded remarkably reasonable and calm. 'I've promised to partner Mr Crabbe, and I won't disappoint him.'

'Why not?' Marcus demanded dulcetly. 'You constantly disappoint me.'

'If you wish me to dance with you, my lord,' she breathed, glancing up in to his harsh dark features, 'come and find me later, and I shall try to fit you in.' Too late she knew it sounded provocatively insulting when all she'd intended was to lure him back inside. She felt too emotionally fragile to want to argue with him now. A lump was clogging her throat and heat burning behind her eyes.

'What the hell were you thinking of coming out here

with him? Are you trying to stir gossip by flirting with every man in sight?'

'Of course not!' Jemma choked. She hadn't been flirting with Robert. But if she wanted to flirt, she would flirt with whomever she pleased! She would talk to whomever she pleased! Despite chaotic thoughts about her family disturbing her mind, she was rational enough to know that, however much she might want to do so, now was not the time to impress on him his hypocrisy. He had a mistress. Almost everybody present tonight believed he also had a fiancée. Yet he had the nerve to sound outraged and disapproving because he thought she'd been flirting with a man.

'You've no right to interrogate me!' she snapped in an angry undertone. 'You don't own me, although I know you think you do.' She swallowed the rest of the bitter accusation. Now was not the time, she reminded herself. 'I must go; the set will soon be starting,' she coolly told him. She again attempted to walk away although her right arm remained anchored behind her. She rotated her wrist in his long fingers, but they became crueller and she ceased straining.

'We've a while yet,' Marcus told her with deceptive softness. 'The musicians are taking a break. There's time enough for you to explain to me why you were out here with Burnham. After that you can tell me why it is you arrived on Crabbe's arm. Are you playing them off against each other?'

'If I thought it to be any of your business, perhaps I might tell you,' Jemma stormed, blinking back tears. She spun back to face him and tilted up her chin. Eyes that glittered like silver stars relentlessly engulfed hers, made her breathing cease, then recommence in a shallow gasp.

'It's my business if you start stirring gossip that you're a trollop,' he said silkily. 'I like my mistresses to be discreet and refined.' A sardonic gleam fired the backs of his eyes as he added, 'When clothed.' A long finger traced the low scoop of her bodice, making an unbidden, delicious shiver race through her. 'I imagine I'm not the first to tell you that you look ravishing tonight. But you need something… Emeralds, I think.'

'I won't ever be your mistress, so don't waste your money buying me emeralds,' Jemma choked.

'Don't be naïve, Jemma,' he drawled mockingly. 'You know, but for my very gentlemanly, unnatural restraint, you already would be my mistress. And you can have diamonds if you prefer…'

'I want nothing from you, least of all your lechery.'

'Is that so?' Effortlessly he turned to trap her back against the balustrade. A hand planted on iron either side of her slender body. 'I could take you now if I wanted to, down there in the garden on a bench. A couple of kisses and you'd beg me to finish what I'd started.'

'You beastly, arrogant—' She got no further; a swooping kiss stopped her words and the more she struggled, digging her nails spitefully into the biceps blocking her escape, the more brutal he became. Finally she stopped straining, and it was her downfall. His kiss became courteous, wooing, and a sob broke in her throat because she knew she was succumbing pathetically quickly to his skilful seduction. From the depths of her being she dredged the pride to whip aside her head. Her breathing was coming in fast, hard pants that grazed her nipples tantalisingly against the hard wall of his chest. He didn't force her face back to his as she'd expected. He nuzzled the ear she'd presented to him, lazily coaxing her to relax as his tongue traced delicate contours to the sensitive spot that made her shiver and sigh. Closing her eyes in frustration, she angled her head, melting in to him, as the soothing fingers stroked at her nape, luring her closer to defeat. As his hot mouth trailed a path back to tease the corner of her lips, she turned towards him, waiting…waiting… Her lids flicked up and she found sardonic silver eyes watching her.

'One kiss—what would you do for me for another, Jemma?' he demanded huskily. He easily caught the fist she swung at his face, mid-arc. 'Don't ever tell me you don't want me, or I can't have you,' he gritted. 'You're mine.'

That was it! She had no more will-power to draw on, and as their gazes grappled the shimmer in her eyes increased, then spilled wet on to her cheeks. Through splintering vision she saw his expression change, soften, as he tried to fathom what was wrong. He'd seduced her with bruising kisses and harsh truths before and released a tigress, not a kitten.

With a groan of apology Marcus tugged her in to his arms and five fingers speared in to soft hair to cradle her scalp.

'I'm sorry. I never mean to hurt you, but always I do. I'm a jealous fool.'

'It's not all your fault—not on this occasion,' she admitted with a choke of anguished humour.

'What is it?' he asked fiercely. 'Has Burnham done something? Said something? Has he propositioned

you?' From a pocket he withdrew a large linen handkerchief and touched it to her wet cheeks.

'Thank you.' She took the cloth and pressed it to her
damp eyes. 'Robert's done nothing wrong. In fact, he's
done me a great kindness,' she mumbled against his
shoulder. A moment ago she felt she hated him; now she
gratefully took his comfort.

'Why were you out here with him, Jemma? Why did
he come to your home? Tell me!' Marcus roughly
pleaded. 'Do you still love him? Does he still love you?'

'No, it is nothing like that. Robert is happily married.
He told me so.'

'And are you pleased about that?'

'Yes,' Jemma whispered. 'I'm not sure I ever really
did love him. But I think we might again be friends.'

'But something has upset you. If it's not my buffoon-
ery... What is it?'

'I can't tell you,' she whispered. Her eyes clung to
his, and she knew she was sorely tempted to confide in
him. She wanted to draw on his undeniable strength. But
how would he react to knowing her secret? She longed
to see her mother again and be introduced to her brother.
She didn't even know his name! But others would not
be so keen to see them. She knew that even the most
liberal-minded person would be shocked to hear that her
adulterous mother was coming back to beg charity for
herself and her bastard son. The fact that Mrs Bailey
expected shelter from the estate left by the husband
she'd shamelessly cuckolded would add to the scandal's
piquancy. But there might yet be some mistake about it
all, and that was another reason why Jemma was loath
yet to divulge what Robert had told her. Until she'd

spoken to her mother, and gained the full story, she must proceed warily lest she stirred trouble where there need be none.

'Burnham has been to France recently,' Marcus said. 'He went on Whittington's yacht.' He gave Jemma a penetrative look. 'Once you all were neighbours in Essex, weren't you? I expect he knew your mother well. Has be brought you news of her from France?'

An astonished gasp acknowledged his perception. She gave a single nod and begged, 'But please don't ask me to say more. Not tonight. I was so looking forward to enjoying this evening.'

'As was I, despite the necessity of acting out the deceit over my betrothal,' Marcus said quietly. 'It is a ridiculous farce.'

'Can you really enjoy this evening knowing such a lie exists?'

'Of course—you're here,' he said simply.

Marcus raised a gentle hand, cradled her cheek before drawing her arm through his. 'The music is starting,' he said softly. 'If you intend to keep your promise to Stephen Crabbe, you should return to the ballroom. I swear not to do any worse than hate him from afar.'

Jemma gurgled a watery laugh. 'He too has been very kind to me tonight. He has withdrawn his proposal. I think Theo probably badgered him into it in the first place.'

In gratitude at knowing it, Marcus swept a stroking thumb leisurely back and forth on the satiny skin of the hand resting on his arm. But his mind was turning over what Jemma had said. He brought to mind the trip he'd taken to France with his uncle when they'd seen Pierre

Devereux and Veronica Bailey out walking. There was something neither of them had commented on that day many years ago—though he was sure Solomon had noticed, just as he had. Veronica had either grown quite fat or she was with child. His musings were cut short by a sound of female voices.

They had moved away from the shadowy corner at precisely the right time. Several ladies, warm from being whirled around by their partners, had tripped on to the terrace, giggling and briskly fanning their feverish complexions. Jemma withdrew her little confection of ivory sticks and lace, and waved it in front of her face as they casually promenaded past into the ballroom.

The ladies might have assumed another of their sex had simply sought to revive herself by taking the air with a courteous escort, but one person had observed much more. He'd seen everything that had taken place between Jemma and the two gentlemen who had been with her in that shady corner of the terrace. He was stationed in the garden below, watching the proceedings from a bench that was backed against a wall and enclosed by a trelliswork tangled in jasmine. On the seat beside him were a half-smoked cigar and a depleted bottle of champagne that had been smuggled out to him beneath the skirt of one of the kitchen maids. The girl had also compounded her disloyalty to her employers by ensuring that a side entrance was left unlocked so the fellow could come and go as he pleased during the evening of this grandest of affairs.

A grand affair indeed it was, but one to which Graham Quick naturally had not been invited as his wicked infamy excluded him from being wanted where young innocents might be forced to breathe the same air. He might not be an invited guest, but it pleased Graham no end that he would tomorrow have more tattle than anyone else, even those right in the thick of things.

He upended the bottle again and swigged from it before plonking it down on the planked wood of the bench and drawing on the cheroot. He stretched out his legs in front of him and blew lazy smoke rings up at the night sky. A rustling in the bushes alerted him to somebody's presence. Indolently he turned his head, unperturbed at the prospect of being challenged as an interloper in the Clevelands' garden. Lucy, his little fancy, crept forwards with a plate of food for him.

'Here, got you this,' she hissed, and giggled nervously.

Graham ignored the delicacies and instead pulled her on to his lap and immediately dragged up her skirts. A moment later he'd pushed her away, his eyes again riveted on the terrace.

'Go back to your duties,' he whispered to Lucy with a perfunctory smile. 'If you're missed, they might come looking for you, then there'll be trouble.'

Lucy nodded. She knew she'd taken a dreadful risk letting such a devilishly disreputable fellow into the grounds of her employers' mansion. To ply him with fine champagne and pastries, and even one of the master's cigars from the box in his study, might be a hanging offence for all she knew! She wished she'd never let him bully her into being bad; but Mr Quick was too dangerous to deny when he wanted something.

Lucy hastened away in a whisper of skirts, leaving Graham smiling with sinister satisfaction at the distant figure of a young woman silhouetted by candle flame from the ballroom. She was pacing towards the balustrade, looking this way and that as though seeking someone on the deserted terrace. He knew that soon others might join her, so he must act in haste or not at all.

Swiftly he got to his feet and strode silently over the lawn towards the steps. He knew that Wyndham was here tonight. Damn the thieving miser! He'd still not paid over a penny piece of what he owed in loans and interest. Graham was now reduced to coercing kitchen wenches to pilfer him a fine cigar and one paltry bottle of champagne when he should have funds enough to buy cases of such luxuries.

But a stroke of luck had just been pitched his way, and he intended snatching at it. Graham wondered how loose would become Wyndham's purse strings once the fellow realised his sister was compromised by a debauched blackguard. It would be up to him whether the *ton* ever came to hear that Wyndham's sister was ruined. And that was a powerful bargaining stake. He stepped into the partial glow of a wavering garden flare so that his blond hair made him recognisable and in a soft voice called to Maura Wyndham to come down to him for he had something vital to tell her.

Chapter Nineteen

'Have you seen Maura?'

Lucy Duncan ceased attending to her friend's chatter and concentrated on the question Jemma had just murmured close to her ear.

'I know she went outside looking for you,' Lucy whispered back. 'She believed you were strolling on the terrace with Mr Burnham,' she added with rather a pert look. 'I expect she was hoping to spy on you.'

'We were taking the air,' Jemma explained lightly. 'But that was some while ago now.' She moved away a step, frowning, as she looked about. 'She isn't in the ladies' withdrawing room; I've checked and there's no sign of her. The Sheridans haven't seen her since they sat together at supper. Perhaps Theo has taken her for a stroll in the garden.'

'She's not with her brother. Mr Wyndham's over there.' Having had a helpful look about, Lucy nodded in the direction of a cluster of gentlemen.

Jemma saw her guardian was hovering on the fringe

of a particularly gregarious circle of fellows, partially obscured by a monumental potted palm.

Throughout the evening Jemma had noticed that Theo had seemed to skip from one group of gentlemen to another. He would single out a person and look very intense whilst conversing with him. Apart from having heaped high his plate in the supper room, then wolfed down the delicacies to return to the table for more, Theo had seemed to take little notice of the enjoyments on offer. Mr Crabbe, on the other hand, appeared to be having a splendid time. Since he'd danced the quadrille with Jemma he'd approached several other ladies and jigged, jovially, upon the dance floor with them. Every so often Jemma would sense his eyes upon her and would send him an encouraging smile. In return she always received a beam that seemed to stretch from one of his ears to the other.

Jemma acknowledged one such sunny salute from Mr Crabbe now, then immediately turned her mind back to Maura. She realised, with a pang, that she had not seen her cousin for some while, and she began to feel a niggling uneasiness. She hoped that Maura was not feeling out of sorts. Maura disliked making a fuss. She would suffer in silence rather than feel she was being a nuisance at such a scintillating occasion as the Clevelands' ball. As she pivoted slowly to fruitlessly scan the room for a glimpse of Maura's sherbet-lemon dress, Jemma's eyes swept over Marcus. Immediately she snapped her gaze back to him and their eyes entwined. Although a great space separated them she felt herself sway with the intensity of the emotion he aroused in her. He continued watching her discreetly whilst standing centrally within a group of gentlemen that included

Gregory Cleveland and Bert Sheridan. She knew he had spent most of the evening with sedate gentlemen rather than the dashing young bucks closer to his own age. Rather sweetly he had taken Mr Sheridan with him from one group of gentlemen to the other, obviously aware that the fellow might otherwise feel a little out of things. Bert was rather retiring and rarely socialised. Yvette Sheridan, however, being some years younger than her husband, had danced and flitted from one group of ladies to another to chat. Marcus had danced only a few times: with Deborah, with the Viscountess and lastly with her.

Jemma looked away just for a moment, concerned that they might be spotted staring at one another. In a second her eyes swung, as though magnetised, back to his and were immediately engulfed. She noticed the question in his gaze as though he had sensed something was wrong. Almost imperceptibly she shook her head to reassure him before she tore her eyes away and began wandering back to the terrace doors to search outside for Maura. Just as she reached her destination Debbie appeared at her side. Her friend looked flushed from her recently ended gavotte with Randolph.

'Are you enjoying yourself, Jemma?' Debbie asked breathlessly, her face a study of happiness.

'Indeed I am,' Jemma said with a smile as she looked about at the gay scene. 'It is the most wonderful party. I hope Maura is enjoying it too.' She paused, not wanting to convey her uneasiness to Debbie. 'I am just going to step on to the terrace and look for her. It is very warm this evening. I expect she is probably taking a stroll to revive herself.'

'I'll take the air too,' Debbie said, fanning her face

with her fingers. 'Randolph is a very good dancer. Did you see us?'

'I did,' Jemma confirmed softly. 'You make a handsome couple.'

Debbie dimpled prettily, but restricted her pleasure at her friend's compliment to a secretive, 'I know!' and linked arms with Jemma. The two young women walked out into refreshing evening air. Despite the high temperature a breeze had sprung up and was stirring the boughs of trees into soft soughing. Jemma angled her head, allowing the balmy air to sweep beneath her glossy curls and cool her skin.

They had been strolling slowly and had almost reached the steps that led to the garden when a noise alerted Jemma to somebody's presence. But they appeared to be the only people occupying this end of the terrace. The leaves shivered on the mulberry tree under which she'd whispered with Robert, and then with Marcus, and she turned her face towards the wind, straining to listen. 'Did you hear something?' Jemma asked with a frown.

Debbie shook her head and gazed up at the twinkling stars studding velvet-blue heavens. 'It is such a beautiful evening! Look at the huge moon—'

'There it is again,' Jemma said urgently. She slipped her hand from her friend's arm and walked swiftly towards the steps. 'I think I heard a woman's voice, coming from below.'

Debbie joined her at the top of the flight. 'Perhaps a romantic tryst?' she suggested with a scandalised smile. 'We'd best not interfere.'

'It *is* Maura,' Jemma breathed as she squinted to the

right and caught a glimpse of her cousin's pastel gown, a stark flag of cloth billowing against shrubbery silvered here and there by moonlight. 'What on earth does she think she's doing?' Jemma said in a horrified mutter. 'If she's with a gentleman…' Jemma turned a disbelieving gaze on her friend. 'Surely she would not be so stupid!' The noise wafted on the air again. Now they were closer it could be distinguished as a female giggle that sounded very much like Maura's. 'Oh, my!' Jemma gasped in a mix of astonishment and anger. 'She *will* be in shocking trouble if this gets out.'

No scrap of sauciness shaped Deborah's expression now. The idea of a couple of her parents' contemporaries canoodling in the bushes was one thing; the thought of a genteel spinster being caught in the dark with a man who was not a relative was another matter entirely. Maura had only one male relation present tonight and he was stationed indoors. She turned a stunned gaze on Jemma. 'She would not be so silly as to meet a fellow out here alone?'

'It seems she is,' Jemma said bleakly. A moment later she again caught sight of a scrap of pale skirt blowing, and heard a woman's guttural sigh. Jemma's face flooded with blood. Now she needed no further confirmation of what was going on! She'd recently emitted very similar noises when Marcus had caressed her in to insensibility. 'I'm going down to get her,' she rattled off in a whisper. 'She will be ruined if ever this gets out.'

'I'll come too,' Debbie breathed bravely.

'No!' Jemma hissed as she descended a step. 'Stay here, please. If someone comes this way you must distract them—take them back inside, anything—just keep them away until I can get Maura safe and sound.'

Without waiting for her friend's agreement, Jemma hoisted her flimsy skirt free of her satin slippers and sped lightly down the stone steps. Once on the grass she ran towards the spot where she'd caught a glimpse of her cousin's clothing, uncaring that the springy turf was dewy and dampening her footwear.

As she rushed in to the jasmine-scented arbour the sight that met her eyes made her freeze and gasp aloud in amazement. Had Maura been caught with a personable young buck it would have been bad enough. For her cousin to be discovered sitting on Graham Quick's lap with her arms around his neck was immeasurably alarming. Swiftly Jemma turned her head away from the pair of vicious eyes that had immediately challenged her presence. 'What on earth are you doing, Maura?' Jemma hissed in a voice rendered almost inaudible by shock. 'Are you intent on ruining yourself and your family too?'

Maura had scrambled up with a muffled shriek and yanked together the edges of her gaping bodice. Despite the dusk giving her some modesty, Jemma could see that her cousin's face and throat were stained scarlet. With her free hand Maura attempted to shove her dishevelled hair back into its pins. As Jemma lunged at her cousin and grabbed her arm to physically put distance between her and Mr Quick, she noticed that the small amount of rouge Maura had applied to her mouth had been smudged to grotesquely outline her lips.

Nonchalantly Graham Quick stood up and an idle hand began adjusting and brushing his attire. 'You seem to have come at rather an inopportune moment, Miss Bailey. Another few minutes and Miss Wyndham and I would have finished our little chat and I would have returned her to the party.'

Jemma flung at him a look of pure loathing. 'I do not think that you would have done that, sir. In fact, I do not think that you are welcome here at all in or out of doors.'

'I think you miss my point, Miss Bailey.' Graham's eyes sparked dangerously. 'I *am* here. And as you witnessed, Miss Wyndham has been keeping me very good company.' His eyes slid to Maura, lingered with evil contentment, as he softly suggested, 'Why do you not help Miss Wyndham to make herself presentable, then escort her back inside before all manner of scandal and gossip ensues?'

It was a moment before the cause of his sinister satisfaction penetrated Jemma's stunned mind. Scandal and gossip was exactly what he wanted. It seemed that Maura too was slowly regaining her senses. She peeked at him with pained, ashamed eyes.

'You meant to dishonour me and cause a scandal?' she whispered, agonised by the possibility. 'You said you were falling in love with me. You said since you saw me at home that day you could not forget me.'

'Go back inside,' he snapped in irritation. He turned away from her as though she had served her purpose and her continuing presence was irksome.

The full force of her imminent disgrace suddenly hit home and Maura let out a wail. A moment later her pride had rallied and she took a lunge at the man who had callously tricked her. She flew at Graham with her fingers curled and aimed at his face.

Neatly Jemma caught Maura about the waist and prevented her launching an attack on the man who had hooted a beastly chuckle.

'Oh, no! Someone is coming. Two gentlemen!' Over Maura's shoulder Jemma could see two tall masculine figures racing across the grass towards them. Immediate, instinctive relief flooded her as she realised that one of them was Marcus.

'What the devil…?' Marcus gritted out as he came to an abrupt halt with Randolph close behind. His eyes skipped from person to person, but no words needed to be uttered for him to guess what had happened. His eyes whipped back to Graham. 'You'll pay dearly for this night's work, Quick.'

'Not I…' Graham sneered. 'But I think Wyndham might, and quite willingly for a change. I want no more than is my due.'

'You think to sink to this level to get back your cash?' Marcus coldly bit out, his tone dripping disgust. He knew, as did most of his peers, that Wyndham and Quick were at loggerheads over money. He knew too, of course, that Graham Quick was an inveterate rogue. But setting out in cold blood to deliberately sully the virgin sister of an acquaintance seemed outside even Quick's devilry.

Graham slanted a sly sideways look at Marcus, no hint of remorse apparent. 'This need not concern you, Speer. Fetch Wyndham for me and we'll reach a solution, I assure you.' His eyes swung slowly and significantly between Jemma and the Earl of Gresham. 'And before you think to moralise, let me tell you that I've been here, in this very spot, watching people on the terrace for some while. I've observed all that's gone on, if you catch my meaning.'

Almost before he'd finished speaking Marcus's fist

slammed in to his mouth, spoiling his smirk. Quick was sent reeling back against the bench where he collapsed in an undignified heap. 'I hope you've caught my meaning,' Marcus enunciated icily. 'Don't ever try to blackmail me or it'll be the worse for you.'

He pivoted on his heel and looked at Maura. She tried to avoid his blazing eyes by hanging her head and allowing drooping coils of hair to cover her features. Jemma continued buttoning her up with shaking hands. Once she'd done with straightening her cousin's bodice, Jemma's nervous fingers set about tidying Maura's hair and complexion. She unpinned, combed with her fingers, re-pinned, then wordlessly accepted the handkerchief that Marcus held out and scrubbed her cousin's face clean of tears and smears.

'Miss Wyndham will go back inside with you, Jemma,' Marcus instructed with quiet, calming authority. 'Randolph will escort you both back to the ballroom. You have all been taking a stroll together. Then Randolph will find your guardian and tell him that Miss Wyndham has been taken ill whilst in his company. Like it or not, Wyndham will take you all home earlier than expected.' Marcus's eyes had been on his friend as he spoke. Randolph nodded that he understood what was expected of him, and why.

'I'll make sure Wyndham does as he's told,' Randolph said, quietly adamant. 'Even if I have to accompany him to the door and assist him into his carriage I'll make sure he escorts the ladies home.'

'But he…' Jemma's eyes darted past Marcus to the odious creature lounging, panting, on the bench. Graham Quick was eyeing Marcus resentfully whilst his hand cradled his bruised jaw. 'He wants to speak to Theo so he might extort some money from him to keep quiet about what he's done,' Jemma whispered urgently to Marcus, her voice shaking with a mix of fury and despair. 'If Theo doesn't immediately come out to speak to him, heaven only knows what he might do. The swine means to cause grave trouble if he doesn't get his own way.'

'I know,' Marcus replied gently.

Their eyes locked for a moment and beneath his quiet adoration Jemma felt soothed.

'I'll deal with Quick. Go home, Jemma; don't worry any more about any of it.'

With utter trust that Marcus would sort things out, Jemma positioned herself on one side of Randolph. When Maura simply stood glaring at her tormentor as though preparing to launch a fresh attack on him, Randolph impatiently wound her arm into his and jerked her into motion. They set off with Randolph leading them at a brisk pace, for he knew time was of the essence. At any moment inquisitive people might come down into the garden to see what was going on. They were in full view of several couples promenading on the terrace. At the top of the steps, Debbie, conscious of spectators and the need to defuse the situation, greeted them with a bright enquiry about the scent of the night jasmine. Jemma answered her in the same happy tone, but a wordless message conveying the gravity of the situation passed between them as the little party trooped back in to the ballroom.

When the knock came at the door Jemma was still feeling too deeply wounded by her guardian's bawled vituperation to pay heed to it.

She had ten minutes ago returned to the house and told Polly to retire for the night. Polly had seen straight away that some disaster had befallen. Miss Bailey had gone out, looking like a beautiful angel, in the happiest of spirits. But she'd returned earlier than expected, with a face as white as a sheet and the hem of her gown and her pretty slippers soaking wet. Jemma had refused Polly's insistence that she make her a nice hot drink. Sounding more querulous than was her intention, she'd firmly instructed her maid to retire for the night.

She wanted to be alone to lick her wounds and to think; in her shock and distress she had started to believe that perhaps there was truth in Theo Wyndham's demented ranting. Had her father expected that by now the Bailey inheritance would have passed to his male heir? Would she die a sour old maid because no man would tolerate her selfish arrogance? Did she deserve every bad thing that Theo had fervently wished might come down upon her head?

On the journey home from the Clevelands' ball Theo had guessed straight away that something other than a physical ailment was wrong with Maura. Whilst his sister had sniffed and tried to withdraw in to a corner of the coach Theo had bullied her mercilessly, despite Jemma's protestations that he leave her be, until finally she'd blurted out that she was disgraced. From there it was but a minor task for Theo to forcefully shake out of Maura all that had gone on to necessitate their early departure from the ball.

'This is all your fault!' he had roared at Jemma with such volume and violence that Maura had jumped out of her seat and screamed. With specks of spittle flying from his mouth he had called Jemma all manner of vile names. She was out of the mould of her hussy of a mother. She was a grasping shrew who, had she taken a husband as was the duty of any right-minded, decent woman, would have prevented his sister being cast into the wilderness. Maura, he'd barked out, was now besmirched for her lifetime and Jemma deserved the same damning fate.

Jemma's reasonable protestations that he had created his own disaster by allowing Quick into his house when Maura was at home, and by taking loans from a man he knew to be a reprobate, were met with pop-eyed fury. Theo had unleashed a fresh torrent of abuse concerning her outrageous impertinence in daring to speak to him so.

As soon as they had reached Pereville Parade Theo had leaped out of the coach and practically dragged Jemma out by an arm as though he could no longer bear her presence. Jemma had been equally glad to be away from him. With a brief farewell for Maura she had hastened in to her house and for a good few minutes had stood shaking just inside the closed door.

The rap at the door came again, with more volume and insistence this time. Jemma started to attention, thrusting her miserable memories momentarily from her mind. She hastened to the window to peek out into the darkness. If it were Theo returned to start on her again now he'd dumped Maura at home, she would most definitely not let him in. Was it Marcus? She doubted it would be him. He was probably still locked in negotiations with vile Graham Quick to save Maura's reputation. What would Marcus do to seal the black-guard's lips? Threaten to expose Quick as a blackmailer? The rapping came again with an urgency that made Jemma's stomach lurch and sent her into action. She did not want any neighbours hearing a commotion and coming to investigate. Swiftly she left the parlour and hastened to the door. In a voice that quavered she demanded to know the visitor's identity.

'It is your mother, Jemma,' a woman's voice softly called. 'Please open the door, I must speak to you.'

For a moment Jemma was struck dumb. The drama that had closed the evening had wiped from her mind what Robert had told her earlier: her mother might already be journeying to London with her son. What a time of the night to come calling! But what better time would there be for a disreputable woman to present herself? Her mother had, sensibly, chosen to arrive under cover of darkness rather than run the gauntlet of the neighbours. With shaking fingers Jemma fumbled with locks and chains and eventually jerked open the door to stare at a thin, middle-aged woman, darkly dressed, who was holding the hand of a young boy.

'Please, come in,' Jemma croaked. She swallowed, trying to moisten her parched mouth. Instinctively she peered into the street and was relieved to see that nobody was about.

'I waited till it was dark,' Veronica Bailey said. 'It is not my intention to embarrass you, my dear, I swear. But we have nowhere else to go. I'm sorry…'

Her mother's soft lilting voice was so achingly familiar that Jemma felt tears sting her eyes. Quickly she closed the door, then turned and led the way from the gloomy hallway into the candle-lit parlour. Once in the room she turned immediately and a hungry gaze roved her mother's face. She then turned her attention to the boy. He kept his dark head bowed as though he were shy or very tired.

'Would you like some refreshment?' Jemma asked.

Veronica nodded immediately. 'We have had nothing to eat since this morning. Jacob is very hungry. If you could arrange for a light supper, that would be very nice,' her mother said gratefully.

Jemma took a step closer to her mother. She looked into her solemn eyes, scanned her wan face. Veronica Bailey looked as Jemma imagined she might do having heard Robert's description of her. In the flickering candle flame she could see the silver threads in her hair and the creases around her eyes and mouth, worsened no doubt by her obvious travel fatigue. Jemma put out a hand tentatively, then suddenly she grasped her mother's upper arms and enclosed her in an embrace emboldened by many years of pent-up longing.

'Oh, my dear,' her mother sobbed against her shoulder, 'I'm so pleased, so pleased to see you. I wondered if you would turn us away. I know you have every right to shun us. I wanted to take you with me, Jemma, but he would not allow it. You were young enough to start a new life. I pleaded with John…'

'Hush,' Jemma soothed with a watery sniff. She knew there was much they had to talk about, but this dreadful night was not the right time. Plans would have to be made, a journey to Thaxham House arranged. In the countryside, away from prying eyes, they could decide on their futures. She knuckled the wetness from her eyes as she stepped away from her mother. She bent down to the little chap who was still silently standing by his mother's side. She felt a rush of pity and affection for the boy. None of this was his fault.

As their faces became level Jemma became quite still. A wobbly finger turned up his chin so she might gaze in to Jacob's adorably sweet face.

'You have spoken to Robert Burnham, I think,' her mother said huskily. 'You are not *very* surprised to see us. You know, don't you, that on disembarking at Newhaven Robert was kind enough to purchase for us a meal.'

'I have spoken to him this evening,' Jemma corroborated quietly. 'I bumped in to him at a very fine party. He told me…'

'He told you about Jacob?'

'Yes,' Jemma murmured, as the suspicion in her mind made her gasp. She fumbled on the table for the candlestick and slowly brought it closer to the child's face so she could see his features quite clearly.

Jemma turned her head to look at her mother with astonished, almost fearful, enquiry.

Veronica Bailey simply nodded, the tears filling her eyes tipping on to her cheeks. 'I'm sorry,' she whimpered. 'John should have let you come with me.'

It was enough of an answer to chill Jemma and prevent her replying for some minutes. She stayed as she was as though frozen in position, half-crouching in front of her brother. Eventually, and without straightening, she listed out what they must do. 'We have Thaxham House still as a retreat. I shall rouse Polly from her bed. I know you are exhausted from the journey, but if you take just a short nap and help us to pack a few things we can leave very early in the morning for Essex.' She looked back at her brother and a gentle finger swept his smooth cheek. 'But first let us see what we have in the larder to eat. Would you like some supper, Jacob?'

Chapter Twenty

'Hold tight, *chéri*,' Jemma warned, laughing, and with a shove she set the swing swiftly into motion.

Jacob did as he was told and his knuckles showed bone as he gripped the stout weathered ropes. With all her might Jemma propelled the seat higher so the boy was sailing towards the lowest of the ancient apple tree's gnarled branches. She stood back, hands planted on her slender hips, watching as her brother hooted a joyful laugh.

'*Encore une fois*,' he shouted his plea as the swing began losing momentum and height.

Squinting up at him through afternoon sunlight, Jemma stepped in neatly and gave the seat another hefty push just as he let go with one hand to point.

'*Regardez!*'

Jemma looked up to see what had caught his attention. In the distance she could see a vehicle driving at speed along the shingle track that led to Thaxham House. The carriage and horses appeared as a blur of black, but suddenly the driver reined back and they separated into a sleek curricle and a fine matched pair.

Before the equipage was properly at a standstill the dark figure had leapt out of it and thrown the reins to the tiger balanced on the back.

Possibly as much as a furlong separated them, but Jemma had recognised him, just as she knew that he'd seen her. She wasn't sure if she were pleased or disquieted to know that a first distant glimpse of her was enough to bring him to a halt in a cloud of dust. He was on the move again, striding through meadow grass towards her, and every pace he took seemed to heighten a painful thumping beneath her ribs.

Of course she'd known he would come.

Since they'd arrived at Thaxham House she'd lain many times in bed at night, staring up at her bed canopy with her turbulent thoughts denying her the comfort of sleep. During those dragging hours she'd attempted to rehearse what she'd say to him when he arrived. But now the moment was here her mind refused to cooperate and battle through a fog of anxiety to find those neat phrases she'd stored away.

Had he guessed her abrupt departure from town might have something to do with her mother? On the Clevelands' terrace he'd suspected Robert Burnham had given her news of Veronica Bailey. It had been the last time she'd seen him and seemed now eons ago. Yet barely one week had passed since she'd left Pereville Parade at dawn to journey with her family and Polly to Thaxham House.

One fact did emerge from the clutter in her mind and was clung to as a drowning person might use driftwood in a stormy sea. *She owed him her gratitude.*

Jemma had received a note that morning from her

cousin Maura. It had been redirected to Thaxham House from her London home for the Wyndhams didn't know, and she hoped would for a while remain in ignorance, of her quitting town. She hoped they remained unaware, too, of their Aunt Veronica's return from France with a cousin they'd never met. Eventually they would find out, as would everyone, that the passing of the years had not mitigated but added to Veronica Bailey's infamy. But Jemma was grateful for the respite of these early days. A volcano of scandal was simmering, but thankfully had not yet erupted and smeared them all.

In her note Maura had asked Jemma to please forgive her brother for his appalling temper and insults on the journey home from the ball. She'd requested, too, that Jemma quickly come to visit her. She badly needed a friend to talk to, she'd written. In punishment for her having disgraced herself, Theo had banned her from leaving the house, and she had no idea how long her incarceration might last. It seemed odd to Jemma that Maura could find the nerve to launch an assault on the stranger who'd tried to ruin her, yet still could not brave her tyrant of a brother. Maura had carried on to describe her regrets at having been such a fool as to be swayed by beastly flattery, and her great relief that the Earl of Gresham had managed to silence odious Graham Quick. But there was no indication of how Marcus had done so. Jemma realised she might today find out.

'*Regardez l'homme!*'

Jemma's frantic reflection was abruptly curtailed by Jacob's shout. She swivelled about to see that the seat of the swing was now swaying close to the ground, and Jacob was making ready to jump off it.

'*Non!*' she gasped. '*Stay there!*' But it was too late. The boy had flung himself on to the grass and set off on his spindly legs.

Instinctively she chased after Jacob, her light cotton skirts gathered away from the swaying reeds that hampered her progress through the orchard. She slowed to an easier pace as she saw her brother reach him. It was pointless to now snatch him away, and nor did she know why she had striven to keep them apart. Had it subconsciously been her intention to reveal her secret to him a little at a time in the hope of diminishing its enormity? A worldly man such as he would, in any case, be well acquainted with the likely consequences of a lengthy liaison between illicit lovers. That truth was joined to another, and the combined force of those suspicions constricted her chest until she felt quite giddy.

Marcus had a mistress. Did he also have a family life with Lady Vaux? When she'd taken a drive with Debbie to the Park she'd learned twice within the hour of the role Pauline Vaux had in Marcus's life. Jemma had imagined simple jealousy caused her to look so sour. But perhaps that bitter expression had been due as much to the woman's fear of her children being ousted by legitimate heirs as to her unwillingness to share her lover with his wife.

She stood still, chest heaving with laboured gasps, watching as Marcus crouched down to greet the boy. It seemed to Jemma that for a moment she ceased to breathe at all. An indrawn hiss of air cooled her burning throat as he lithely stood upright again. Marcus ruffled the lad's dark locks with a careless hand then he was again approaching her, Jacob jogging at his side to keep up with his long stride.

Usually he looked sartorially immaculate; today his riding boots were covered in a film of dust that also powdered smudges on his tight buff breeches. The sleeves of the white shirt he wore had at some point been carelessly pushed back on muscular forearms, and the top unbuttoned to expose to summer air a column of strong brown throat. As Jemma watched his unfaltering approach both of his hands were plunged deep into his pockets, completing the picture of moody masculinity he presented.

Unable to compose herself enough to boldly meet his eyes, she stooped, plucking several long blades of grass to fiddle with. 'I thought you might come,' she blurted out, drawing sharp edges against the soft skin of thumb and forefinger. She was aware of his steady regard warming the side of her face more fiercely than was the summer sun. Unable to bear it any longer, she swung her head around and up so that their eyes collided.

There was nothing in his gaze to alarm her; nothing that she'd not seen before and conquered in their many passionate skirmishes. Desire was there, blackening his pupils as they roved her face with such intensity it seemed he would imprint each of her features on his mind; she could read too a question in his eyes. But it wasn't the one she'd apprehensively anticipated. Perhaps, despite his ill humour, he was too gallant to yet ask about a small boy who spoke French and looked like her.

'Why didn't you let me know you were shutting the house and going away?' he demanded so tonelessly it was obvious he was very angry indeed. 'I wasn't sure if you might have set off for France until I went after Burnham and made him tell me what news he had of your mother.'

'You have sought out Robert?' Jemma breathed. That she had not expected! When they had all stood together on the Clevelands' terrace she'd realised immediately that no love was lost between the two men. She hoped they hadn't clashed violently over her. She owed Robert gratitude, not trouble. 'Was he still in London? What did you do? What did he tell you?' she whispered. Aware Jacob could understand from her tone of voice, if not from her rapid words, that something was wrong, she gave the solemn-faced child a faltering smile and drew him to her side. 'I should like to introduce you to my brother, Jacob,' she blurted her voice trembling with a mix of defiance and pride.

'He introduced himself in French,' Marcus replied easily. 'Although he tells me he speaks some English.'

'Yes, he does,' Jemma said quickly. 'Mama wants him to practise his English so we encourage him to use it. I take it you know a little French?' She let go of her brother's hand as he wriggled his fingers to liberate them and collapsed in the clover.

Marcus smiled, that devastating tiny movement that barely curved his mouth yet had the strength to squeeze her heart.

'I've been to France a few times,' he told her.

'Jacob!' Veronica Bailey waved at them from the door of the elegant pale-brick house set off to the right. Immediately interpreting her signal her son jumped up from where he'd been lounging in the grass and set off towards his luncheon. A moment later he sped back and, as though remembering his manners, he stuck out his hand, and gazed up at Marcus with large green eyes.

'*Au 'voir, monsieur.*'

Marcus extended his hand; having given it a single, manful shake Jacob was again racing towards the orchard and his mother.

'You must be thirsty after the journey. Would you like some tea? Perhaps a glass of wine instead…' Jemma had felt suddenly too shy and confused to be alone with him. She set off at a brisk pace in Jacob's wake. It was only when she'd reached the shade of the stately old apple tree, and would have carried on towards the house, that Marcus restrained her and backed her against wood. Her feeble attempts to evade him were defeated as he lifted her off the ground and placed her again before him. A large hand was planted either side of her on the rough bark so that she was kept sheltered from view between his arms beneath its cool canopy.

'A moment ago you wanted to know what Burnham had told me. Have you changed your mind, Jemma?'

She shook her head so violently she felt apple bark spitefully abrading her scalp. Shimmering emerald eyes scanned his face, probed his steady grey gaze before skittering away. Had he guessed all of it, or did he just know that her brother was a bastard?

She understood now what it was that Robert had felt unable to tell her on the night of the ball. She understood too why he had looked so utterly miserable to be the un-willing keeper of such thoughts. Jacob Devereux was the image of her—and with good reason: they had the same father. On the journey to Thaxham House her mother had wretchedly admitted what Jemma had suspected from the moment Jacob had turned his face up to hers and stared at her with mournful jade-green eyes: she was Pierre Devereux's daughter, and not a Bailey at all.

Marcus cradled her chin in the fork of his hand, then tilted it so she must look at him. 'I went to Berkshire to find Burnham. Unfortunately he'd gone home directly after the ball. Had he still been in London I'd have been here so much sooner. We were civil to one another,' he reassured her with an ironic inflection tingeing his eyes and voice. 'Burnham explained that far from being in France, as I imagined, your mother was again on English soil with her son. On learning that I guessed straight away that you'd bolted here to give them privacy and shelter. He told me, too, that Devereux had died, leaving your mother impoverished.'

'It was not his fault.' Jemma immediately jumped to the Count's defence. 'My mother has said that he did not intend her to be left destitute after his death. They were never able to marry, but she insists he was always good to her and treated her no differently to his wife.' A far-away look clouded her eyes as her mother's descriptions of her life in France played over in her mind. Only Jemma knew what she'd suffered; but oddly it seemed natural to her to trust Marcus with the information. 'Once she had a fine apartment in Paris, in a very nice *quartier*. They had all they could wish for and lived sumptuously. The Count resided with her and Jacob much of the time as though they were a proper family.' She paused, stared off at an angle towards the mellow-hued house into which Jacob and her mother had disappeared. She was conscious of Marcus's quiet attentiveness. He was waiting for her to enlighten him further about the disaster that had befallen her mother and forced her back, penniless, to England. After a deep breath she continued quietly telling the tale.

'The Count was involved in some commercial ventures that unluckily went awry at the beginning of this year. His merchant ships foundered and the cargoes were lost in high seas. My mother's apartment was sold and a smaller property leased for her and Jacob. That home had to go, too, when the Count's many creditors continued to clamour for their dues.' She agitatedly twisted together her fingers, unsure whether she wanted to yet draw a comment from him or would prefer he continued to quietly listen. 'My mother believes the financial disaster took its toll on the count's health. He died quickly and unexpectedly of a heart attack before he could recoup his losses or pay back all he owed. Following his death my mama thinks the Count's wife too was under siege from angry people, although neither of them had help of any sort to give. By that time my mama and Jacob were confined to just one room and had very little cash left to live on.' Jemma blinked back the heat that was attacking her eyes at the thought of their hardship and distress. She had grown to love Jacob very quickly. The idea of him hungry and scared, and much more so than he had been when he arrived at Pereville Parade, was hard to bear. But, with youthful resilience, he'd soon regained confidence and was revealing a sunny nature since he'd moved to Essex. Aware that she'd been silent for a while she quickly concluded her story. 'My mother had secreted away a few pieces of jewellery and sold those to purchase passage for her and Jacob on a ship back to England. Mama believes that the Count's wife and legitimate offspring will fare little better than will we.' She dipped her head, her slender body held tensely as she waited for his reaction.

Marcus touched his lips to her cheek in a way that was pure comfort, but Jemma flinched from him as though he'd tried to force a passionate kiss on her.

'You must know that everything is very different for me now,' she cried in tone that mingled determination and despair. Both her hands sprang to curl about a solid tanned forearm that was barring her escape. She pushed and pulled and lastly shook it violently when he simply flexed warm sinew beneath her fingers to thwart her futile attempt to move him. 'You must leave me alone and go back to your life in town.' She flung herself back against the bark again and turned on him imploring green eyes that seemed to float in tears.

'You know I can't do that, Jemma,' he reminded her softly as a hand cupped her cheek.

'You're so…so…' Jemma cried, unable to articulate her anguished frustration that he couldn't divine a scandalous truth and save her telling him of it.

'Persistent?' he supplied quietly. 'Why do you think that is?' he probed. 'Or do you still think me an arrogant lecher out to ruin you to salve my wounded pride?'

In all the turmoil of the past week she had almost forgotten that once, years ago, she had treated Marcus Speer as though he were of little consequence. Now it seemed absurd to suppose that this powerful aristocrat had once fallen foul of a teenage girl's silly whim to run off to Gretna Green with her childhood sweetheart. 'I know you pretended not to be embarrassed when I rejected you. I know afterwards you had lots of lady friends to make it seem you weren't wounded by it all…' When he denied none of it, and continued looking at her with overpowering intensity, she whispered, 'I never intended to hurt you.' An entreating look willed him to believe her. 'I know I was young at the time but…that was no excuse. I feel ashamed to have acted in such a way. But it was *not* callousness,' she offered her defence quite vehemently. 'It was just that you seemed, much as you do now, I suppose, self-assured and invincible and so very popular with the ladies.' She twisted a bitter little smile. 'I thought you would soon forget me and find someone else to propose to.' She looked down, avoiding his relentless silver stare. 'I know that's not a proper apology and you do deserve one.' Again her eyes glanced off his to settle on a spot over his shoulder. 'I considered writing to you to let you know how sorry and guilty I felt for having led you on.' Still he was silent, allowing her uninterrupted time to describe her regrets.

Jemma took in an inspiriting breath and forced her gaze determinedly to his. 'So, I'm very sorry for having behaved like a common tease, and for having led you to naturally believe that I would marry you.'

'There's no need to be sorry for that, Jemma. I thoroughly enjoyed it when you were leading me to believe you would marry me.'

Heat fizzed beneath Jemma's cheeks at his sultry amusement. 'You think me a shameless wanton, don't you?' she said, striving to sound careless.

'I think you're wonderful,' he whispered against her brow as his arms moved around her, easing her against him. His hands travelled caressingly over her back, soothing her quivering. 'You're brave and honourable and faithful to those you care about. You thought you were in love with Burnham, and you stayed true to him

despite my best efforts to drive a wedge between you.'
His lips touched gently at a cheek. 'I have a confession
to make too, Jemma. I knew you were trying to resist me
and I guessed why. It wasn't your fault that I set out to
seduce you into agreeing to be my wife instead of his.
You were young; I was old enough to know better than
to try to use sensuality to get you.' He chuckled huskily.
'But you defeated me, and my despicable strategy. The
shame was mine, sweetheart, not yours. You stayed loyal
despite my low tricks and went home, unattached, just
as you'd promised Burnham you would.' Marcus ran a
smoothing finger along her jaw line; it was joined by
others to cup a blushing cheek before his fingers speared
into her hair and angled her face up to his. 'I loved you
the more for it. I hated Burnham the more for having
captured such an exquisite prize. I was mad with jealousy
and thought philandering might protect my pride if not
my heart. But I didn't deserve you then. Now I do. That's
why I can't let you go. You're mine this time, Jemma.'

'You implied you had no fine feelings for me then,'
Jemma said, astonished at what she'd heard. Had he
really loved her, yet not told her so? 'You said you only
wanted to sleep with me.'

'I lied. When you told me you had considered it a
pointless flirtation, my damnable pride wouldn't allow
me to admit how different it had been for me.' He eased
her back a little from him so he could see the expression in eyes as brilliant as precious stones. 'I could have
told you five years ago that I loved you, but I'd sensed
a secret part of you was longing to be elsewhere…with
another man.' He swiped a hand over his jaw, looking
appealingly bashful as he admitted huskily, 'I've never

stopped loving or wanting you, Jemma. If I'd had your courage I would have come and told you so years ago when I found out that Burnham had betrayed you.'

'I wanted you to come.' She moved her fingers to touch his abrasive jaw in a way she'd done at seventeen. Her lids dropped as sandpaper skin tickled her palm. 'I hoped so much that you would,' she achingly murmured. 'Despite feeling cross and shocked about Robert leaving me, it didn't stop me thinking about you, wanting you. When I was staying in town I used to dream that we might bump into one another and you would again woo me.'

'I thought about coming to Thaxham House and speaking to your father that Michaelmas…'

It was as though an unseen hand had dashed cold water over Jemma. Her low lids flicked up and her fingers slowly withdrew from fondling his angular jaw. *Her father…* Marcus still didn't know that John Bailey was not her father, even though the man himself had been aware he was bringing up his rival's by-blow.

John Bailey, Jemma had come to realise, had been a very kind and forbearing father. Never before had she appreciated just how tolerant of her he had been. She knew that she would always think of him as her papa, despite knowing none of his blood flowed in her veins. Only her sisters could claim to be legitimate offspring of the Bailey marriage.

Despite hating his youngest daughter's sire with a maniacal intensity, John Bailey had bequeathed her his assets, to protect her until she married. Blame and bitterness had never been directed her way. She could recall no nasty, snide remarks, even when they had bickered or she had annoyed him. And she had greatly annoyed him when she'd turned down Marcus Speer's marriage proposal. Marcus said he still loved her, but would he ever have proposed marriage to a Frenchman's bastard?

'It is all different for me now,' she blurted huskily. 'You must go back to town, Marcus. A scandal will break when it is known that my mother has returned and has Jacob with her. I have already written to my sisters, preparing them for the worst.'

'Do you think I care what people say?' he interrupted quite harshly. 'It mattered not a jot to me five years ago when I knew your parents' marriage was a disaster and your mother had gone off with her lover. Do you think gossip worries me now?'

'Pierre Devereux was not just my mother's lover…' She closed her eyes, sucked in the breath to eject the words that seemed to stick to her tongue. 'He was Jacob's father…and mine, too,' she finished in no more than a whisper, yet sounding appealingly defiant. With all her strength she tried to break free of his lulling embrace, but he held her fast.

'I know…'

In her anguish Jemma still struggled to escape, the blood pounding in her head, deafening her to his two quiet words. When he repeated them a moment later with an added endearment and a brush of his cool lips on her feverish brow, she froze into immobility.

Glittering green eyes slanted up at his face. 'You know?' she squeaked in a daze. Her bosom was heaving with the effort she'd put in to attempting to get away. 'Did Robert tell you what he suspected once he'd seen Jacob? I'm sure he'd noticed how very much alike we are.'

'No,' Marcus said, soothing her with a slow, devastating smile. 'I didn't need him to tell me what he'd seen, my love. I used my own eyes…years ago.'

Chapter Twenty-One

'When?' Jemma demanded in a gasp. 'How long ago did you see?'

'It was perhaps seven years ago. I was in Paris with my uncle. We passed your mother and Pierre Devereux walking by the Seine. He had remarkably green eyes. Your mother looked to be with child, so your brother's existence is no great surprise to me either, Jemma.'

'You had guessed I was illegitimate when you proposed marriage to me five years ago?'

'It would've been an odd coincidence for you both to have eyes of such an unusual and startling colour and yet not be related by blood.' The disbelief in her eyes prompted him to demand huskily, 'I know my behaviour was reprehensible, Jemma, but please say you don't think me mean enough to shun the woman I adore because of an accident of birth. Knowing you were Devereux's child never made a difference to how I felt about you.'

'It would have made a difference to someone marrying for status or convenience rather than love.'

A noiseless chuckle grazed his throat, drawing from Jemma a startled look that demanded he explain what had caused such wry amusement.

'My uncle said something similar to me during our last conversation,' he said. 'Solomon thought I shouldn't marry Deborah and hinted as much on his deathbed.'

'Did he not like her?' Jemma asked in surprise.

'He liked you better. Or rather he understood me better than I realised. We were talking of wives and weddings, and just before I left him to the care of his doctor and his mistress…' Marcus paused before resuming with a throb of emotion in his voice he made no attempt to disguise, '…he told me I knew where happiness was. His dying wish was that I return to you. I understand that now.' He paused to reflect. 'He wouldn't advise me directly because he knew that breaking my betrothal to Deborah would cause her and her family embarrassment and ridicule. He was telling me it was up to me to find a way. And I would have done so. Even before Deborah kindly jilted me I was investigating ways I might wriggle out of it as decently as I could.'

'You were?'

'I considered doing it as soon as I received Wyndham's letter begging me to take you off his hands. If I'd been free, I'd not have propositioned you, sweetheart, I'd have made Wyndham a very happy man.' With a rueful smile that bordered on apology he admitted gruffly, 'It had to be one or the other, Jemma. Wife or mistress.'

'And Lady Vaux?' Jemma asked boldly, her eyes capturing his challengingly. Polite society might consider it an outrage for a young lady to discuss a gentleman's *amours*—especially with the fellow himself—but

Jemma knew their love had freed her from such constraint. 'What position do you intend she will take?' Jemma demanded huskily.

'Neither,' he answered gently, but with a spark of amusement shading his eyes and voice. 'Pauline was my mistress, but she isn't any more, and had I ever wanted to marry her I would have done so by now.'

'When we saw her in Pall Mall she was staring at us and looking very bitter. She was jealous of Debbie, wasn't she?'

'Yes, although you and I know she missed her rival. Whereas you don't have one,' he said, lowering his lips to touch hers. A sweetly determined kiss pursued her evasive mouth, finally convincing her of his sincerity. 'I've never loved her and I've not wanted her since you came back into my life,' he murmured against her skin. 'I swear that's the truth.' As though he'd already guessed her other fears he pre-empted the question. 'And I've no children, I swear that too.' He tilted up her chin, sweeping long fingers on the satiny skin of her jaw to make her look at him. When she continued to shield her thoughts behind lowered lids, he ordered huskily, 'Look at me, Jemma.'

She raised long curly lashes so their eyes merged. He was gazing at her with such fierce longing that she felt her bones melt with tenderness for him.

'Do you believe me?'

'Yes,' she whispered. 'I do.'

'Who told you about Pauline? Wyndham?' Marcus enquired with a deceptive quiet that Jemma knew all too well. He was subduing the anger he felt for Theo.

'Yes…well…no…not really,' she stuttered. She might

dislike Theo, but she wouldn't accuse him of making trouble when he'd intended none. 'I think he might have spotted you in the vicinity of her home and made a cryptic comment on it. I expect he imagined I wouldn't understand what he meant. But Debbie knew Lady Vaux was your mistress and so…it made sense suddenly.'

'Wyndham did pass by as I was coming out of Pauline's house. I hadn't seen her for a long while and I knew formally ending our relationship was long overdue. That was why I was there and for no other reason.'

'You don't have to explain to me, Marcus,' Jemma piped up with forced nonchalance and a flounce of her chestnut-coloured curls.

'Yes, I do,' he said with sardonic gravity. 'If we're to have any peace in our lives at all.'

Jemma's prim look collapsed and a musical little laugh escaped. He knew her too well! She would have probed mercilessly to find out if he'd been sleeping with another woman whilst also intimately kissing and caressing her.

A moment later her smile had faded as her mind returned to her cousin Theo. 'I know Theo deserves to hear some unpalatable truths about himself, but…you won't go and impress on him he's a swine, will you?'

'It's a little late to ask me to desist on that, Jemma,' Marcus said, mock solemn. 'Although I'm not sure I used an epithet as mild as swine.'

'I hope he thanked you for dealing with Graham Quick.'

'He did, although it almost choked him.'

'I must thank you, too, for protecting Maura's reputation from dreadful damage. She wrote to inform me you have managed to sort things out. Poor Maura—she almost scratched out Graham Quick's eyes, but it seems she cannot withstand her obnoxious brother. He has punished her by locking her in her room.' She glanced up at Marcus. 'Did you threaten to expose Graham Quick's devilry to make him keep quiet?'

'Quick's not averse to exposing his own devilry,' Marcus returned drily. 'I gave him what he wanted.'

'Was it a lot of money?'

'It doesn't matter, Jemma,' Marcus said softly. 'Forget about it.'

'I can't,' she said honestly. 'I think you have laid down a lot of money to protect Maura, and you hardly know her. I'm so glad she is not in disgrace. Despite her foibles I do like her. Once she is able to defy Theo, I think I will like her even better.'

'I did it for you, Jemma,' Marcus said with a smile. 'I'd do anything for you…'

'Anything my heart or body desires?' she reminded him saucily.

'Exactly,' he growled.

He would have plunged his mouth to hers, but Jemma put a finger to his lips. There was more to be said before she gave herself up to a sweetly anticipated torrent of entrancing kisses.

'So now Theo owes you the money?'

'I imagine he does, unless you consider it's worth writing off the debt to buy his absence.' Marcus kissed the fragile finger that held him at bay.

'Would you do that for me?' Jemma cried, quite jauntily. 'Heaven only knows, if there is something to be grateful for in all this it is knowing that Theo

Wyndham is no kin of mine. Actually, he is not full-blooded kin of my papa either. Our fathers were only stepbrothers.' She sighed. 'Of course Theo will sue to try to take everything I have when he discovers I'm not a Bailey. He'll think I was never entitled to my inheritance, and yet my papa knew the truth and still left it all to me.'

'I expect John Bailey thought as do I that it's who you are rather than who'd sired you that is important. I expect in turn you loved him dearly.'

'I did,' Jemma avowed huskily. 'He was an excessively good father, if perhaps not such a good husband. I know it was not all my mama's fault that they got divorced.'

'It's wise to see both sides,' Marcus said gently. 'As for Wyndham, he won't sue. He won't need to.' He paused for what seemed an inordinate amount of time before concluding gruffly, 'I understand he gets the estate legitimately when you marry.'

Happiness began to filter in to every part of Jemma's being, gaining in strength until it was an unbearably poignant ache. 'Is that a proposal, Marcus?' she whispered.

'Not a very good one,' he admitted with a boyish bashfulness that tweaked at her heart. He drew from a pocket a small velvet box. 'I brought this to give to you. Please say you'll take it this time. I refuse to put it back in the safe. It's been there already for five years.' Slowly he lifted the lid to reveal a superb gem nestling on white satin. A huge oblong emerald of the deepest, richest colour formed a centrepiece. Diamonds, radiating fiery sparks from dappled light, surrounded the glowing green gem.

'You bought me this when I was seventeen?'

'Yes…would you have liked it then?'

'Probably not as much as I like it now,' she gulped through the tears clogging her throat.

'Will you marry me, Jemma?' he asked hoarsely. 'I love you so much and want you always by my side as my wife. I promise to care for you and your mother and Jacob. There'll be no scandal for any of you, I promise. I'm the Earl of Gresham,' he said with wry persuasion. 'Who would dare…?'

She raised glistening eyes to his face and, incapable of speech, nodded her head before throwing her arms about his neck and hugging him tightly. 'I love you, I do, I do so love you,' she mumbled against his shoulder.

'I know,' he said gently, threading tender fingers into loose coils of chestnut hair that had lost their pins. 'I was almost sure of it five years ago, sweetheart. You just took a lot of convincing before you believed it too.'

'I like your convincing,' she whispered impishly, lifting her head a few inches from his collar. She brushed away her teardrops from his bare neck.

'Good,' he purred wolfishly.

Immediately she was angling her head, her lips were parting, her breathing slowing in anticipation of the first proper kiss he would give her today.

'God, I've missed you, Jemma.' His mouth swooped to hers, moving almost roughly at first before he tempered his desire to woo her with savage tenderness. Her lips parted willingly, widening as his tongue probed to touch the silk of her inner lips and tantalise her tongue. Shyly Jemma returned his kiss until, emboldened by his grunt of pleasure as her teeth nipped his lip, she raised herself up on tiptoe to taste more of him.

Marcus felt his body heating, tightening with desire at her uninhibited response. Fire raged in his veins, increasing the buoyancy at his pelvis to a throbbing ache. His hands streaked from her back to the full ripeness of her thrusting breasts. They swelled to fill his palms and, as he brushed the hardening nipples through the light cotton of her gown, she moaned and chafed against him, wordlessly pleading he give her more pleasure. Desire exploded in Marcus. His kiss became fiercely erotic. His tongue retreated and plunged in a way he yearned to mimic with the rigid part of him that was pulsating against her soft abdomen. With a groan he lifted her so apple bark was at her back and his solid body at her front. He parted her thighs to wedge his muscular frame between them. Instinctively Jemma coiled her calves about his hips, holding him close so she might rock her pelvis against him and sweetly soothe the need at her feminine core.

A moment later she was gasping in disappointment as Marcus lowered her swiftly to the ground and flicked down her clothes. He slammed an arm on the tree trunk to one side of her, giving her a necessary few minutes to compose herself before her brother streaked in to view.

'*Maman* says guest come in, have…' He frowned, his lack of English defeating his attempt to invite Marcus to lunch. '*Manger, s'il vous plait?*' he offered brightly, then smiled.

'*Merci beaucoup*,' Marcus replied, and, following a sidelong smouldering look at Jemma, politely offered her an arm.

With a hand shielding her fiery cheeks from her brother's probing gaze, Jemma came out from under the apple tree and slipped her hand on to Marcus's arm.

To ease her self-consciousness Jemma burst into conversation as they started to walk. 'Were the Clevelands very upset about you and Debbie breaking your engagement?'

'They only want Deborah to be happy. She told them she feels too young to yet marry,' he explained. 'It was enough for them to accept our decision.'

'You know about Deborah and Randolph, don't you?'

'Yes,' Marcus confirmed.

'Did you know when you proposed to her?'

'I had no idea. He says he wasn't sure himself until he came back from overseas and realised he might lose her.'

'Will he propose?'

Marcus pulled her closer, brushed a thumb, with sensual slowness, over her passion-bruised lips. 'I want to talk about us,' he said softly. 'Just know that I'm glad Deborah will find happiness elsewhere. And she will. Eventually Randolph will give it to her...when the time's right.'

'Do I look like him? The Count?' Jemma asked wistfully as they strolled on through the meadow grass, Jacob a few steps ahead of them. 'I've never seen him. My mama says she thinks that I don't...apart from the eyes.'

'No. But apparently I do,' Marcus said with a grin.

'You?' Jemma gasped in surprise, angling her head to stare at his face.

'My uncle told me, just before he died, that he thought I had a look of Pierre Devereux about me. Needless to say he was a handsome devil!'

Jemma raised her eyebrows at that conceited quip.

'Or he wouldn't have had such a beautiful daughter,' Marcus finished huskily and, dipping his head, he skimmed his lips discreetly against hers.

'I'd like my mama and Jacob to live with us.' She glanced up, her eyes asking permission even if her bald statement had not.

'Your mother might prefer her own residence, Jemma,' Marcus answered diplomatically.

'You'd prefer she had her own residence, you mean,' Jemma contradicted, but with a smile.

'Well, it might be wise till after the honeymoon, sweetheart,' he muttered.

'How long will that be?' Jemma asked brightly.

'About thirty years.'

She chuckled and in sheer joyfulness enclosed him in a fierce hug about the waist that prompted him, in retaliation, to lift her and spin her around.

When Jacob realised what was going on he scampered back, keen to join in. As Jemma's feet again touched grass Jacob clung to his breathlessly laughing sister's skirts.

'Who?' He pointed at Marcus and squinted at Jemma for a reply.

'*Ton beau-frère*, Jacob,' Jemma told him proudly.

If he wasn't quite sure what brother-in-law meant, Jacob had grasped the important part. '*Vraiment?*' he asked, wide-eyed.

'Yes, truly…' Marcus confirmed and, as Jacob

darted off to excitedly tell his mother his brother was coming for lunch, Marcus gave his fiancée a lingering kiss before they walked on towards the house.

* * * * *

HISTORICAL

Regency

THE DARK VISCOUNT
by Deborah Simmons

Wilful Miss Sydony Marchant is not one to be afraid, even in the looming shadow of her imposing new home. But if the vast mansion doesn't shock her, the arrival of Viscount Hawthorne will! No longer the boy she once kissed – Bartholomew is now a man with a ruthless glint in his eye...

LORD PORTMAN'S TROUBLESOME WIFE
by Mary Nichols

Normally self-controlled Harry, Lord Portman is unsettled by his attraction to his convenient wife Rosamund, so keeps her at arm's length. When Rosamund falls into danger, Harry must let go of the past and fight for the woman he loves.
The Piccadilly Gentlemen's Club mini-series

THE DUKE'S GOVERNESS BRIDE
by Miranda Jarrett

Dreading the end of her Grand Tour, former governess Jane Wood nervously awaits the arrival of her employer, Richard Farren, Duke of Aston. Widower Richard is stunned by mousey Miss Wood's transformation into the carefree and passionate Jane!

On sale from 1st October 2010
Don't miss out!

Available at WHSmith, Tesco, ASDA, Eason and all good bookshops

www.millsandboon.co.uk

0910/04a

HISTORICAL

CONQUERED AND SEDUCED
by Lyn Randal

Two years ago former gladiatrix Severina had no choice
but to flee from her beloved Livius Lucan. Now she needs
his help. And in return Lucan is determined to conquer
this runaway woman – and claim the wedding
night he never had!

THE LAWMAN'S BRIDE
by Cheryl St John

All Sophie wants is to be left alone to build a new life.
Town marshal Clay Connor is upright and honourable; he
deserves more than a woman with a tainted past. But
if Sophie learns to trust again this lawman could
make her new life complete...

THE NOTORIOUS KNIGHT
by Margaret Moore

Sir Bayard may be handsome and secretly make
Lady Gillian rethink her vows never to marry, but she
has no intention of giving in to this presumptuous knight!
Sir Bayard must protect Lady Gillian, but he doesn't
expect to do battle with the lady herself!

On sale from 1st October 2010
Don't miss out!

2 FREE BOOKS
AND A SURPRISE GIFT

We would like to take this opportunity to thank you for reading this Mills & Boon® book by offering you the chance to take TWO more specially selected books from the Historical series absolutely FREE! We're also making this offer to introduce you to the benefits of the Mills & Boon® Book Club™—

- **FREE home delivery**
- **FREE gifts and competitions**
- **FREE monthly Newsletter**
- **Exclusive Mills & Boon Book Club offers**
- **Books available before they're in the shops**

Accepting these FREE books and gift places you under no obligation to buy, you may cancel at any time, even after receiving your free books. Simply complete your details below and return the entire page to the address below. You don't even need a stamp!

YES Please send me 2 free Historical books and a surprise gift. I understand that unless you hear from me, I will receive 4 superb new books every month for just £3.99 each, postage and packing free. I am under no obligation to purchase any books and may cancel my subscription at any time. The free books and gift will be mine to keep in any case.

Ms/Mrs/Miss/Mr _____ Initials _____

Surname _____

Address _____

_____ Postcode _____

E-mail _____

Send this whole page to: Mills & Boon Book Club, Free Book Offer, FREEPOST NAT 10298, Richmond, TW9 1BR